Long Island Slayer

Dark Mafia BWWM Romance

Long Island Mafia Romance
Book 3

Jamila Jasper

Thank you to all my patrons for your support with this story.
www.patreon.com/jamilajasper

Thank you to my most supportive readers:
Amna, Nysta, Fayola, Ty, Shyra, Andi-Mariee, Keisha, Jennett, Fredericka, Candece, Lydia, Sabrina, JM, Jackie, Mo, Ashaunte, Tolu, Lori, Dionne, ZLB, Nicol, Elbert, Jesi, Brenda, Desiree, LaShan, Only1ToniD, Debbie, Tiffanie, Shawnte, Lisema, Christine, Trinity, Monica, Juliette, Letetia, Margaret, Dash, Maxine, Sheron, Javonda, Pearl, Kiana, Shyan, Jacklyn, Amy, Julia, Colleen, Natasha, Yvonne, Brittany, June, Ashleigh, Nene, Nene, Deborah, Nikki, DeShaunda, Latoya, Shelite, Arlene, Judith, Mary, Shanida, Rachel, Damzel, Ahnjala, Kenya, Momo, BJ, Akeshia, Melissa, Tiffany, Sherbear, Nini, Curtresa, Regina, Ashley, Mia, Sydney, Sharon, Charlotte, Assiatu, Regina, Romanda, Catherine, Gaynor, BF, Tasha, Henri, Sara, skkent, Rosalyn, Danielle, Deborah, Kirsten, Ana, Taylor, Charlene Louanna, Michelle, Tamika, Lauren, RoHyde, Natasha, Shekynah, Cassie, Dreama, Nick, Gennifer, Rayna, Jaleda, Anton, Kimvodkna, Jatonn, Anoushka, Audrey, Valeria, Courtney, Donna, Jenetha, Ayana, Kristy, FreyaJo, Grace, Kisha, Stephanie E., Amber, Denice, Marty, LaKisha, Latoya, Natasha, Monifa, Alisa, Daveena, Desiree, Gerry, Kimberly, Stephanie M., Tarah, Yolanda, Kristy, Gary, Janet, Kathy, Phyllis, Susan

Thank you to my Patrons, *Shawnte and Damzel for allowing me to use your names to name some supporting characters after you!*

I offer this fun little option for patrons who are at the $10+ tiers behind the scenes.

Thank you also to everyone who helped name the other characters in this book. 🖤

Contents

Mafia Playmate

Forced To Surrogate

ISBN: 979-8-3303-3511-4

* * *

This is book three in an interracial mafia romance series with dark themes and potential triggers. If you enjoy steamy and spicy BWWM romance with a black woman/white man romance, you will enjoy this story. For readers of the Pagonis family or Doukas family series, strap in... You'll enjoy this deliciously wild ride.

❀ Created with Vellum

Description

His daughter-in-law, Melanie, is pregnant.
His son dead.

The slayer, Sammy Zagarella, faces his biggest challenge…
Keeping Melanie from bullets or blades.
His son had enemies… and they want blood.

One problem…
Melanie's the most mischievous pregnant woman he's
ever met.
And Sammy falls for her.
Hard.

* * *

If you enjoy WMBW mafia family romance stories with
action and dark themes, you'll love this enemies-to-
lovers dark romance story. Get Book #3 in this series of
interconnected standalone stories.

Series Titles

Long Island Executioner
Long Island Butcher
Long Island Slayer

https://bit.ly/longislandseries

Content Awareness

dark bwwm mafia romance

This is a mafia romance story with dark themes including potentially triggering content, violence, frank discussions and language surrounding bedroom scenes and race. **All characters in this story are 18+.** Sensitive readers, be cautioned about some of the age gap material in this dark but extremely hot romance novel.

* * *

Enjoy the steamy romance story…

* * *

This book comes with two free samples of other dark mafia romance stories that you may enjoy.

Note From Jamila

Hello Reader.
Are you ready for the third book in the series?

If you enjoy the bad boys who are truly fucked up… welcome.

I've been in the lab with Sammy's book for quite some time now and this is the book with some of the most controversial scenes…

But the love scenes in this book are not going to be the same old cookie cutter bedroom scenes. Melanie and Sammy have intensity in their relationship unlike any other couple in this series.

The age gap, the shared grief and Melanie's circumstances create an erotic energy between them that is explosive AF.

All characters are 18+

If you find the good in the bad boys and enjoy stories with

these possessive alphas who completely melt for the **black
women they love...** *welcome.*

Be warned, the content in this story may be sensitive to some
readers but if you want to walk with me on the wild side and
dare to have dark fantasies about twisted alpha heroes and
black female leads — turn the page and begin the third
installment in the series...

The completed series:
https://bit.ly/longislandseries

* * *

Chapter 1
My Villain Origin Story
Melanie Stevens

Melanie's last day of freedom before she falls into the clutches of a dangerous and violent mobster twenty-two years her senior.

* * *

The worst day of my life begins like every other day. It's funny how horror always collides with the banal. I love that word. Banal. My best friend thinks it looks too much like the word "anal", but I think it sounds fancy. She's the first person I text when I wake up.

Me: Hey hoe.
Shawnte: We gon beat her ass today fr
Me: Who, lol?
Shawnte: Damzel. Duh.
Me: What she do?

Shawnte always wants to beat someone's ass. It can get exhausting being her best friend, but as my mom likes to point out, getting into fights seems to be the only thing I'm doing to stay in shape. Shawnte is my ride or die so if she says we're beating up Damzel, I guess that's what we're doing.

Speaking of my mom…

"MELANIE!" she shrieks. "GET YOUR BIG FAT ASS DOWNSTAIRS."

The floor to my bedroom rumbles when my mom yells her usual morning wake up call. She's the main reason I've been spending as much time as possible at Enrico's place but… we broke up. I couldn't take all the secrets and lies about strange men showing up in the middle of the night, or his odd disappearances for weeks at a time. He's either on drugs or he's selling drugs. I might throw hands, but I want nothing to do with them. I've seen what they can do to a person, how drugs can change them. *Sigh.*

"I'M UP!" I yell back at my mother, who stomps around downstairs, loudly yelling 'to herself' about what a lazy piece of shit I am.

I pull on a pair of black leggings, my tan Ugg boots and throw on a giant hoodie over a black t-shirt. There is seriously no point in overdressing to go to my lame ass high school. Shawnte says we're beating up Damzel today? I hope she doesn't show up so I can get out of supporting my friend. Shawnte pulled a couple guys off me last week who wanted to fight me in the halls, so I owe her. I cannot fucking *wait* to graduate. I just turned eighteen last week.

My ex was grown and I am so over this high school mess. Enrico was my hope for escape, but our relationship ended, which my mom probably would have predicted. He was too good to be true and then, of course, I discovered his lies and everything fell apart.

"What's taking you so long?" my mom calls up the stairs. "I know you're not trying to look nice for school, you never have so why start now?"

I try not to let her get under my skin. I have enough problems, especially if Shawnte means what she says about beating Damzel's ass. *Damzel could probably kick us across the freaking street. Maybe there's a way out of this.*

I wish I could wear headphones downstairs the rest of the morning but if I show up downstairs wearing them, she'll smack the shit out of me again. I would move out, but the last time I saved up enough for a security deposit and a couple months rent, she broke her foot and I spent all the money I had taking her to the ER.

I don't even have Enrico to rely on anymore...

I shove my books and homework into my green backpack and hurry downstairs before my mom can come up with another somewhat hurtful zinger. By now, I don't really let her jabs get to me, but it's impossible not to be hurt when your mother's hobby seems to be coming up with insults to take you down a peg.

I get downstairs to see her holding a broom and half-dressed for work. Her hair is still in its curlers, her face sour, but done up with makeup. She won't tell me where she works exactly, but I think she must be back waiting tables or something like that. She has enough money for whiskey, which is the most important thing for her.

"You're wearing that to school?" she says. There she goes. I just need to get my breakfast and get the hell out of here. She's so difficult, but if I leave her alone, what the hell will happen to her? The last time I tried, she nearly died.

It would be a dream come true if I never had to come back to this stupid house, but I can't handle the guilt of abandoning her.

I try to act boring, so she doesn't get excited from getting a rise out of me. "Yes, mom. It's the same outfit I wear every day. Leggings and a hoodie. Nothing special."

She inspects me and sets the broom aside, washing her hands and then reaching for her e-cigarette.

"At least your hair doesn't look like shit," she says, puffing on the little blue e-cig and filling the room with a cloud of menthol scented smoke. It's as close to a compliment as I can expect from her.

"Thank you."

She glances at my empty bowl with concern. "What are you eating today?"

I haven't decided yet because eating in front of her is the worst part of my day.

"I don't know. Cereal."

She scoffs, which she would do regardless of what I answered. She has over seventy pounds on me, but she won't stop pestering me about my weight.

"You still seeing that Italian boy?" she asks. This is the fourth time she's brought it up since Friday.

"I told you, we broke up," I grumble. There's no point talking to my mom about Enrico, how much he hurt me, or how much I miss him. I haven't been the same since we broke up and it's not just my emotions that are all over the place.

"I bet he found a nice white girl," she says. "A *skinny* white girl."

She emphasizes the word "skinny" with an odd smirk on her face. I tune her critiques out while I pour myself a bowl of cereal and finish off my breakfast with half a cinnamon raisin bagel coated in cream cheese.

She's still going on about her theories on why Enrico and I ended things. I don't bother correcting her and let her ramble on until I finish my bagel.

"Are you done?" I grumble when I'm ready to head out

the door after finishing up. She doesn't bother with the dishes, so I just leave them until I get home from school. My little comment is enough to trigger her.

"What the fuck was that tone?"

"Good bye, mom," I mutter.

"Get your ass back here by six," she says. "This place is a mess and I'll be working late. I know you enjoy living like a pig, but I don't."

"Okay."

I walk out the door and feel the tightness around my chest unraveling slowly. The longer I spend at home, the harder it becomes to cope with her. I don't miss when my step-dad was around for other reasons, but I miss having a buffer between the two of us. Sometimes.

I look at my phone for Shawnte's response as I walk down the street towards my school. It's only a ten minute walk, but it's only recently I started walking instead of taking the bus. My mom keeps getting on me for my weight. She won't help me get any healthy food, and she *hates* the idea of me going to the gym where she claims thuggish men on steroids with small dicks and huge egos hang out.

When I point out I've never seen her go to the gym, so how would she know... well, let's just say that never ends well.

Shawnte: She made out with Javier, first of all.
Me: Who dat?
Shawnte: From last Friday...

Keeping track of Shawnte's conquests is harder than keeping track of all the characters on *Game of Thrones*. I text her back that I'll talk to her at school and that I'm almost there. I thought Javier and Damzel were an item, but I guess I don't keep up with gossip at our high school. I'm too busy trying not to get the shit kicked out of me or get into another fight. *I won't be able to avoid one today. This place is hell.*

As I walk to school, I slip my headphones on and try to drown out the shitty, awful and completely boring world around me. I shuffle through my playlist until I hear a song that will help me dissociate with the world for the next few minutes of my walk before I have to deal with the god-awful students at my school. As I walk, I try to envision I'm in a music video and not on my way to living hell.

I avoid a group of pigeons picking apart pieces of smushed white bread against the pavement as I close in on our school compound. Not quite a music video moment. I step around a few splatters of pigeon shit and see a couple people I recognize walking into the school gates.

This place is my worst nightmare. Thinking about meeting up with Enrico was the only thing keeping me going in this shithole and I don't even have that anymore. It'll be a damn miracle if I graduate. Why do I even care? My own mom thinks my life is worthless. What's the point? I don't have a boyfriend, a mother who loves me… I don't have anyone except my best friend, Shawnte. And she has her own problems.

Shawnte hangs out in the student lounge every morning, so if I make it past the pack of student athletes, I can get to safety where we can talk about the school day and whose ass we need to beat. Hopefully I can talk her out of the Damzel thing.

I walk through the school gates and, despite having my hoodie up, I can't make it in undetected.

"The whale has landed. The beached whale has landed," he repeats, curling his hands around his mouth to make a fake megaphone. Alex sits at a lunch table with his buddies. They're all douchebags, but Alex is the biggest douche out of all of them. He's not even attractive, but he acts like he's the hottest guy in school because he's the second string varsity quarterback.

His buddy Mike follows up with whale noises and the table hoots with laughter. I just need to keep walking past them and pretend they aren't saying anything. Their opinions don't matter… *Don't let them get to you.*

"Hey, Melanie," Alex calls. "Are you seriously ignoring me?"

Yes. Obviously. I keep walking past them, but Alex won't let it go. He jumps away from the picnic table and runs up to me, yanking on my hair… *hard.* I scream as searing pain shoots through my scalp. I only got this sew-in done last week and the woman who does my hair doesn't believe human beings are capable of feeling pain. I've been on a regular dose of Advil since my hair appointment, but my scalp is still tender as fuck.

"What the fuck is wrong with you?" I yell at him.

"Get out of our fucking way," he says as he pushes me. "Fat bitch. Keep it fucking moving."

I'm not in the mood to fight a gang of obnoxious school bullies so I settle for smoothing my clothes and telling Alex and the rest of his idiot buddies that they can fuck off with their tiny dicks. They seem to find my comment hilarious.

"Every dick must look tiny to a fat bitch like you," Alex calls after me. It's not even an intelligent or funny comment, but his collection of bandits clearly doesn't give a fuck.

I walk into the school hallways and immediately see Shawnte leaning against her locker. My heart pounds. I hate them, but at least I made it.

She doesn't notice me at first, but when she does, she screams my name and runs towards me to give me a hug. You would swear we don't see each other every day the way Shawnte acts. She seems like she's in a good mood, which means I have a good chance of talking her out of beating up Damzel. It's just not worth it.

Shawnte lifts me off the ground and screams, "Happy fucking Monday, girl!"

The world around us disappears, and our distraction becomes an opportunity for Damzel to strike. I feel Shawnte ripped out of my arms and she screams as Damzel yanks her by her hair and drags her to the ground. Apparently, Shawnte's hair wasn't sewn in, so her wig goes flying as Damzel knocks her own.

"I know you weren't texting my man, you trifling ass hoe!" Damzel yells, slamming her Fila Disruptor into Shawnte's stomach. I can't stand by and watch my friend get into some mess like this. I push Damzel against the locker and slam my fists into the side of her face as hard as possible. She is *much* bigger than me and it only occurs to me how fucking stupid a choice this was when she pushes back and sends me flying across the room.

No one at this school gives a crap when a fight breaks out, but we probably only have a few minutes before one of those guards that's supposed to stop us from stabbing the fuck out of each other shows up. Damzel grabs my hair and that searing pain shoots through my skull again.

She slams my head against the locker and the room threatens to go black. Oh hell no. I can't let this hoe win in a fight. I push back against Damzel and try to kick her as hard as I can. She hits me in the head again and I hear a loud crack somewhere in my face. I hit her in the stomach and I hear Shawnte yelling, "Beat her ass, Melanie!"

Beat her fucking ass!

Damzel grabs me by the strings of my hoodie and then shoves me against the locker again, hitting me in the face with another well-formed fist. I cry out as I lose consciousness completely...

．　．　．

WHEN I WAKE UP, I'm in the nurse's office lying on one of the beds for students who have the flu. Yuck. I hope this place doesn't make me sick. I sit up and groan. My head hurts and my face… There's something on my face. I walk to the sink and mirror in the room and fuck, I look bad. My mom will kill me when she sees my face. My nose hurts so much. I stupidly try touching it and wince as I do.

I open the door and the nurse notices me right away. She was just leaving one of the other rooms and turns to me with a smile.

"You're awake. Thank goodness. We had a team come look at you. The principal wants you in the office once you feel ready to head over there on your own."

"My face still hurts."

"Yes," the school nurse says. "That would be the broken nose."

She takes my blood, and disappears for a few minutes before coming back with some Tylenol.

"What was the blood for?"

"Just standard, hun," she says, and I leave it at that.

Once I get to the principal's office, I knock on the door, hoping I lucked out and that there's no one inside.

"Come in, Melanie."

I open the door and take a seat next to Shawnte, who's looking pretty bad. My best friend holds her wig in her hands and gazes down at her knees in shame. Her wig cap holds securely to her head, but she doesn't exactly look glamorous in this position.

"Don't even think about speaking to each other."

I know from the nurse's office that I look like absolute shit, so the two of us together probably look like a couple of mafia members.

"We have a zero tolerance policy for violence at this high school. *Zero.* This isn't the first time both of you have been in my office but this time, you have both gone too far."

"Melanie was just trying to defend me," Shawnte says. "Whatever consequences there are should be mine and mine alone."

The principal steams ahead, ignoring Shawnte's pleas for my freedom.

"I saw the footage of the fight. There were no efforts made to de-escalate the situation and when I spoke to Damzel, she provided significant evidence that her move was defensive."

"She defensively pulled my friend's wig off?" I blurt out. It's not a good idea to push back against the principal considering our predicament, but it doesn't make any sense. We didn't start the fight. How can starting a fight be considered a defensive move?

The principal glares at me. Shawnte glares at her right back. This isn't fair and everyone in this room knows it.

"Listen, we will help you enroll in new high schools so you can graduate on time, but both of you are expelled effective immediately."

"What?" The principal's tone sends panic shooting straight through me. There's no way they can expel us without a hearing, right? Don't we get a chance to defend ourselves?

As if reading my mind, the principal continues. "This is a final decision and is in complete alignment with school policy. Clear out your lockers and leave campus immediately. Thank you."

She purses her lips and stares down at her desk as if we were somehow forcing her to go through this difficult experience, and as if her awkwardness about the situation could match the horror faced by both me and Shawnte. I'm eighteen. I don't have a job and I was counting on graduating high school so I could enroll in a nearby college to get an even better paying job.

There's nothing I can do as my world spirals. Nobody speaks to me or Shawnte as we clear out our lockers. They feel sorry for us and it absolutely fucking sucks to be the object of someone's pity. Not even Alex and his idiot goons say anything as we walk past the pool of our peers with a free period gathered in the hallway to soak up as much of the gossip as possible to spill to their group chats. They snicker, but say nothing. It's humiliating.

Where do I go after this? I wanted to get out of high school, but I needed that damn diploma. How will I ever escape my mom, or escape Queens without a fucking high school diploma? *I'm screwed.*

When Shawnte and I get to the sidewalk, she offers to walk me home since I live closer. Shawnte spins her wig around on her fingers and cracks jokes, avoiding the subject of our expulsion. When we get about a block away from my house, she sighs and turns to me.

"So. Wasn't fair what happened to you today," she says, sounding genuinely sorry, but all too calm. Doesn't she worry about the future? I wish I could be as carefree as Shawnte sometimes.

"I know," I tell her. "It's fine. I'll handle it."

She keeps twirling her wig around her finger, the wig cap glued to her head peeling off a little due to sweat. "You need help dealing with your mom?" she offers.

"The type of help I need could land us both in prison," I mutter. My mom will probably add to Damzel's blows. It would probably be a good idea to plan my defensive moves in my head before heading back there.

Shawnte laughs at my dark joke. "If you need anything, call me."

"What about your parents?" I ask. "Aren't you worried?"

Shawnte chuckles. "Are you crazy? Of course I'm worried. My mom will kick my ass when she finds out. I'm packing my bag and getting the hell out of there before she's done with work. I'm going to live with my brother in New Jersey. He loves surprises."

I'm tempted to run away with Shawnte. We could either get jobs or go to public school in New Jersey, which would most likely be a far more favorable outcome than facing my mother's wrath. She might freak out even more if she heard I was in New Jersey, though and who knows what crazy shit she would do then.

"Call me when you get there."

"I'll be back once she calms down," Shawnte says, wrapping me in a big hug.

As we stand there, I can't see how the next few months of my life are going to go without her. To help me through this break up, the expulsion, and dealing with my psychotic mother. We finally reluctantly let go, and Shawnte gives me a sly grin.

"At least we got her ass," Shawnte says as we pull away from each other. "Taught that hoe a lesson."

"We sure did, girl."

Although, I'm pretty sure Damzel did more damage since I ended up unconscious with a broken nose and a completely effed up face. Shawnte walks away towards her house and I knock on the door to my mom's place. She doesn't answer, so I use my key to get in, hoping desperately that she's not home.

The second my foot steps on the welcome mat, my mother screams, "Hello, dropout! Welcome home."

Fuck. I hope I can slip around her, but she rounds the corner before I can get away and puts her hands on her hips, blocking my way. My chest tightens once I see the look in her eye. She has the ass-whooping look about her, and I know from the last incident I had with her that she hasn't ascended above a good ass-whooping.

"Hey."

There's a part of me secretly hoping that she'll notice the bruises on my face and scoop me into her arms, telling me it will all be okay. I desperately want to cry and I want this shitty day to end because no matter what I do, it keeps getting worse. My lower lip trembles and my mother scoffs.

"Wipe that look off your face. I just got off the phone with the nurse at your school."

"Great," I say to her, trying not to break down in front of her. That would only make her mood even worse than it already is. "Then you know I broke my nose."

"Yeah, I also know you're pregnant."

Her eyes turn to hard black beads as she stares at me. It's not quite a glare, but it's penetrating, cruel and filled with absolute disgust.

"What?" I whisper.

"They tested your blood as part of their standard procedure. You're pregnant."

Now I want to collapse and die on the spot. I wish there was a way I could just will myself to spontaneously combust, but not even the redness rushing to my cheeks and pressure building in my skull seems to force me to explode.

"I'm not..."

"Yes you are, you dirty little hoe. Do you at least know who the father is?"

"I–

Of course I do. It's Enrico. He's the only guy I've ever been with and he... *Oh God...* I bend over, hyperventilating as the reality of my situation hits me. I'm pregnant from my ex. This is the worst-case scenario and I can't get any oxygen into my lungs. No sooner do I take in that first full breath of air than my mother hits me in the stomach with a curled fist. I double over and cry immediately despite myself.

It's all the pressure building up in me. It's the news that I'm pregnant. It's the expulsion from school and the bullying that made school miserable in the first place. Losing my best friend to New Jersey doesn't help either. She hits me again and I scream at her to stop which only gets her angrier.

"You're hitting my stomach!" I yell at her, trying to dodge her blows. I've never felt more protective in my life, even if the news hasn't hit me, a strange instinct activates and I shield myself from her next fist.

"You don't have a baby daddy," she says calmly, swinging at my head and missing as I start to realize I'll have to fight back again and get the hell out of here.

"It's for the best that someone knocks that baby out of your hoe ass." She manages to get out in between swings. I keep dodging her, stumbling backwards and tripping over objects and furniture in the room. I don't want to hit her, but the only way out of here might be fighting back. *Where the hell will I go? I can't let her kill me.*

I push her back as she tries swinging at my head again. Her body moves easily and my strength surprises me. I'm terrified she'll hurt me. My nose throbs from earlier and I'm sore from the fight, but I have to escape. My mom screams as she stumbles over in a manner far more dramatic than the force I used to push her.

"You tried to kill me!" she shrieks. "You tried to kill me!"

I push her again and sprint up to my room. She falls over and even if I feel guilty, my heart races so fast that I can't stop and think about it. I just have to get out of here. I barricade myself in my bedroom, knowing I'll have to leave eventually and that it'll be hell once I do. I drag an Adidas duffel bag out from underneath my bed and stuff it with clothes, my cell phone, my laptop, a few chargers and a couple days worth of clothes. Lots of underwear. And all the money I have left. My hands shake as I pack as quickly as possible. My mom keeps yelling downstairs and threatening to call the cops on me for being a "violent little bitch".

She's still yelling when I'm done packing, but I have to get past her and this is my only shot. I grab the chair from beneath the door and walk down the stairs as calmly as I can.

"Oh, your bitch ass finally decided to face me, huh?" she says once she sees me appearing at the foot of the stairs. "Where the fuck do you think you're going?"

Enrico. He's the only person I have and even if I dumped him… it's different now. I'm pregnant with his baby and I don't want much from him, I don't need him to look after the baby. I just need a place to rest my head for a few days until I figure out how to get on my feet.

"I'm staying at a friends."

"Not that slut, Shawnte, I hope," she hisses.

My mom hates Shawnte, but she also hates most people, so I don't take her shady little statements seriously.

"No. Not with Shawnte."

"I'm not letting you leave this house," she says, stiffening her body.

As I TRY to make my way towards the door, my mom barricades herself in front of it.

"Get out of the way," I tell her, trying to sound forceful, but ultimately fearing that she'll throw her hands at me and make the injuries from my previous fight worse.

"Or what?" she says.

The force in my voice surprises me.

"Or nothing," I snap at her. "I just need to leave. I need to get out of here."

My desire to escape this hell, of always being under her control, always having to listen to her rants and always feeling so damn small trump everything, including my fear. I have to leave and I don't care what she says or does to me.

"If you leave this house you're never allowed back."

If I do this, there's no going back.

"I don't care."

"Nobody will ever love you the way I do," she hisses at me.

I hope not.

"Good bye, mom."

I TAKE the subway to the Upper West Side and head over to Enrico's place. I know I should have called first but I didn't exactly have time and this is the type of news I should give in person. I'll build up to it slowly. Enrico will understand...

I get to the front door of his brownstone and knock. And knock. Nobody answers. I call Enrico, but he doesn't answer. I ring the doorbell, knock some more and then call him three more times. I know we broke up, but this isn't like him. I keep knocking and calling his name until his neighbor pops out of her house. I've met her a couple times before, but this time she has a black hoodie pulled up to hide her face and she glances around furtively before pressing her fingers to her lips.

"Melanie, quiet," she hisses.

"Zariyah? What's wrong."

She looks terrified.

"Everything," she says. "You looking for Enrico?"

"Yes."

"Enrico's dead. He's been missing since last week. I asked around and..." Zariyah's eyes water. "It's mob related. Trust me, girl. He's gone."

She squeezes my forearm. I appreciate her effort to comfort me, but it's like offering a band-aid to someone you just smacked with a wrecking ball. I don't want this to be real, but Zariyah keeps talking, describing a suspicious detective who stopped by, a couple tattooed guys dressed in black and then even more tattooed muscular Italian men moving furniture and tarps out of the place.

"I left Boston to get away from people like this, but it's safer for me to move back. Don't stick around. Go back to wherever you came from and forget you ever heard the name Enrico Zagarella."

I have a million questions to ask Zariyah, but the door to Enrico's apartment thrusts open and I see a man who looks exactly like my ex-boyfriend, only two decades older. He can only be one person...

He scowls at me. "What do you want? Who are you?"

Zariyah disappears back into her place and slams the door shut, sliding the bolt through the door. Damn, girl. Cold. Once she disappears, the man in Enrico's apartment reaches out and grabs my forearm. The first thing I notice about him is how big his hands are. He squeezes and drags me towards the door.

"Come inside."

HE DOESN'T GIVE me a choice and frankly, I don't have one.

* * *

Chapter 2
Unruly Teenager
Sammy Zagarella

Present Day

I don't know why the fuck my cousins and my brother think I need *therapy*. I lost my son. What the fuck is a therapist going to do about it, bring my son back? There's no therapy for this shit. There's nothing that can heal the absolute fucking heartbreak I'm going through. There's only one fucking way to get through this shit and it's to go through it.

But my brother insists... so here I am. In a fucking psychotherapist's office. All I can think is that I fucking hate this place and it doesn't matter that the therapist is a knock out because I don't want to fucking be here.

Dr. Rebecca Gabriel sits across from me in a tight-fitting red dress that should be fucking illegal. She has heels to match the dress and a dog curled up next to her vintage leather chair. John swears this is the best therapist in Long Island. I don't know. The best fucking therapist in the world couldn't help with my problems because most people, no matter how fucked up they are, didn't grow up with a mobster's life.

I'm older than John and Lucky, I've seen far more shit than they have, and I don't have any more reasons to live. I don't need therapy, I need a fucking .22 and three bullets. One bullet could do the trick, but you want to get the others in before the shock gets you. I've been shot before, so working up the courage to take the bullet wouldn't be the problem.

There's something odd forcing me to cling to life, like I'm not done here yet despite my desire to end the whole fucking pony show and finally sink into peaceful fucking blackness.

"HOW LONG HAVE you had this suicidal ideation?" Dr. Gabriel asks. The pit bull sleeping at her feet yawns. The collar around her neck jingles and I read the name on it – Taylor Mae Davis. Strange name for a dog.

"I never said I was suicidal."

"Right. You just want to… shoot yourself in the head?"

I hate it here. These people make regular fucking shit sound so dramatic. Everyone wants to off themselves at one point or another.

I shrug. "You seen the shit I've seen, you'd want to do the same."

She purses her lips. Red lipstick. This woman must love the fuck outta the color red. Everything in here is so red it makes my head hurt. I thought therapy ought to be fucking soothing. With the red and the black leather, this place looks like a pleasure palace.

What the fuck, John? This head shrink had better be fucking good.

"I've worked with a lot of men like you, Sammy," she says. "I sense you're holding back."

Holding back is a survival strategy in our world. You talk

too much, you open your fucking mouth and someone puts a bullet in your head. It happened to my son. I should have taught him better. If I'd taught him better, this shit would have never happened. He failed the test of loyalty. The Vicari family holds no sympathy for rats, for the disloyal. I raised a rat. That hurts. I could have saved his life if I hadn't been such a fuck up…

Does this head shrink understand how hard it is to love the people who killed your son and to blame yourself, even if you weren't anywhere near him when they put a bullet in his head? Lucky promises they were respectful but… *I should have been there during his last moments.*

"There's nothing for us to talk about. My son died. I'm fucked up…" I grumble.

"You reported in your intake form that you thought you were having auditory hallucinations."

Or as we say on planet earth, hearing fucking voices. John's overreacting to what happened. I squeeze the leather arms of the chair and try to focus on Dr. Gabriel. *Ignore the red walls, the red lips, the red tongue hanging out of the fucking dog's mouth.* It's like there's a necktie getting progressively tighter around my neck. They should serve beer in therapy.

"It's not a big deal. My cousins… they got me to a doctor. I got sleep medicine and that all went away."

"Are you sure, Sammy?" she asks. "Are you sure you don't hear voices telling you what to do?"

"Yeah. I think they're gone."

She uncrosses her legs and then runs her tongue over the red lipstick. None of it comes off. Dr. Gabriel's eyes return to mine. They're large, dark and intense. What is the fucking point of this?

"Can you describe these auditory hallucinations to me, Sammy?" she says, scribbling notes on a stupid clipboard. The sound irritates the fuck outta me but I don't want to act all jumpy in here and give her a reason to prescribe me some other shit that forces me not to drink. If I was still drinking, I wouldn't have any of these fucking problems because I would be asleep or dead or whatever the fuck.

I describe the hallucinations to her and she nods, taking more furious notes and then staring at me for far too long when I stop talking. I will run this fucking hour out if she makes me. Unfortunately, Dr. Gabriel doesn't have any intentions of letting me off scot-free.

"Is that the only thing going on, Sammy?"

"No. My dead son's girlfriend is pregnant and she's staying at my place for a while. It's driving me nuts. How could he... How could he be such a fucking idiot as to do that, huh? But I can't exactly ask him, can I?"

I realize I'm talking to myself, but ain't that what I'm paying for? It's not like this doctor with all her fancy credentials has any of the necessary skills to survive the life that I live.

"How is she driving you nuts?" Dr. Gabriel asks. "Difficult house guest?"

"No. Perfect house guest. A little too quiet maybe. It's just that... She's pregnant and a high school dropout, and I don't know what the fuck to do about her. She ain't ready to be a mom, but I'm supposed to send her out into the world and... I dunno."

"What do you want to do, Sammy?"

I can't confess that – not even to a fancy therapist paid to hear mind fuckery like what's in my head.

"I want my bloodline to be cared for. I want this girl to be a suitable mother. She's the last person I would choose for my son to settle down with, but now, I'm stuck with her."

"Is there any way you could make the best of the situation?"

I've thought of what my therapist has suggested before.

"You mean force her into my bed?"

Dr. Gabriel purses her lips. "No, Sammy. That's not what I meant."

"How else could I make the best of it?"

"Molesting her certainly wasn't what I had in mind."

"It's a trade, not molestation. I'm offering her copious amounts of care, and honestly, she is rather difficult..."

The girl comes to me with a broken nose and my heir in her womb... What sort of high school girl gets into such violent fights that they end with a broken nose? I don't know what kind of girl this is, but I doubt I can survive the duration of her pregnancy without some salve for putting up with her attitude.

"Perhaps she's difficult because she's been through something traumatic," Dr. Gabriel says. "Listen, Sammy. She's a young girl who just lost her boyfriend and found out some devastating news. I know you want to help her, but you have to try listening to her. Have you asked her how she feels about the situation?"

This is why everyone fucking hates therapists. All this feelings talk makes me instantly sick to my stomach.

"Has anyone ever mentioned you should serve beer here?"

She won't let me change the subject.

"Sammy. Answer the question."

"Her feelings don't matter. She got herself into this situation when she went to bed with my son. It's only out of the goodness of my heart that I haven't left her to her fate."

Dr. Gabriel shifts uncomfortably, but she doesn't seem upset. She seems fascinated and I hate feeling like a bug trapped beneath a clear jar. This vintage leather chair has to be worse than a straitjacket.

"I don't have to ask how she feels. She lost someone she

loves. She feels like shit because the whole world is shit and it doesn't take a fucking genius to figure that out."

Dr. Gabriel stares at me blankly. Taylor Mae Davis stares too with creepy yellowish eyes. If you showed that dog to the wrong Zagarella, Taylor Mae would likely spend her whole life ripping other dogs' throats out. It's probably for the best that she stays right here with Dr. Gabriel.

"That's how *you* feel, Sammy," she says. "You're projecting how you feel onto her, but you have no idea how she feels because you didn't ask. She's your only living connection to your son, but you're afraid to let her in."

"I have no reason to let her in. My son and I… We weren't close. If we were close, maybe he wouldn't have died."

"You can't blame yourself for what happened to him."

"Hm."

"I sense your resentment, Sammy."

Does she also sense my desire to drown in a bottle of tequila? I don't know how she expects me to face Melanie, much less talk to her. I haven't talked to her since I met her outside of Enrico's place ten days ago outside of exchanging pleasantries and the bare minimum.

"I would expect as much considering the cost of this appointment."

Dr. Gabriel ignores my comment. "Your assignment for this week is to get to know Melanie. Find out her likes and dislikes. She's carrying your grandchild and she's a scared teenage girl. She needs to know that she isn't going through this alone."

How the fuck do I break it to Dr. Gabriel that the kid is absolutely going through this alone. She won't tell me how to find her parents, she claims she had to drop out of high school, and she won't tell me where her school is. She's difficult and all she does is cry all day and… she's nothing that I want to deal with. I have my own problems.

Dr. Gabriel raises an eyebrow like she can read my mind. "You have your own problems, yes. But it might help you to focus on someone else for a while and take your mind off things. You never know."

I grunt in response and let Dr. Gabriel carry on the conversation in a more idle direction. I talk to her about work, the construction business I'll be carrying on with Aiden Murray in Jamaica, Queens and then the business we'll work on together in Boston if our partnership works well. Talking about business is far easier than talking about my personal life or the frustrating teenager I have at home. Dr. Gabriel reminds me of my assignment when I leave her office, and I think about how the hell I'm supposed to talk to some kid I barely know about their life problems while dealing with mine at the same time.

WHEN I APPROACH MY HOUSE, I regret not driving off a bridge instead of coming here. I can hear Big Tex barking loudly and Melanie yelling at him even louder.

"BIG TEX GIVE ME MY UGGS BACK."

Yes, I can hear both of them from *outside*. I've thoroughly enjoyed the peace and quiet of living with only my retired greyhound up until this point. He *used* to have a calm and settled personality until Melanie moved in and turned him into a hyperactive monster. I hear Melanie shriek and then the sounds of Big Tex crashing into something.

Christ.

"Melanie! Big Tex! What the hell is going on here?!" I yell as I walk through the front door.

Melanie lies on her back with her hands gripping the leg of her Ugg boot. Big Tex has his mouth wrapped around the sole of her shoe, tugging with all his might. She shrieks and tries to drag it away from him, but Big Tex thinks she's playing a very exciting game and successfully gets the boots away from Melanie.

She cries out and hits her head on the ground as Big Tex tears off to the other end of my house with her boot.

"UGH!" Melanie shouts with exasperation, trying to stand up and nearly rolling over. I extend a hand to help her up, which she reluctantly takes. When she stands up, I struggle to hide my amusement. She looks like a mess. Her hair is everywhere, her sweater is shifted to the side, and her face is slick with a thin layer of sweat.

"He got you worked up, huh?"

"I'm fine," she responds defensively. "Your dog needs obedience school."

I have to try to get to know her. *Be kind.* It's hard and unfamiliar.

"Did you order anything to eat?"

"You won't let me have any fast food, so no. I haven't ordered anything," Melanie says huffily. She's only eighteen. Teenagers are unruly. I can't take it personally.

"You're pregnant. You can't have fast food," I remind her. "I want you to do what's best for the baby and I'm responsible for your well-being."

"Whatever."

Melanie storms off to the guest bedroom downstairs, a few feet off the kitchen, and shuts the door behind her. I guess that's our conversation for the day and it isn't exactly a glowing success. I walk to the door of Melanie's bedroom and knock a couple times.

"Do you want me to order dinner?" I offer.

"No," Melanie calls back. "I'm going to bed."

It's only 7:30 P.M. We've been through this before, so I just leave her alone. She won't change her mind and she'll probably sneak to the fridge at midnight like she did the other nights she's been here and needed something to eat.

I ORDER delivery from the Jamaican vegan restaurant a few blocks away and enjoy fried plantains, rice, and kidney beans with a delicious sauce along with a side salad. It's amazing and I order an extra plate for Melanie in case she gets hungry in the middle of the night. Eating alone sucks, but there's no point in calling John or Lucky.

I don't want to talk about the shrink, or Enrico, or how fucking hard it is to close my eyes and see anything but blood. *They followed orders, just like I would've done.*

We've always done what we were told, especially my cousins. I can't fault them.

I can't worry about them now, anyway. I have a bigger problem, a pregnant and very *curvy* problem. It's not like I think about her curves, but it's hard not to notice them. I'm a man, not a robot. She has very large breasts for a girl her age, and a nice bum. I rather like the extra weight on her. Her round, soft-looking cheeks, although currently bruised up, make it much easier to deal with her frustrating attitude. Pretty girl, for an eighteen-year-old.

I've kept Melanie out of trouble by some fucking miracle, and now I'm alone in a peaceful city with no one in the world who I can really trust. I sigh to myself as the thought leaves, and stand up to head to bed. I pass through the kitchen on my way up, and take my sleeping pills from the bottle in the cupboard. I have to take the new pills Dr. Gabriel prescribed before bed.

It's the only chance I have of falling asleep.

* * *

Chapter 3
Night Terrors
Melanie

Sammy doesn't know what happens to him in the middle of the night. All the time I've stayed with him, his new sleeping pills from his therapist turn him into a raving maniac. I swear, the problem started with the pills. It was the night he left the vegan food from the Jamaican restaurant in the fridge for me, the night I saw the little orange bottle in the kitchen and tried to remember the name – I couldn't.

He talks to himself all night and I can hear his footsteps in his bedroom above me along with his guilt-ridden ramblings. I don't know how much of what Sammy says is true, but if even half of what he says has a basis of truth, *he's a monster and the pills make it worse.*

My body curls up on the memory foam mattress in Sammy's guest bedroom as I listen to him start his ranting for the night over the sound of the storm outside. Last night, he talked to some vision of Enrico's mother and ended the night screaming at himself, calling himself names and all types of crazy shit. Enrico told me her name was Maria, so I recognized the name as Sammy spoke.

He scares the crap out of me, especially when he doesn't stick to his crazy man routine. Tonight is different and I feel it. He isn't loud or obnoxious like he was before.

His footsteps slow down and he isn't talking to himself, just walking across the top floor of his house. There's nothing inherently wrong with that, but I notice everything about Sammy's habits and how they change. It's in my best interests. I know he wants to do right by me. He can't help that he's terrifying. I hear Sammy walk down the stairs and while I think it's strange because he doesn't come downstairs once he retires to his bedroom, I mustn't think much of it because I close my eyes and drift into temporary sleep.

I can't have been asleep for long. My door swings inward and my eyes snap open. I know he's in my bedroom even before my vision adjusts to the darkness. My body paralyzes in fear. Rain pounds against the window. Thunder booms outside and lightning flashes, illuminating Sammy's silhouette in my doorway. He's a beastly hulk of a man, towering over 6'7" tall and thick with muscles. He must eat an entire cow a day to stay that big. He has a raw, chiseled jawline with a beard that he doesn't shave regularly so he looks like a wild man. The thick brown hair spilling down his neck in an unwieldy tangled mess reminds me of *Tarzan*.

Even Tarzan had more inborn civility than Sammy. My chest tightens in fear as he stands in the doorway. *He's naked. Holy fuck, he's naked.* Well, he has underwear on, but other than that, he might as well be naked. His underwear shows everything – the dick *and* the balls. I've never been exposed to a guy this way before, without knowing it was coming and without expecting to see the shape of his ass and entire package lewdly before me as I'm trying to sleep.

If I say anything, he'll know I'm awake and right now, he doesn't seem to be aware of anything. With another flash of lightning, I can see him staring off into the distance, his eyes appearing to not be fixed on anything. He doesn't speak, he just stands there and the bulge in his pants expands before me as my eyes adjusts. *He's hard. He's naked, hard and standing in my bedroom.*

I don't think he's awake, either. Even if it scares the crap out of me, my only way out of this is checking to see if he's awake. He could be sleepwalking. I already know he's crazier than a bat out of hell, so sleepwalking could surely be on the table. My heart races. *He's Enrico's father. He has to have some of the good parts of Enrico in him.*

"Sammy," I whisper. He doesn't move. He just keeps staring. I don't know how to react to his strange behavior aside from trying to wake him up and guide him out of the room. I say his name louder in case he isn't hearing me because of the rain. He doesn't respond. I start to sit up in bed, hoping the movement will wake him up, but he doesn't even look towards me. Instead, Sammy slips his hands into his underwear and touches his dick.

I freeze halfway up.. My ex-boyfriend's dad is sleepwalking and sleep… touching himself?

"Fuck…" he groans as he strokes his shaft in front of me. Now I really don't know if I should wake him up. I don't know how he'll react or if I'll make the situation worse by drawing more of his attention to me. Sammy throws his head back and groans with pleasure as he strokes his shaft. My thighs twitch. It's strangely hot watching him stroke himself with reckless abandon and vocalize his pleasure. He's jacking himself off in his sleep and letting himself go more than he ever does when he's awake around me.

I freeze and stare at the outline of Sammy's body. His hair brushes the back of his neck, and I watch as he pumps his shaft. He moans again and the sound of it sends a shiver straight to my core. What the fuck is wrong with me?

I bite on my lower lip as he changes pace and lets out a

low growl. I can feel a puddle of wetness pooling at the apex of my thighs and my lip might burst if I bite down on it any harder. I need to get a fucking grip.

"Oh, fuck," Sammy groans. "I need this... I need this..."

He stops stroking himself suddenly and I think he might have finished, except his dick is still way too hard and his underwear seems to be dry. *Maybe this is the best time to wake him up.* I turn on the lamp on the bedside table. Sammy doesn't react and I can make him out more clearly. His body is completely fucked up with a mixture of scars and tattoos. He's so jacked that he could probably break me in half and I'm no skinny minnie.

Holy fuck he's hot. I hate comparing him to Enrico, but right now, they couldn't be more different. Sammy's older. More scuffed up by life. He's rugged and so fucking sexy. But he's still asleep. His eyes are open but completely glazed over. If I had the lights on in the first place, I would have never mistaken him for being awake.

"I need a *cunt*. Fuck, I can't stand it."

He's still asleep. This is another one of his crazy rants except instead of confining himself to his bedroom upstairs, Sammy's half-naked ass wandered into my bedroom and I'm fucking terrified of waking up a man twice my size with an erection that's unreasonably big. I shouldn't compare it to anything but it's the biggest cock I've ever seen.

"Maybe you should go to sleep," I tell him, trying to act naturally and go along with the sleepwalking man's madness. Hyping him up can't exactly work out in my favor.

"No," he says, his hands returning to his underwear. "I need to... It's been so long..."

"What do you need?"

"I told you..." he sounds gruff and I almost don't believe he's asleep.

I climb out of bed and wave my hands in front of his face. He doesn't react. I'm so scared that I can feel my stomach start to churn. I freeze once I'm sure he's asleep. I'm too close to him and he's too hard. This is dangerous for both of us, but most importantly for me. I'm pregnant with this man's grandson, I can't have him rearranging my guts with his ten inch dick.

"Tell me again," I say to him confidently. *This will work. I can talk him out of this.*

"I need to cum."

"You have your hand down your pants. Just do it."

I can't believe I fucking said that to Sammy. Just saying it makes me want to throw up, but I don't want to wake this man up and escalate the situation, if it's even possible for this to get worse. Sammy makes a low growl in the back of his throat and strokes his cock a bit.

"That never works," he mumbles bitterly. "I've never been able to without... a *real* woman. I never... Fuck... I can't..."

He takes his hand out of his briefs again. His ass is ridiculously big for a white guy. There isn't any sagging at all, just pure muscle bulging through the fabric. His thighs are equally muscular and defined. Sammy's cock bulges forward lewdly, his erection showing absolutely no chance of subsiding.

"You should go call up one of your girls then."

"I don't have any," he growls. His hands are back in his pants and he's jacking himself off furiously. I can't take my eyes off him. He's just so passionate and fucking wild about it because he's asleep and doesn't have any reason to feel shame or inhibition about what he's doing.

"Sammy..."

"Yes..."

He shows no signs of slowing down. I move closer to him,

hoping that maybe I can slowly guide him out of the room. I press my hand to his chest in an attempt to push him out, but he takes his free hand and grabs my wrist the second it touches his chest. I gasp loudly, but that doesn't wake him up. He still has that blank stare. His pupils are wide, covering his murky green eyes. His other hand is still in his pants, but he's slowed down stroking himself.

He grasps me tightly and holds me in place.

"Cunt," he whispers. "Give... me..."

"No," I say to him. "Sammy... *no!*"

The terror in my voice does something to him and his hand falls away from me. I stumble back a few feet. He takes his hands out of his pants and his breathing starts to slow down. I can't tell if he's falling deeper into sleep or waking up. *Please, just leave.*

"I can't hurt her," he murmurs. "She has the hottest ass I've ever seen but I can't hurt her."

He seems unaware of my presence again, which I definitely prefer.

"Who are you talking about?"

"Pregnant Melanie," he mutters. "Great fucking tits. Nice ass. Can't touch her. Can't even fucking think about it."

"Go to bed, Sammy," I whisper. "Please... go to bed."

I'm trembling with terror, but mostly surprise. Great fucking tits? Nice ass? Sammy's barely looked twice at me. I don't take my eyes off him, just in case he pounces. He sighs and pulls back. *I'm safe.*

"Yeah. You're right, kid," he whispers. "I gotta go to bed."

He walks out of my room. The second he's gone, I run to the door and slide a chair under it so he can't get back in. My heart's beating so hard I can't control my shaking hands. Tears slide down my face. What the fuck.

What the fuck just happened? I feel like I just escaped something horrible by the skin of my teeth and I don't know what in the world it even was. This is worse than his night terrors or whatever keeps him screaming upstairs.

I feel like I need to call someone for help, or to just tell someone what happened, but I don't know who. I don't have anyone in this world anymore, and have a baby on the way. What the fuck am I supposed to do?

Chapter 4
Pounding Headache
Sammy

I can't stop thinking about killing. I wake up with a pounding headache and I'm fucking cold. I don't know where my clothes went, but eventually I find an old *Islanders* hoodie and a pair of black sweatpants. It ain't exactly glamorous, but whatever. I throw my hair up in a low bun at the back of my head and feel around for some painkillers. I want something stronger than ibuprofen, but I don't have the luxury of ending up like Lucky.

I need to fix my fucked up head. My phone buzzes with a reminder of my appointment with the therapist today. Whatever. I'm itching for John to call me with a job, even if I know there won't be any more jobs. I don't know what my fucking deal is. I think about killing the way I used to think about sex.

It's been ages since I've... done it. Sex. Cum. Masturbation. Whatever. When I'm awake, I don't think about sex anymore. Just murder.

I head downstairs for breakfast with Big Tex on my heels. As I walk into the kitchen I look over at Melanie, who's sitting at the counter. Already she's avoiding eye contact with me.

"G'morning, Melanie," I grunt after several minutes of her pretending I don't exist while I meticulously weigh out the ingredients for my morning protein shake.

"Good morning," she mutters. Why the fuck does she sound so mad? It must be the pregnancy. I remember my therapist's advice when I glance over at her and notice that she looks about twice as mad as she sounds. *Fuck.* I don't know how exactly I fucked up, but I should try to fix this. If I want to get out of therapy, I have to make some changes. I have to keep taking the fucking pills and listen to this doctor lady because she's gonna fix my head. Or whatever.

"Are you feeling… morning sickness?"

I want to show her that I care. She doesn't look at me. I haven't done anything wrong, have I?

"No," she answers curtly.

"Uh… Right. Would you like to go out to Lucky's place? He has a big house in Westhampton with a pool and a lacrosse field and his wife is–

"I don't need to go anywhere," Melanie says. Christ. Why is she being so fucking difficult today?

"Is something wrong?"

"No. Nothing."

I am in my fucking forties which means I'm smart enough to know that when a woman says that, she means something is definitely wrong and if I don't figure out what the fuck it is, she's going to put her foot up my ass.

"I can tell you're upset about something."

"Your behavior is completely unacceptable," she says huffily.

"What behavior?"

I just got out of bed and she's giving me lectures on my behavior. Can I get a cup of fucking coffee before I have to hear this? I scowl and wait for the coffeemaker to belch out the last of my *Folgers* while giving Big Tex a head scratch as he sits next to me . I pour in twice the necessary hazelnut creamer and add an extra two spoonfuls of sugar, stirring it all around and taking a few sips before turning back to Melanie, who continues ignoring my question. I stare at her, hoping my interrogation tactics will crack her under the pressure, but she doesn't look up from whatever the hell she made for breakfast. It's a pancake with anchovies and butter on top. Ah. One of her pregnancy cravings.

"Well?" I ask her again.

"I'm not fucking stupid, Sammy."

"I didn't think you were."

Although I have wondered why she got into so many fights at school, how she got kicked out, and why her mother was all too willing to send her to stay with me. I didn't have to work hard for her to sign the necessary paperwork and although I neglected to share this with Melanie, she tried to get even more money out of me than I originally offered.

This girl is a mystery to me…

"Good," she says. "You try that shit again and I'll cut your dick off."

I nearly spit out my mouthful of coffee. It's a hell of a lot more urgent now to understand where the fuck I went wrong. My dick is on the line.

"I should probably admit exactly what I did," I tell her. "In detail. And take full responsibility for my actions."

"That would be a nice start."

"Well, I do that."

"Do what?"

"I take full responsibility for my actions and admit all the details."

Her eyes narrow. I don't have any more clues about what the fuck she's talking about. I suspect it's completely obvious that I don't know shit about shit. There's no way I'm getting away with this. *Fuck.* I don't even know what "this" is.

"What actions were those?" she huffs. "Be more specific."

"I... I don't... Just being a crazy nutjob or whatever the fuck. I think... Listen, my psychiatrist gave me new meds. She just called this morning, so I won't be screaming in the halls anymore."

"Well you weren't screaming this time, that's for damn sure," Melanie grumbles. What the fuck does she mean by that?

"Right," I mutter. "I'm sorry. Once my medication kicks in, I won't bother you anymore."

"I know you won't," Melanie snaps back. "Like I said, you come near me, say goodbye to your dick."

"Can you stop talking about my dick? Please?" I grumble. "This is not the sort of conversation I need to have with a teenager."

Melanie snickers, but I don't get the impression that it means everything is okay between the two of us. "Whatever. I can stop."

I try not to sound growly and angry with her despite temptation. I don't understand a word she's saying this morning.

"I have to go to work today. Can I trust you to stay out of trouble?" I ask her. I have to trust her... or at least try.

"Probably not," Melanie says, crashing my hopes of trusting her completely.

"Find a way to change that answer, Melanie."

She shrugs. "Just being honest. I'm pregnant, I'm bored and I'm tired of putting up with your shit. I wasn't meant to be cooped up in the house like this."

"You could always go back to your mother's house," I grumble.

I wonder if the comment pushes her too far because

Melanie's lips tighten and her gaze drops away from me. I saw where she lived and what her home was like. I've heard the way her mother spoke to her…

"That's a great idea," she says sarcastically. "You are *so* helpful."

"I didn't mean to be a dick."

"Whatever, Sammy. I get it. You want me here because you want to protect Enrico's kid. That has nothing to do with me. I'll look after myself and your grandkid. I don't need you watching over me like a hawk."

"It's worked so far."

"I *need* fresh air."

I wouldn't call any of the air in this city fresh and the thought of letting Melanie out of my sight doesn't bring me any joy.

"Can I trust you to stay in this part of the city? Don't take the fucking bus, don't take the fucking train. Stay close where I can have people watching you."

"What type of stalker shit is that?"

"I need to look after you, Melanie. That's all."

"Why?"

"Because I didn't look after my son and he's dead."

She flinches. This hurts her too. It's something we share that we can't exactly talk about.

"That wasn't your fault," she responds quickly. I can tell that she means it from the heart, but it isn't true. I avenged my son, but it hasn't made the pain go away. Doesn't matter how much I made Alfonso beg and scream throughout the hours of torture, Enrico's death won't get off my mind. *He's gone. My only son.*

"This won't be my fault either," I tell her. "Stay close and stay out of trouble. I don't want more problems than I already have."

"I'll be fine."

Sammy

. . .

SHE CAN'T KNOW the extent of my problems. Melanie wouldn't understand how precarious things are now that John has taken over the mob. I've made a public show of forgiving him and I've hoped the other Zagarella family members would fall in line. I love my son, but his death isn't worth causing even more bloodshed.

There are still people I can kill who no one will give a fuck about. I don't need to kill other people in this life. The city is teeming with creeps and criminals who deserve more than a shot to the head. They deserve a worse fate than what happened to my son. Fuck, John's gonna kill me if he finds out I'm still thinking of this shit.

My cousin's right. I need help. Coping with my son's death should be getting easier, but each day it gets more difficult and even Melanie has had just about enough of me.

DR. GABRIEL SITS with her legs crossed at the ankles. Her dog sits there with its large head between its paws, glaring at me. At least I think it's glaring. I'm probably fucking paranoid.

"How did you sleep last night?" Dr. Gabriel asks, gazing at me beyond tortoiseshell glasses. She's staring at me as if she expects a specific answer, but I dunno what the fuck she wants me to say. I don't feel like I slept. I'm frustrated. This medication should be working but when I'm awake, all I can think about is killing people and death and all the gory shit I've seen. I want to push these images out of my head, but with Dr. Gabriel asking more questions, the images just seem to get more vivid. .

"I don't know."

"Are you taking your new medication?"

"Yes."

"Did you make any progress on your relationship with Melanie?"

The question forces me to shift uncomfortably in my seat. We don't have a relationship. I take care of her and make sure she has a fucking roof over her head until I get my grandkid, and then figure out what to do with her. But her attitude this morning was different than usual.

"I don't know."

"Did you try to get to know her?"

"Yes. She doesn't like me very much. It doesn't matter what I do."

I'd much rather sink a knife into a man's chest than talk about my fucking feelings any more than I'm doing already. I pierce my fingernails into the arm of the chair in Dr. Gabriel's room. Her expressionless face makes me sick to my stomach.

"I see."

What the fuck does that mean? She scribbles more in her notebook. I couldn't even read her handwriting if I tried. So I don't. I just stare at her and try to read her, try to see what the fuck she wants from me or what I need to say to fix my bullshit.

"Have you had any disturbing thoughts since you started your medication?"

She gazes at me with knowing eyes and hot shame courses through me starting from the tips of my ears and covering my entire face in a humiliated flush.

"What kind of disturbing thoughts?"

"Sexual thoughts. Sexual behaviors. Sexual desires."

Our eyes meet. *Is this traditional in therapy?* I don't know how to answer the question, but I shrug.

"Nothing different from normal."

"I see."

"That has nothing to do with Melanie," I blurt out. "She's

pregnant with my dead son's child and I would *never* hurt her."

"I understand. You *have* been taking your medication?"

"Yes."

"I'll increase your dose," Dr. Gabriel says in a soothing voice. "That should help you sleep better and maybe next time, you'll have something different to report."

"There are other disturbing thoughts," I tell her, before she waves me off too quickly with her little prescriptions.

"Like what?" she says, leaning forward with her pen pressed to her notebook eagerly.

"I can't stop thinking about killing. Death. Hurting people."

"I see. But no changes in your sexual behavior?"

I give her an annoyed look and she purses her lips before giving me a terse explanation.

"It's a professional inquiry, Sammy. Men have very inter-connected highways between sex and violence. It's genetic, scientific, as old as men themselves."

"Hm," I grunt. "No changes. What about the fixations?"

"I don't need to tell you that killing people is illegal, right Sammy?"

"You don't," I reply. That doesn't change the fact I want to do it. I want to hurt someone and I'm starting not to care who it is. The pit bull whines and raises its head, staring at me even more intensely than when I first entered the room. Dr. Gabriel doesn't react to the dog, but my instincts rush to the defense. I should have brought a gun in here.

"If you take a higher dosage of your medication, these problems should go away. I'll write you the prescription now."

She writes the prescription, and as she hands me the paper Taylor Mae Davis shows her teeth and snarls at me. The snarling turns to barking as I shift in my seat to shove the prescription into my pants. Dr. Gabriel can't get a hold of Taylor Mae Davis as she yaps towards my ankles. I make an excuse to leave a few minutes early and burst out of the room.

My head hurts like fuck, so I'd better get those fucking prescriptions. I head to the nearest Duane Reade and as I'm standing in line, when I'm not thinking about rivers of blood, I picture Melanie's face. Where the fuck did she want to go so badly today? I have a tracker in her phone which I'm sure she doesn't know about. Once I'm done here, I'll find her.

I told her to stay out of trouble, but I was a parent. *I am a parent.* I know kids get into all kinds of fucking trouble. I don't need her ending up hurt. Life has been hard enough to that poor girl. She's too sweet despite herself to have the life she's had.

ONCE I GET MY MEDICATION, I'll track her ass down and make sure she's obeying my damn instructions.

Chapter 5
"I Killed For You..."
Melanie

I know it's stupid, but I'm going to Shawnte's house to see if she's come back yet.

I miss her and she won't answer any of my phone calls. Where the hell is she? If her mom has found out about her expulsion, maybe things have already calmed down between them. Unfortunately, to get to Shawnte's house, I have to walk past our school, which means taking a huge risk.

Damzel got kicked out of school too. She won't be there to make my life hell, but that doesn't mean I'm safe.

"Hey Melanie!"

I'm three blocks away from school, in a part of the city I thought would be safe from anyone I knew. I tried to disguise myself with a white pompom hat. But I guess that wasn't enough. I keep my head down and keep walking. If I turn around, he won't notice me.

I didn't know Damzel's boyfriend lived in this part of town because why would I? But I know her boyfriend, the guy who Shawnte was apparently fighting over. I know his name, what he looks like and his voice because he has a thick Puerto Rican accent. Javier Romero.

He won't do anything stupid. I hear another boy with him say something in Spanish. This time, I make the mistake of glancing over my shoulder. It's a blessing and a curse. I have almost enough time to react, but it's not quite enough. The hand reaching for my shoulder doesn't come as a complete surprise. I throw my elbow into Javier's stomach and miss. His friend grabs me and as I flail around, I recognize Alex...

They're going to beat the shit out of me.

"Hey, whale," Alex says. "Where the fuck do you think you're going?"

"You got expelled," Javier sneers. "You don't belong here."

"Where I'm going isn't a concern to you, now get your hands off me!" I scream loudly, hoping to attract the attention of some bystanders so they intervene and get these boys hands off me. They're gripping me tightly and way too strong for me to break away. I keep fighting and yelling, but they just drag me down the street and pull me away onto a more isolated side street. None of my yelling attracts any attention and anyone around decides it's better for themselves to not intervene.

Once they're away from any prying eyes, Javier slams my back against a wall.

"Shut the hell up!" he yells. "Shut. Up."

I can't yell at all because my back hitting the wall knocked the fucking wind out of me. Alex blocks my only avenue of escape.

"Come on, man. She's scared," he says. "Just take her fucking bag and let's get out of here."

"No way, man," Javier says. "We have a great opportunity on our hands."

Alex is half-Puerto Rican. He never mentions what his other half is, but he speaks fluent Spanish. He says something pleadingly with Javier who chuckles.

"Who gives a shit, man? My girl told me to fuck her up. I'm gonna do that."

"Please, just leave me alone. I'm pregnant!"

"Dude," Alex says. "Damzel didn't tell you to do this. She said to scare her."

"Once I'm done with her, she'll be more than scared. Come on, man. Help me."

I see a gap and try to dart between them to run away. Alex reaches out and grabs my arm before pushing me back against the wall. He wants to stop Javier from doing *something*, but he also won't let me go. My heart races. I have to get out of here, but I don't know how. Alex hits Javier in the shoulder.

"I'm out of here, man. I'm not gonna fucking rape her."

Hearing that, I freak the fuck out, rushing Javier to push him out of the way since he's leaner than Alex and by my estimates, the easier one to get around. This ends up being a miscalculation. As I launch myself at Javier, Alex disappears. This is going too far for him and he can't stand it. I know Damzel and there's no way she asked her boyfriend to do this. *She had a problem with Shawnte, not me... Or maybe this asshole has been manipulating her.*

Javier throws a fist at my face with all his strength. If I hadn't just been in a fight, I might have been able to take the punch. My mom wasn't above throwing her fist at my face after a night of drinking, but my face is still bruised up, so the searing pain nearly knocks me unconscious. I scream and Javier pushes me face first against the wall, shoving his hands down the back of my pants.

I scream loudly and try to kick him despite my pain.

Melanie

"You are such a fat slut," he snarls at me. I scream again and try to kick him in the balls but he's too large for me to fight against. He wraps his forearm around my neck and I bite him hard. I want to pierce skin, but he's sweaty, gross and I only end up choking myself, not to mention inhaling the scent of some *Playboy* cologne.

"Get off me!" I scream. "Get off me or I'm calling the police!"

My terror excites him more. I can feel something hard along my backside as Javier holds me against him with his chokehold, and my fear intensifies. *He's going to rape me and there's going to be no one there to help me. No one to save me.*

I shriek as he rips a giant hole in my pants and I bite Javier's forearm again. This only infuriates him more and he slams my head into the wall. I can feel my consciousness waver as I try any movement I can to get him off of me. Once he has my pants and underwear down to my knees, I start to give up hope of fighting him off. With the last of my consciousness hanging on by a thread, I wriggle against him to try and break free, but there's nothing left in me. With all my adrenaline spent, my body lies there in a shameful heap as he readies himself to hurt me.

I WANT TO PASS OUT, but I don't.

A VOICE ECHOES across the street. A bystander...

"Get away from her," the bystander growls. *This isn't a bystander. It's Sammy. But he sounds different. He has the voice he uses at night. The crazy fucking voice that means he's not okay.*

"Back off, man. That's my girlfriend."

He distracts Javier enough for me to barely shove him off

with what's left of my strength. I scramble away from Javier while trying to pull my pants back up and race behind Sammy. How the fuck did Sammy find me out here? He throws a punch at Javier's face and Javier *immediately* hits the ground. What in the fucking Floyd Mayweather just happened? It's more than enough for us to get away, but Sammy isn't done.

Sammy starts to reach into his pocket for something that's making a slight bulge. I realize as he's pulling it out that it's a sheath for a long knife in his pocket. He glances around him furtively and before I can tell what the fuck he's looking for, he slams the knife straight into Javier's chest. I scream and my knees wobble, threatening to take me out of consciousness. I brace myself against the wall and I think I beg Sammy to stop.

He kneels next to Javier's body and the knife makes an ungodly crunching sound as he pierces Javier's flesh again. Blood spurts up from his body and I stumble back with my back against the wall, trying not to get any of the gushing blood on my clothes. I'm too frozen to scream anymore. Sammy slams his knife into Javier's abdomen again and I double over, getting sick all over the sidewalk.

Sammy yanks his knife out of Javier and tosses it to the ground. There's no one around. Javier knows these streets like the back of his hand and picked this spot on purpose. The restaurants and businesses around here won't have the opening shifts show up for a couple hours and this cut off only has foot traffic.

Javier's dead. Obviously. Sammy turns him over and empties his pockets. He grabs his school ID and shoves it in his pocket. *His eyes.* There's something wrong with Sammy's eyes.

"Sammy?" I yell at him. "Sammy?"

He looks asleep, but this isn't possible. It's broad daylight and he was fine this morning. His bizarre night terrors are *night* terrors. Blood pools around Sammy's knees and he turns his head towards me, the blank expression on his face sending terror straight through me.

"Help with the body. Come on. John's gonna fucking kill us."

What? He isn't making any sense?

"You just killed someone!" I shriek at him. "I'm not helping you move the body. I'm going to the p–

I don't finish my sentence before Sammy wraps his bloody arms around me and drags me screaming to his car. He shoves me in the backseat and locks me in. My head swims with terror and a million other emotions. I'm covered in sweat, my mouth tastes like bile, and my clothes are still ripped from Javier's attack. I can already tell by the pain in my face that my slightly healed black eyes will probably be dark purple again tomorrow..

I try to get my body to move so I can make another effort at escaping, but nothing works. I'm in shock, or there's something else wrong with me and I don't feel entirely in control. *He's crazier than I thought.*

Sammy returns a few minutes later. He opens the trunk of his Escalade and I hear a very loud thud. I glance behind me and see Javier's wide opened eyes set upon mine.

"I'll have someone clean up the blood," Sammy mutters.

Is this motherfucker going to get behind the wheel?

"Are you sure you should be driving?" I ask him, although that ought to be the last question on my mind. *Are you going to kill me next? That might be a more relevant question, Melanie.*

"He asked for it," Sammy growls. "He hurt Melanie."
I'm Melanie.

He drives us out of the city. My panic only increases the

further away from my old neighborhood we get. It's Queens, so there are sirens every thirty seconds and with a dead body in the back of Sammy's fucking car, you could say I'm paranoid. The vision of being pregnant while in prison flashes before my eyes as we race through Queens.

"When we bury him..." Sammy says, trailing off and then running his tongue over his lower lips. A nervous shiver undoes me. Sammy continues. "I will finally... *finish*..."

I don't have a fucking clue what that means. We drive for about thirty minutes, and the entire time I'm hiding my phone on my lap, debating on calling the cops but... I don't see any way I could get out of this without getting my ass in even bigger trouble. I had my suspicions about Enrico Zagarella, but now that I see his father, I wonder...

"Why did you kill him?"

"Because I needed to."

"That's not an answer."

"My family killed my son," he whispers, his grasp on the steering wheel so tight his knuckles have gone white. "That motherfucker hurt... He can't hurt Melanie."

I reach over and touch his cheek with a shaking hand. There's blood on his cheek, his hands, and soaked through his clothes.

"You killed him in the street, Sammy. You're gonna get caught. You're gonna go to jail."

He glances over at me. He's definitely awake, but he has that faraway look in his eye from the night he was sleepwalking. Whatever is happening now might be some mental state in between the two that I don't quite understand. My throat tightens as I wonder what to make of it, but it's hard to keep a coherent thought in my head with Sammy's murky green eyes fixing me in place.

His gaze is more analytical than reactionary. He considers

me slowly, even if he's definitely out of his mind or on some-thing. *On something.* I've never seen him doing any illegal drugs. Maybe he could do them in secret. That's a possibility. I don't know...

The smell of blood is starting to make my head hurt. My stomach battles the nausea from the intense copper smell, and I can feel sweat start to break out on my forehead. Sammy's still looking me in the eyes as he reaches over to push hair out of my face.

"I'll be fine," he says. "We're burying him out on my land."

He drives the car for a while before taking a turn that takes us off the main road. After a while, we arrive at a place that seems too isolated to be a part of Long Island. I know we didn't drive for too long, so we must still be in Long Island or somewhere close to it. When I get out of the car, Sammy has already started to pop the trunk and haul the body out. I don't want to think this is really happening, but of course it is. He drags the body out and disappears for a while. I wait a few minutes before risking everything to follow him.

I don't get very far before I see Sammy returning. I'd just about given up on him coming back when I saw his hulking body appearing in the distance. His shirt looks ripped and it billows open as he comes over the dirt path with his long messy hair stuck to his neck. He still has that far off look in his eye, the one that whispers his secret to me – he isn't all the way "there" mentally.

"Were you trying to run away?" Sammy growls.

"Where would I run?"

He gives me a knowing look and then grabs my cheeks. The sudden action surprises me. This isn't like Sammy to touch me like this, and having him seize me somewhere so intimate with his bloodied, dirt-covered hands sends a forbidden thrill through me.

"I killed for you," he whispers. "Now I get to fuck you..."

It hits me why he's holding my cheeks, but before I can wriggle away from this horrible decision, Sammy Zagarella pulls my face against his and kisses me deeply. His lips are rough and his scratchy stubble-covered face is the most grown man face I've ever kissed.

He makes a low, growling noise in the back of his throat as he thoughtlessly grabs my face and kisses me. I can smell the dirt and the blood, but more importantly the potent scent of Sammy's raw masculinity. Without thinking, I yield to him completely, my lips falling open so Sammy's tongue can slide into my mouth.

He grabs my lower lips between his teeth and bites hard. I whimper as he draws blood but Sammy reacts by letting go of my face and grabbing my hips instead. His forceful hands around my waist cause me to freeze in terror or maybe just surprise. He isn't rough in the way he handles me. His lips and teeth may be rough and exploratory, but Sammy holds me like I'm made of porcelain.

"I don't think that's how that works," I stammer as I try to step away from Sammy's kiss. He won't free me from his grasp completely.

He acts like I didn't even speak. "We need to lay low. Safe house in the Poconos until this blows over."

"Don't you think you need to call someone?"

Sammy's eyes narrow. "No," he says. "I'm fine."

His chest heaves in time with his rapid breathing. He's not acting like someone who's okay. He's acting like a crazed maniac and he's still covered in blood.

"I'm not a monster," he snarls. "That man... He almost..."

One hand rushes to my cheek and doesn't squeeze me this time. I shiver from the contact. His hands are dirty and every sensible part of me knows I should recoil completely from Sammy's touch, but I don't. I look deeply in his eyes, and through the glaze of whatever drug has his mind captivated, I can see the concern he has for me brewing.

"I'm fine," I say to him.

"You will be once we get to Pennsylvania. Now get in the car." Any gentleness I noticed in his eyes quickly vanished as he pulls his hand away and moved towards the car.

"You probably shouldn't drive."

Of course, Sammy ignores me.

FOR THE ENTIRE drive to the Poconos, Sammy blasts the rock classics radio. While he continues to bellow out all these old ass songs that he somehow knows by heart, my mind starts to replay everything that has happened over the last few hours. I can feel the aches start to spread throughout my body from Javier bashing me against the wall, and the overall drain my body has been through today. I come to the quick realization that I never did make it to Shawnte's house, so I have no idea if she ever came home or if she's even okay. As the next song starts to play, I look over at Sammy as he starts to use the steering wheel like it's his own personal drum set.

He's acting like he didn't just kill a man, but he's also just acting like a crazy person. Against all the warning sirens going off in my head, I bite my tongue until we get to an impressive house deep in the mountains of Pennsylvania. I read the road signs as we approach, but knowing where we are doesn't help me. I just have my phone, a couple twenties in my wallet and a man who I... I think made me an accomplice to murder, and I'm carrying his grandson.

Sammy orders me into the house, but the second I take my shoes off, his hand reaches for my forearm and grips me like a vice. *What the fuck?*

"You aren't going anywhere."

I hadn't started going anywhere since I just walked into this house and I don't know my way around it, but there's no point in arguing or even slightly disagreeing with Sammy when he's in this state. *I have to wait for this to wear off and then talk sense into him, but I'm hovering near a dangerous outcome – I can feel it.*

"Now, I get to fuck you..."

I'd like to pretend he hadn't uttered those words a few hours ago, but we both know he did. Every time he glances over at me, those six words haunt me completely. I shoot a quick glance at the grip he has on my arm before making eye contact, knowing what I'm going to see in his eyes.

"You need to call someone. We have cell phones. You killed someone in broad daylight. You're going to go to prison."

My voice tenses as I say it all out loud because the truth is – I could go to prison too. Sammy's face breaks out in a broad, crazy grin.

"No. We're going upstairs, sex pot."

"Sex pot!? Sammy, get a hold of yourself!"

I know I'm not trying to piss him off, but when Sammy wakes up out of whatever hallucinogenic or possibly drug induced haze he's in, he'll regret dragging me off to the fucking Poconos or wherever the fuck we are and treating me like... *a woman.* I've always been For Enrico's girlfriend to Sammy, and if anything happens tonight, that will change and he'll become a man, I'll be a woman to him and we can't possibly share a house after that.

I'm pregnant and if Sammy kicks me out, I'll have nowhere to go except back to my mom's house, which isn't an option. Our last exchange doesn't haunt me exactly, but it's an uncomfortable closure. I had to grow up when I did. I'm not a kid anymore.

Sammy's grasp on me tightens. He doesn't appear to have any plans to kick me out yet considering how tightly he holds onto my forearm.

"Fuck, I'm sick of this. I need to cum. I needed to *kill* and now I need to cum so are you going to help me or not?"

"You're not yourself," I plead with him, trying to shake my hands away from him. He doesn't know what it will do to me if we go through with this. My body is already in a constant flood of pregnancy hormones and getting into bed with a chiseled beast like Sammy Zagarella who kisses me like a grown ass man who knows what the hell he's doing...

I can't want this.

"No," he growls. "I'm not. I won't be myself until I get my dick inside something nice and warm. Something like you."

He pulls me against him by my hips this time, his lips against mine forcing me to accept my fate.

"Get upstairs and take those clothes off. I want to lick your tasty slit before I fuck you."

"We're covered in blood and dirt."

There's that crazy fucking smile again. "Good. That will make it better."

He drags me against him again and plants another one of his crazy kisses that sends an inappropriate chill straight to the center of my thighs. The throbbing between my legs threatens what little remains of my self-control.

I'm not myself with him and that scares the crap out of me.

Sammy's intense green eyes rove over me and in his crazed state, he makes no effort to hide that he's staring directly at my chest. Nope, there's just a low growl in Sammy's throat as he presses his lips to my neck. This kiss comforts me more than the rough biting kisses he passionately delivered before.

"I won't hurt you," he growls in between painfully sweet neck kisses. "I just really *really* need to cum."

His fingers sink into the extra flesh around my hips as Sammy growls the word "really". It's a stupid thought, but I can't help wondering if sex will snap him out of it. Sammy flattens his tongue and runs it along the length of my neck. *Oh my fucking God, who cares if sex snaps him out of it. I'm pregnant and he smells like man and this is bad fucking news.*

Sammy chuckles. "I can smell you getting wetter. Now go on upstairs."

"You'll regret this," I tell him, making one last effort to resist Sammy's lips and tongue, which is an impossible feat.. "I'm pregnant with Enrico's baby and this is very…"

I want to say that it's very wrong, but Sammy sucks on my neck so hard that I moan instead, utterly losing control of myself and giving in to my most inappropriate desires as he chuckles.

"Very wrong," he murmurs. "I know. That will make it so much better when I cum inside you, sweet Melanie."

I push against his chest, but Sammy's ready for me. He easily hoists me into his grasp. I'm a big girl and even Enrico, who wasn't a weak man by any means, could never lift me off the ground like this. Sammy swings me around and slams my back against the wall of the house. I won't even get to see the living room before he completely rips apart my destroyed pants, apparently.

"Fuck the ones who hurt you," he murmurs, kissing my neck. "Curse the ones who abandoned you. And may you forever be safe in my arms…"

He's crazy, Melanie. He doesn't mean any of this because he's a heavily medicated maniac covered in blood and kissing your neck.

I grunt as he slams his hips forward, forcing me to feel

the hardness between his thighs that before I'd only seen from a distance. Holy fuck, he's huge and feeling the thick coiled rope of Sammy's cock pushing against the fabric of his pants, raw and hard with desire for me sends the most infuriating sensations straight through me.

Sammy drags me away from the wall with as much ferocity as when he placed me there. He doesn't know what he's doing, but that doesn't fucking stop him from doing it. Sammy takes my over two-hundred pound behind up the stairs like it's *easy* for him and thrusts the door open to the first bedroom he finds. His safehouse bed isn't made, there's just a white sheet covering the mattress but Sammy doesn't give a fuck.

I glance over my shoulder in an effort to take in *some* information about the area around me, but turning my head only allows Sammy to surprise me by careening into the bed with me. I groan as his body lands on top of mine, but I don't push him away. The first thing I notice is his heaviness. He's a ton of muscle and pinning me to the bed with his body even before putting any effort in.

I can't resist him, so why bother.

Sammy caresses my neck with gentle kisses like he gave me downstairs right after knocking the damned wind out of me.

"Touch my hair," he grunts. "I know you want to. I see you staring at it."

He's crazy. It doesn't matter what you do because he's crazy and he probably won't remember any of this when he stops hearing those voices and becomes the gruff fatherly asshole you're used to.

Sammy commands it, so I listen even if I feel stupid touching him at first. He moans when I sink my fingers into the strands, letting go for once and parting the dark knots of Sammy's thick long hair as he kisses my neck.

"Yes," he groans. "Fuck yes…"

Sammy's hands slide unceremoniously into my pants. I gasp as his fingers spread my lower lips without any warning and he slips one rough digit between them. His invasion forces me to notice how wet I am and the shame forces me to buck my hips up in a last ditch effort to stop him from rubbing between my lips and noticing the effect his kisses and crazy fucking words had on me.

I'm only wet because I'm pregnant. It's not because a crazy mobster dragged me to his bedroom planning to have his way with me. Sammy rolls his finger in slow circles around my clit. I gasp as his touch sends a sensitive thrill through me. He moans with pleasure as he touches my clit as if the softness of my body and my responsiveness to him were enough pleasure for him to get along.

My pussy soaks his finger as he strokes my clit. Sammy slows down and my core tightens as I get ready to climax. He just keeps softly kissing my neck and then plying me with kisses along with the slow rubbing between my legs.

"You have a nice clit," he whispers. "It's soft, round and very sensitive. I love listening to you moan…"

He pushes me to moan louder by sinking his teeth into my neck as he removes his fingers from my clit and shoves two of those fingers inside me. I cry out. I've always struggled with sex and feeling *anything* up there. Sex has always hurt and the sudden invasion from Sammy's fingers causes a genuine flush of pain.

His cheeks redden as he observes my reaction.

"You are *tight*," He growls. His tongue teases my earlobes gently. "Does sex hurt for you, honey bun?"

Honey bun?!? That's new, but I can't push back against Sammy's pet name because he slowly eases his fingers deeper and a new sensation between my legs causes a sound halfway between a scream and a moan out of me. Sammy grunts as he pushes his fingers deeper.

"I can feel your tight black pussy grabbing my fingers like a vice grip. We'll have to be gentle."

I've seen Sammy's dick and there's no way stuffing a 12-inch pole in my pussy that can barely fit two fingers won't hurt like hell. I squirm against him but only end up drawing Sammy's fingers into me deeper and stimulating a moan of pleasure that I wish I could have stifled. My pleasure only prods him forward and I despite my pleasure, especially knowing that Sammy isn't in the right state of mind to do this.

I shouldn't let him put his fingers in my pussy or press his raging cock against my thighs through his pants.

"You are so fucking wet," he whispers. "But I'll still take my time."

He eases his fingers out of my tightness. I'm sore around the elastic edges of my entrance, but my depths throb with excitement. He kneels between my legs after forcing them apart to splay me at his mercy on the bed and to keep me right where he wants me. Sammy thrusts his fingers into his mouth and wraps his tongue around them, vocalizing pleasurably as he sucks my juices off his hands.

"Fuck, that's good," he growls. "It's been a long time since I've tasted some good ass pussy."

I've never heard Sammy talk like this, but I'm long past a way out of this. He kisses my neck and then lifts my shirt.

"Take that off," he growls, leaving me to untangle myself from the fabric as he presses an unceremonious kiss to my exposed stomach and works to remove the rest of my pants. *Monster, he's a monster. I don't know why his touch does this to me.* I gasp with excitement and allow Sammy to strip my lower half as I obediently do the rest of the work for him.

I'm vulnerable, exposed, soaked between the legs and too emotionally shattered and confused to stop Sammy's unhinged ass from having his way with me. He kisses me like a lover, not like a madman. It doesn't matter how much control I think I have, I'm still a woman and he's a red-blooded man who unfortunately knows exactly how to kiss me, finger me and push me devastatingly close to the edge of an orgasm.

He's made me so hot that I want to cum. I offer Sammy no resistance as he gets my underwear off and when he pushes his nose between my legs to sniff his prize, my legs spread wider. His son was my first. This is so fucking *weird* but Enrico's gone and my life has been one fucking shit show after another.

Sammy spreads my lower lips with his tongue and runs his tongue over the clit he stroked to the edge earlier. I whimper as he gets my clit and pussy lips even wetter and then fixates his energy entirely on my clit. His enthusiastic tongue forces another moan out of me and Sammy hikes my legs up over his shoulders so he can better access my wetness.

He slides his tongue from the top of my clit to the base of my pussy, teasing the hole he spread open with his fingers and then slowly easing his tongue back up to my clit where he swirls his tongue in deliberate circles. Fuck, this is incredible. I moan Sammy's name and he increases his attention, flicking his tongue over my clit until I whimper his name and then slide my fingers through his hair.

"Yes..." I moan despite myself. Sammy wraps his lips around my clit and sucks on it until I finally release.

I've had orgasms before but I've never had back breaking orgasms like this. My body contorts and writhes out of my control while my limbs buckle like I'm going through an exorcism. I can feel my pussy throbbing out of control as Sammy drags me by the hips to his lips so he can keep lapping at my pussy after I cum.

"You're an angel," he growls. "Cum again for me..."

He licks my pussy again until I cum and then he kisses the top of my mound before tracing kisses up my mound all the way to my navel. Once his lips get to my navel, he kisses me in a circle and then growls, "I need to cum, honey bun and I want to cum with that sweet, sexy ass jiggling around my cock."

Sammy was already a raw, untamed version of a normal man, but when he's like this, he's something worse. His beastly body hulks over mine and he flips me onto my stomach before sliding my ass cheeks apart and running his tongue along the length of my slit before rubbing his tongue around my asshole.

I moan as Sammy's tongue invades my back door, but he doesn't linger there before running his tongue back along my pussy lips. He nibbles and sucks my lower lips a while longer until I feel like I'm going to burst.

This is pure fucking torture. Sammy reaches his tongue to my clit and pushes a finger inside me as he teases my clit with his tongue. I moan again and ignore the initial searing pain from his finger entering me. Sammy grunts vocally. "Fuck, you're tight. Still so fucking tight."

He eases his finger into me as he teases my clit and within a few seconds I cum again. Sammy pulls his finger out of me slowly and then removes his tongue from my lower lips. I feel bare and desperate for his touch again. It's far too painful to be there without his tongue between my legs.

I arch my back instinctively, hoping for more of Sammy's soft tongue but I feel something the size of a modest apple pressing against my entrance. The muscles in my arms freeze, holding me in this tense, arched position and leaving my pussy easily accessible for the monstrous dick preparing to enter me.

Sammy kisses my butt cheeks, rubbing his hands along the soft flesh and then he presses the tip of his dick along my entrance again. He rubs his dick head along my slit and I moan as he slowly coats the head of his cock in a mixture of my precum and his juices.

"Mmm," Sammy growls. "Your pussy gets my cock nice and wet, honey bun. I love it…"

He pushes forward and I cry out as the wide head of Sammy's cock spreads me open. He doesn't even slide inside me right away. That would probably break my tightness in half. Just the head stretching me open sends pain straight through me as I struggle to adjust to Sammy's size.

"Yes…" he growls. "You must be the tightest… *holy fuck I want to get you pregnant.*"

My skin flushes nervously. He's out of his mind, so I know I can't take him seriously, but my ex-boyfriend's father has his gigantic bare dick pressed against my pussy and he's muttering about how he wants to knock me up.

"I want to watch my cum drip out of that sweet little pussy," he whispers, running his hand down the length of my spine and then stopping with his thumb hovering over my asshole. He growls as he rubs a slow circle around my asshole.

"I could cum in there too," Sammy grunts, pushing his cock into me an inch. I cry out and he moans with pleasure.

"Fuck that was good," he whispers. "Moan all you want, honey bun. I want to hear you scream while I make love to your sweet ass pussy."

He slides another inch inside me. The girth of Sammy's cock stretches me wide. I shut my eyes and attempt to spread my legs to take more of him in easily. It doesn't work. Getting Sammy's big cock between my legs won't ever be easy. He pushes his thumb against my butthole but doesn't enter it as he slides in more. His giant shaft stretches me out and I feel him pulsing inside me. Sammy's dick is so big that every inch of me can feel him.

I feel so much pain along with the pleasure. He groans as he pushes half his cock into me. He moves slowly as he tries to fit the rest of his dick inside me. Just half hurts, but he needs more. *I want more.* It hurts to take him, but my body responds with desire regardless. My hips thrust upward to meet him.

"I need you to cum," he growls. "Cum for me, honey bun…"

Sammy thrusts into me deeper, slowly teasing my arousal and pushing me to the edge of orgasm without forcing me to take the pain of his entire dick yet. I feel that enormous round head thrusting deep inside me even with his attempts at gentle strokes. He's so big and I feel so full having him inside me. Pain pierces the base of my abdomen as he shifts his weight slightly.

I've never been this full before and I've never felt so tight. There's no gentle with a dick like Sammy's. He grabs my hips tighter and thrusts the rest of his big dick between my legs. I close my eyes and cry out in pain as Sammy's dick thrusts into me. The ache in my pussy spreads through my body and the tingling in my thighs turns to something else.

I cry out Sammy's name without meaning to and my voice sounds weaker than I intend for it to sound.

"Heaven," Sammy growls, leaning over me to press his skin to mine as he keeps me in place with his large dick thrust into my pussy from behind. Sammy wraps a large arm around me, his muscular bicep clutching my body to his. This is the first time a man has held me against his body and made me feel precious.

Sammy growls and sinks his teeth into my shoulders.

"So fucking soft," he growls…

With his free hand, Sammy reaches around in front of me and rubs my clit as he thrusts into me. I don't need more stimulation than having Sammy's big dick thrust between my legs. He moves his hips slightly and then brushes against my clit, forcing me to explode with unexpected pleasure. I moan and bite my lower lip, tilting my head back and leaning into Sammy's muscular body, pushing him deeper inside me inadvertently.

Pushing back against Sammy's cock as I cum only makes me cum harder and I scream his name again as I feel a gush erupting from my tightness, coating Sammy's dick in my essence.

"Holy fuck," he grunts. "Your cum is all over me…I fucking love it."

Sammy sinks his teeth into my shoulders again and gently wraps his hands around my hair, grabbing it and tilting my head back as he uses my hair to control me.

"I know women like you don't like guys like me touching your hair but too fucking bad," he whispers. "I love taking your sexy ass from behind with your hair wrapped around my wrist…"

He pumps into me faster, forcing me to cry out in pleasure instead of chastising him about potentially damaging my hairdo. As Sammy pushes into me from behind, he kisses my neck and teases me with his tongue while taking me from behind until I climax again. Once I climax again, I lose track of how often I cum.

Sammy rubs my clit as he eases his cock into me and forces my tightness to adjust to his invasive member. Just when I think he's about to finish inside me and coat the walls of my tight pussy with his thick cream, he pulls out of me with a loud groan. A very vocal Sammy flips me onto my back. He caresses my face with his hand and then forces my legs open with his other hand.

"I'm getting you pregnant tonight," he growls, even more proof that he's not himself. Sammy definitely knows I'm pregnant. My throat tightens and I draw my hands over his muscular back. If I can just let him fuck the sense out of me, I don't need to worry about the fact that he's out of his fucking mind.

Sammy runs his tongue over my nipples and then eases his weight over mine so his eyes lock with mine and the giant head of his cock rubs purposefully along the length of my soaked and reddened slit.

"Your pussy is so swollen and delicious," Sammy murmurs, stroking between my legs with a rigid index finger between kisses.

"I like watching your tight little pussy all wet and fucked up from my dick. I almost want to taste her again, but... not tonight... Tonight, I want to watch my cum spill from your tight ass pussy and fuck, that's gonna keep me going for a while..."

My nails dig harder into Sammy's back. At least I'm already pregnant. It's not exactly the most comforting thought considering my predicament but... what choice do I have? I can try to enjoy Sammy's big dick and a night of mind-blowing orgasms or I can overthink and ruin the first burst of pleasure I've had in ages.

"Mmm," he growls again, pressing the head of his cock against my entrance now that he has me laying flat on the bed in missionary position. "I like your nails..."

I squeeze them into his muscles and Sammy groans again, sliding his dick a couple inches inside me. Even after a few rounds of climaxes, it's not easy to get his cock between my legs. Sammy eases his hips forward, his well-formed ass tensing as he pushes into me.

As his cock stretches me out, he leans forward, pressing his muscular body into mine. I cry out and wrap my legs around him, pulling Sammy into me deeper.

"Fuck," he growls. "You want me to cum inside you..."

He bites my shoulder fiercely and I don't help my situation by cumming hard as Sammy's rough teeth tease my shoulder again. As I cum again he holds me against him and thrusts between my legs with reckless abandon.

"I need it… It's been so long…" he growls. "You're so fucking gorgeous, honey bun… I needed this…"

Sammy leans forward and his hair falls out of the loose knot he tied at the nape of his thick, muscular neck. He growls as he pushes into me one last time and his eruption leaves no mistake of his orgasm. Sammy vocalizes loudly as he cums, expressing his pleasure verbally as thick rivers of his cum shoot out of his staff. The warm gush coats my inner walls and I wrap my thick thighs instinctively around Sammy.

He's finished. A rush of satisfied bliss washes over me as Sammy kisses my shoulder gently and withdraws his spent cock from my entrance. He licks his lips and smirks as he gazes between my legs for the prize he was waiting for.

"You look delicious with my cum spilling out of your pussy," he whispers. "Now roll over… let me get some sleep, honey bun."

SAMMY ROLLS over and then grunts until I come close to him for cuddles. He falls asleep holding me, but sleep isn't so easy for me. My ex-boyfriend's dad just came inside me and unlike Sammy, I don't have bottles of pharmaceuticals to numb me from what the fuck just happened. I don't even know exactly where we are. I'm pregnant in the Poconos with a mad man who just filled me completely with his cum and I don't know what the fuck I'm going to do next.

I can't sit here and do nothing. Once I'm sure Sammy's asleep, I hop out of bed and rifle through his clothes downstairs. I'm looking for a cell phone, but I find something better – a new prescription, based on the date, and a bottle of new pills. *Did he take these before everything happened?*

I run my tongue over my lower lips and struggle to pronounce the strange scientific name out loud.

70

WHAT THE HELL is in this shit?

* * *

Chapter 6
The Boss's Orders
Sammy

My head pounds. The last thing I remember completely was the barking dog – that fucking annoying dog – and leaving the office. Wait... I remember the pharmacy and I remember Melanie. I went to find her, didn't I? Fuck... my head. I know I found Melanie and I know... holy fuck...

I lean over the bed and throw up on the floor. As I retch, I hear footsteps. Who the fuck is that? Melanie thrusts the bedroom door open as I throw up again. *Fuck,* I don't want her to see me like this...

I glance over at her from the corner of my eye and immediately wipe my mouth to stare at her.

"Why are you wearing my t-shirt?"

"Are you fucking serious?"

Oh God... something is very wrong here. The room is far too dark for us to still be in New York.

"Where am I? What the hell is going on?"

"What's in this bottle?" Melanie says. "I've let you sleep the last six hours and I haven't had any access to the damned

71

internet to research this crap, so you have to tell me what it is."

"I don't have time for this Melanie..."

I'm naked. And I feel... *better.* It's like there was a coil inside me that isn't wound up anymore and I don't understand what the fuck happened.

"You'd better have time," Melanie says. "Since in your psychotic haze, we had sex."

I give Melanie one withering look to see how serious she is. She's fucking serious, isn't she? This kid is too young to pull some shit on me, so this means she's as serious as a fucking heart attack.

I want to throw up again. This can't be possible, but judging by the look on Melanie's face, it's not just possible. It happened.

No...

I run my hands through my hair and glance down at the scene around me. This is my bed... one of my beds.

"Where are we?" I growl again.

"The Poconos, if what you said is true."

"Fuck..."

"What's in the bottle Sammy?"

"How the fuck should I know? My psychiatrist..."

My head hurts too much. I'm in fucking hell, that's what must be happening to me, because there's no way I did this. I didn't drive my dead son's pregnant girlfriend to the middle of nowhere and then...

"Sammy, you need to get up and call someone. You killed a kid."

"I did what?"

No... I couldn't have killed someone. If I believe Melanie, if I took someone else's life... why the fuck don't I remember it and why the fuck do I feel so good? Well, that has to be the sex. *No, Sammy.*

"You killed someone, Sammy"

"My phone doesn't work?"

"No. I tried."

I give Melanie a disapproving look, which she does her very best to ignore. The phones don't work at my safehouse without *enhancement*. I don't call it a safe house for nothing.

"Bring it to me," I command her, but really I need time to think and clean up the disgusting chunk-filled puddle of vomit on the floor.

THIS IS ROCK BOTTOM, isn't it? Fucking a beautiful eighteen-year-old woman who is nearly half my fucking age, and who is also currently carrying someone else's baby has to be rock bottom, no doubt about that shit.

I get out of bed and can't find a t-shirt. Or pants. At least I find underwear, amongst more evidence that I was completely fucking reckless. I fucked her. I had sex with her. I came… and that's why I feel so fucking good. I satisfied both my urges – I killed and I came, and I don't know why I did either of those things. Melanie returns with a mop bucket, a few towels from the kitchen and a disgusted expression on her face.

"I *really* don't want to clean your vomit."

"Then leave it," I grunt. "We can't stay here long. How did I get here?"

"You drove."

"Fuck… Fuck, Melanie… I fucked up."

"I knew you would say that."

I don't know what she expects me to say. Probably something caring…

"I'm sorry for fucking you. It was very inappropriate and it won't happen again. I'll call my brother and get you away from me and I'll set you up with–

"So you can go out there and kill again?" Melanie snaps, before allowing me to finish. "That's your solution? Give me a million fucking orgasms and then disappear?"

She sounds very upset. Something tells me it's wrong to assume this is caused by pregnancy hormones this time. It's me, I'm the problem.

"I'm not disappearing. Now give me the phone."

"Not until you promise not to do anything stupid."

"Once you have Enrico's child, you don't have to keep it. I'll take the kid and you can get as far away from me as possible."

Melanie throws the towels at me. I catch them, feeling the force and ferocity with which she flung them. *Ouch.* She's very upset, so I should probably try my best not to say anything stupid. My head hurts so bad that I wonder if I should ask her to pour me a stiff drink, regardless of how pissed off she is at me. Whiskey would make it much easier to get through this conversation.

"You are a fucking idiot," Melanie says. I guess we're not holding back with each other anymore. "You're on some mystery drug that knocks you into a semi-conscious state where you *murder* someone and you're worried about the fact that we had sex?"

"I assume I buried the body."

I hope I buried the body. Melanie looks like she wants to strangle me, but perhaps doesn't have the energy to do so. I could easily pry her off me, but judging by the expression on her face, she wouldn't care. She has a pretty face. I understand why I did what I did but... Fucking hell.

My father always told me men were dogs and that we can't help it, but did I have to be a dog with her of all the people in the fucking world? I'm forty years old. I outgrew fucking the wrong people ten years ago.

"Yes."

"Who did I kill?"

"A kid who goes to my school."

"Fuck."

Melanie wraps her arms around her chest and shakes her head. "I'll give you the phone. You're messed up and I don't think that medication is doing you any favors."

"My psychiatrist wouldn't have prescribed it if it wasn't supposed to help."

"Right," Melanie says, handing me the cell phone and then wrinkling her nose as she steps over the vomit. "I'm microwaving a frozen burrito downstairs. I'll give you time to do… whatever."

She scurries away before I can protest, shutting the door behind her. She still seems upset and I don't know what the hell I've done to upset her. Orgasms? I gave her orgasms? That's good, I suppose. It's been years since I've been with a woman, so it's good to know I still have that skill set available to me. I run my tongue over my lips and taste something unfamiliar. Is that her? Fuck, that tastes good. I lick my lips clean and have to suppress a raging erection by the time I fix my phone to call my cousin John.

I fucked up, John.

MY COUSIN JOHN, current boss of the long island mob, hates fuck ups. He shows up reeking like cigarettes with bloodshot eyes and a grim, tight jaw. *He wants to kick my ass, but knows he can't because he already took too much from me.*

I let John into the house and he pulls out another cigarette, lighting it in the house without asking for permission.

"Where's the fucking girl?" he asks with the cigarette between his teeth.

"She's sleeping."

John snorts. "What the fuck were you thinking?"

"I wasn't."

"Where's the body?"

"I don't know."

John's cheeks darken and his brows furrow into a haunted caterpillar over his searing gaze.

"Bring the girl out."

"John…"

John puffs on his cigarette a few more times. "I'm not gonna hurt her, for fuck's sake. But this is a huge problem Sammy. I want to be lenient but *Christ*. What did the fucking kid do?"

I hate that I can't tell John any of the details, especially because it means I can't keep him away from Melanie. John hasn't had his father's habit of spilling blood through our city. I believe in his commitment to peace, but I don't want him to hurt her. I reluctantly draw her from the bedroom. Her tummy is starting to protrude forward in a smallish baby bump, and despite her modest clothes – a hoodie and my sweatpants – I find myself staring at her.

My cock stiffens in my pants as she walks into the room to talk to John, and I struggle to hide my body's instinctive reaction to her. *She's so fucking pretty.* Melanie doesn't look at me. She's smart enough to realize she should watch the person who's the biggest threat to her the closest. John stares at her and then he glances at me with a disapproving frown. Like he's one to talk. Sure, he's several years younger than me, but he fell for a college student. I didn't fall for Melanie.

I screwed up. *And now I can't control my raging erection around her. I can't stop myself from staring at her, and I don't give a fuck if John notices how badly I want her.*

"I need your account of what happened," John says to her bluntly. "I need you to be completely honest with me."

Melanie nods and folds her arms. If John scares her, she

doesn't show it. I love that she's so brave, but I still hate myself for my body's reaction to her. Flashes of what happened between us during my period of memory loss interrupt my thoughts, and my cheeks flush with shame. And guilt. It's been so many years since I took a woman to bed. It's been years since I've wanted anything more than to twist myself into celibate suffering as some fucked up form of atoning for the sins I've committed.

John killed my son, the dam broke and somehow through my grief and my screwed up head, I ended up in bed with her. And damn, it must have felt good because her presence makes me uncontrollably hard.

"I can be honest," Melanie says. "But you need to get him to a doctor again. Soon."

John ignores her pleas. He's here for information, and whatever the fuck he plans to do with me, he's probably already made up his mind. We have rules in *cosa nostra* and they got made in my early twenties, so I know them well. You kill without permission from the boss and you lose your fucking life. John killed my son – he could be just like his father and show neither of us any mercy.

"What the fuck happened? Tell me exactly where the fuck you were, who the fuck he killed and what he did with the body. Then, I need you to tell me how the fuck you ended up in bed with my cousin and exactly what happened."

I look at Melanie, assuming she'll balk at my cousin's suggestion that she expose the explicit details of our encounter. Melanie raises an eyebrow, rising to John's challenge. John must notice the bruises on her face and the signs that Melanie isn't the sort of young woman to back down from a fight... perhaps to her own detriment most of the damn time.

She tells John everything I did and my stomach sinks in horror. Every fucking part of this is bad news, especially the part where I drag Melanie's attempted rapist off her and kill him in broad daylight where there could have been any number of witnesses. If I don't go to prison, I'll be lucky. John has no reason to bail me out of this. He goes through about four cigarettes as he listens to the story, scowling. Once Melanie finishes, quickly summarizing what happened upstairs yet humiliating me completely despite her lack of details, John only says three words.

"Not good, Sammy."

I can't tell if it's a death sentence or not.

"I agree."

"What the fuck do you want me to do about this, huh? I want peace in New York, Sammy. Word gets out the mob is out here killing innocent kids and–

"That kid wasn't innocent. Look at her fucking face. What kind of man hits a woman like that, huh?"

John glances at Melanie's face, but that only deepens his scowl. I don't care about helping my case anymore. Maybe what I did was fucking wrong but the rawest part of me reacted to protect her, and I can't genuinely apologize for that. I wasn't in my right mind but... I kept her safe. My grandchild is safe.

"You weren't conscious for any of this? How the fuck can you drive unconscious?"

"He was conscious," Melanie says. "But he was taking this. It's some weird drug."

She produces the prescription from my psychiatrist, handing it to a skeptical John who holds it up.

"What the fuck is this, crack?"

"You know it's not fucking crack."

"I told you to see a shrink, not become a junkie."

"Dr. Gabriel prescribed it to help with my sleep. I'm not a damn junkie. I just had a bad reaction."

"Bad reaction? Sammy, you dumb motherfucker, you killed someone."

He slips the pills into his pocket. My stomach lurches. I don't want him to blame the pills. I'm just fucked in the head because something in me snapped when my son died… that's all.

"He could go to prison," Melanie says. "Worse, I could go to prison. I'm pregnant."

"I understand, Melanie," John says in his best attempts at a comforting voice. "You don't have to worry about that. This dumb motherfucker forced you into this, raped you and–

"He didn't rape me," Melanie interrupts.

John sighs. "Listen, kid. I don't want to argue. You're eighteen years old, pregnant, bruised in the fucking face and both of you admit that this drugged up criminal cousin of mine took you to bed."

"He didn't hit me," Melanie snaps. "He didn't hurt me at all. I know Sammy wasn't in his right mind and I know everything that happened between us probably shouldn't have happened but he needs help, not your judgment. I don't need your judgment either. I'm not a wilting violet. I can handle myself."

John's voice tightens with anger. Does Melanie know what the hell she's doing talking to my brother like this?

He responds smoothly, "Handle yourself? You're eighteen. I don't care if you're the fighting type, you're a woman and a pregnant woman at that. You shouldn't be getting into trouble."

"I GUESS in your world the men tell the women what to do?" Melanie says. "I'm not stupid John, and I'm not a victim. Sammy did some bad things but he also… he just wanted to keep me safe."

"You are suspiciously comfortable with murder," John grumbles under his breath. I don't know if Melanie hears him. She acts like she doesn't.

"Get him help," she says. "That's what he needs."

"You don't think he should go to the cops then?" John says.

Melanie tightens her lips. "I don't snitch. If that makes me a bad person, then fine. At least now Javier won't be able to hurt anyone else."

John's expression softens and it occurs to me that he wants her scared to get the truth and maybe he doesn't have any intentions of hurting us. That could be wishful thinking.

"I'll help you out of this, Sammy. I'll even take your damn dog until you can get your head right. But after this I want the past behind us. I want us to go back to the way things were."

Fuck. I had completely forgotten about Big Tex in my apparent drug haze…

"John…"

"I don't want to hear it. I know what I did. I know there's blood on my hands but I'm going to give you this pass, get you out of this major fuck up, and then I expect your loyalty for the rest of your fucking life, do you understand?"

"Yes."

"One screw up and you'll start a war that I'll have to finish. Because I fucking mean it when I say I want peace, and if you screw that peace up, you won't give me a choice."

"I understand, boss."

"I love you like a brother," John says. "So while I clean this shit up and you get your head straight, I want the two of you close to Lucky where he can keep an eye on you. I've got a condo in Westhampton with great neighbors and no way for you to get in trouble. I want both of you there for the next six months."

"You expect me to live with him for six months?"

"I'll compensate you well," John says. "But it's not an expectation. It's a command."

"What about–" Melanie starts.

John quickly interrupts. "You already started banging the girl, so there's no point trying to keep you apart. The trouble will be keeping you out of trouble. So I need the two of you to listen to me and hear me loud and fucking clear – no more trouble. You look out for each other. Get that fucking psychiatrist to fix your head or better yet, get another doctor."

"What if I don't want to be trapped with him for six months?" Melanie protests.

"You aided and abetted a murder, young lady. You have bigger fucking problems than my cousin's shit personality and drug use. Believe it or not, you'll be safer with him. My brother lives a few minutes away and… well, I think his wife will understand your problems."

"I don't agree to this," Melanie protests.

You don't understand, honey bun. We don't have a fucking choice. But why the hell is my cousin putting me through this torture? I won't be able to resist that woman… and she will drive me completely mad. How the hell is living with her supposed to fix my head when she drives me insane?

Chapter 7
My Humiliating Crush
Melanie

John makes it clear that our wants don't matter. I know it should help that Sammy doesn't want to be here as much as I don't want to be here, but Sammy's reasons for not wanting to be here are far different from mine. He went back to that stupid psychiatrist of his who changed the dosage of his medicine. He sleeps through the night now and he wants nothing to do with me. I'm worse, because I make it a project of avoiding him.

It's hard, considering this condo is the smallest confined space I've been in with Sammy, and John doesn't want me leaving the house without an escort. All I have time to do is update social media.

I don't want to talk to my only available escort who keeps acting like us having sex was the worse thing that ever happened to him.

I might not have the perfect body, I might be pregnant and yes, he's Enrico's father. I get that. I know what we did was wrong... but he acts like he regrets sleeping with me more than he regrets taking a human life. He has such a low opinion of me and it humiliates me that I opened up to him.

If he wasn't acting like this, Sammy would have been the best sex I've ever had.

He doesn't even want to look me in the eye. I hate that it hurts. Does he think he's the only one who feels guilty about what happened? Enrico and I were building a bond that I had to sever because of all his secrets and lies, but I never hated him. I never loved him either, but I never hated him. If he were alive, I obviously would have never looked twice at his father. Sammy knows the same would be true for him. What happened between us only happened because of circumstances – and maybe those circumstances weren't perfect, but I don't think Sammy's a bad person for kissing me. Or for feeling something.

MAYBE I'M TOO young to understand. That's what Sammy seems to think... That's why he seems to be ignoring me. I'm too young and stupid for him. *He'll never want me. Everything that happened was just a mistake to him and I'm all alone here. Ugh.*

AFTER OUR USUAL morning routine of ignoring each other, the Friday after the *Islanders* lost and he stormed off to his room with alcohol he isn't supposed to drink, Sammy leaves for his psychiatrist's appointment and I sit in the condo... *alone.*

The first three weeks were fine because I caught up on every single TV show I cared about, but after the novelty of binge-watching television wore off and my baby bump started *really* showing, I stopped wanting to sit in front of the TV all day. The baby makes me gassy and also makes me constantly think about the future and what sort of life I'm bringing my child into...

What happens when Sammy stops wanting me around so

he can watch my every move and "keep me safe"? He could easily snatch my baby and leave me high and dry. I don't want that either. The only way out of this is to get on my feet like I planned. My mother took a bribe from Sammy to get me out of the way, so there's no point in feeling guilty about leaving her behind this time. I have a kid to worry about now and the bigger my baby bump gets the more real it gets that I can't have my kid hearing the abusive stuff she would always say to me. Boy or girl, I'll love this baby to the moon and back.

Just when I pull out my phone to read *Lipstick Alley* gossip about a True Crime case Shawnte and I obsess over after scrolling through *Netflix* without finding anything good, the doorbell rings.. I didn't even know this place had a doorbell. A stupid part of me hopes Shawnte's at the door, though she doesn't even know where I am, so that's impossible.

I miss her. She still won't answer her phone and I hope she's okay.

"I'm coming!" I call out.

It takes me a while to get off the couch with my baby bump protruding forward and I groan as I call out again that I'm coming to whoever's at the door. By the time I get to the door, I look out the peephole and don't see anyone. I don't even see a delivery truck. I glance down at the stoop and there's a tiny brown box.

The delivery driver must have been busy and hurried off down the street. I open the door and take the box. There's a little rattling noise. Weird. I shut the door and lock it, taking the box to the kitchen counter. There's no name on the box or indication of the sender, which is weird if this is something Sammy ordered. Maybe John left the box and he just didn't want me to see him.

I don't think John likes me or he wouldn't have stuck me

here with Sammy, who ignores me completely the vast majority of the day when I'm not ignoring him.

I peel the box open and a disgusting smell hits my nostrils. I gag and stumble backwards against the counter in sharp revulsion. *Get the fuck away from that,* nags the voice in my head. I hold my nose but the stench already feels like an infection and I know I have to get closer for no other reason than the fact that I need to throw that box out before the smell spreads.

With a shaking hand, I inch closer to the box again and try not to throw up. Breathing slowly just barely stops my head from swimming. Looking into the box makes things worse. There are three dead rats in the box and none of them have heads. The three heads were included in the box, detached and rolling around. *I want to throw up.*

The white rat is limp and stiff next to the black rat, which has a large incision in its stomach with a tiny rat poking out of the hole. That one is small enough that it's probably a mouse – also headless. I run to the front door and double check the locks. *Who the fuck left this here?*

I grab my cell phone and click the option to speed dial Sammy, wishing that Big Tex were here. Sammy picks up after a couple rings.

"Where are you?" I yell at him. I know I'm overreacting, but my heart feels like it's in my throat and I have three dead rats on the counter that smell exactly as dead as they are. I want to vomit and cry and get the fuck out of here.

"Melanie? What's going on? I'm on the subway and I–

HOLY. Fuck. The line goes dead. I can't deal with this shit. I need Sammy and he isn't here and whoever put those rats on our doorstep clearly wants to send a message that we're dead meat. I need to get the hell out of here. I call Shawnte. She hasn't answered the last few times I called her, but this time… I'm praying.

SHE PICKS up after three rings.

"MELANIE! Oh my God, it finally works."

"Where the hell have you been?"

"I just got back to New York. I… Oh my God, where are you? What's going on? I heard… I heard some bad shit, girl. Are you okay?"

"No. I'm not okay. I need you to meet me in front of Boulevard Pizza. I'm coming from Westhampton, so it'll take a while, but I need you there. Please."

"Okay," Shawnte says calmly, with no questions asked. "But you should know, Damzel's claiming she's the reason her boyfriend went missing and she wants to kill you next."

"What?"

"She thinks you two ran away together because she found out about his other baby mama aside from Angelica, and Damzel claims she took Javier's life as revenge."

"Why would she brag about that?"

"Street cred," Shawnte says. "Duh."

"That never happened," I grumble. Why the hell does this shit keep following me? I'm still nauseous from the dead animals, Sammy won't answer his phone and Shawnte announces that someone wants to kill me. *Could Damzel have sent the rats?* The thought seems unrealistic.

"She doesn't care what happened. I'll meet you in front of the pizza place."

"Got it."

. . .

I BUST out of the house so fast that I don't bother with the box, leaving a note for Sammy or anything else. He's made it clear how he feels about me. I'm a nuisance, a stupid mistake, and once I give him his grandchild, something that's never gonna happen, he'll get rid of me. I throw a few simple outfits into a backpack and hit the streets. I have to get a taxi to the city, which takes a while, but once I get there, I know I'll feel free.

It's too much being in that house with Sammy and acting like our night together never happened.

He might have been high out of his damn mind, but I wasn't. The way he felt on top of me, the way his lips felt against my skin... I can't get it out of my head and it makes me feel crazy because he's two decades older than me. I know it's wrong to even look at him like this, but I want to run my hands over his skin and touch the scars that mark Sammy's years of experience.

He protected me. He made me feel loved for the first time in months. I'm pregnant. Is it so wrong to want someone to give a fuck about you when you're pregnant? My mom never did. I just want to feel that love once in my life, you know? I want to know what it's like for someone to really *want* me. Sammy doesn't want me and I'm tired of pretending that he does just so he can get his grandchild.

As the taxi pulls up to Boulevard Pizza, I notice Shawnte has her own version of a getaway vehicle waiting for us.

"Did you buy a new car?"

"I wouldn't call it new," she says, slapping the hood of the 2007 Chrysler 300. "But it works."

"Where the hell did you get this?"

"A friend of a friend lent it to me. Are you ready to get the hell out of here?"

Chapter 8
The Shrink & My Secrets
Sammy

"How are you adjusting to the new dose, Sammy?"

"I'm fine."

"What about the impulses we discussed before," Dr. Gabriel asks. "Have you had a recurrence of memory lapses and violent thoughts?"

Violent thoughts... She can't know that I killed someone, but she seems to almost wish that I had.

"No. Not that I'm aware of."

"Interesting. And no violent behavior that you're aware of, right?"

"No. I just... I had... an inappropriate encounter with the girl. Melanie."

Dr. Gabriel's grip on the pencil tightens. "What do you mean an inappropriate encounter?"

"During my last memory lapse I might have... touched her."

I don't want to confess my darkest secrets to this woman. I just need to rest and to get some peace of mind. Can a shrink give me peace of mind, or is that something I can only find myself?

"Has that happened since you started your new dose?"

"No. No, nothing like that."

"Then you do have an absence of violent and overtly sexual thoughts?"

I grit my teeth. What's the point in confessing anything to this woman? She'll either raise or lower the dose and what the fuck will either of those things do.

"Sammy?" she asks.

"I'm just not sure how any of this is helping."

Dr. Gabriel purses her lips. "Are you sleeping better? Keeping better control of your impulses?"

"I barely know when these impulses started. I came here because I lost my son and now... I've hurt people. I've hurt Melanie and I don't see a fucking end to this."

"Sammy," she says. "Take a deep breath. You don't need to be so hard on yourself. You need to recognize that losing someone comes with these highs and lows. Tell me more about what happened with Melanie. I can't help you unless you tell me the truth..."

I LEAVE the shrink after skipping around the details and confessing whatever the fuck I could about Melanie without spilling the gory details of my criminal enterprises. I don't know if this shrink is working and all I can think about is heading back to Westhampton so I can be with Melanie again, especially after our call dropped while I was on the subway.

When I get to the house, the front door swings open without me unlocking it.

"Melanie?"

I've warned her about this door. Where the hell is she? It doesn't take more than a few steps into the house for the putrid smell of death to slam into my nostrils and nearly send me doubling over. *Fucking Christ.*

I reach into my pocket for my cell phone. It's not there. What the fuck? It was there when I entered the damn therapist's office, but I pat myself down thoroughly and there's no fucking sign of it. How the fuck am I supposed to get a hold of her now? *Fuck.*

I push past my instincts and follow the disgusting scent to an open box in the dining room. There's something dead in there, that much is obvious. No signs of breaking and entering. She must have let someone in with the box or brought the box in herself and what the fuck is in the box anyway? I take one quick glance inside the box before forcing down another gag.

Jesus fuck.

I NEED TO THINK. My father taught me that panic never helps. You push the panic out of the way, you think very fucking carefully and only then, you load your pistol and take care of whatever you gotta take care of. *I need to think.*

The stench makes it impossible to think, but I'm almost too jittery to clean 'em up and consider who could have sent these and what the hell happened to Melanie. If she were dead, there would be signs. That calms me down. I put on gloves, get the bleach out and start cleaning one of the easier crime scenes I've been a part of.

Sicko. Some sicko sent her a threat.

Once I get rid of the dead rodents and clean my kitchen with bleach, I'm able to get my head together to find Melanie. Forget about Dr. Gabriel's new fucking prescription, I have to find her. She must've been scared out of her fucking mind and fled, but where the hell would she go?

Knowing the girl I've had in my custody, she wouldn't go anywhere sensible. She's still so young, and remembering how I touched her makes me feel guilty knowing just how young she really is.. Parts of me remember how it felt. My skin flushes when she gets near me, and when she walks by me the scent of her lotion alone makes my cock stiffen. I don't know what the fuck John was thinking sticking me in a confined space with her.

She thinks I hate her, but nothing could be further from the truth. I want to protect her from my darkness, shield her from the pain I've already caused and the pain I could cause in the future. I can't look Melanie in the eye because it hurts too much to have the constant reminders of how much I screwed up with my son and then how I made it worse by touching her.

It doesn't matter that she's lonely too. She should be with someone her own age.

I DON'T HAVE my phone, so I drive to Lucky's house because it's closest. I know he'll judge the fuck out of me, but if I go to John with this... Christ, what the fuck was Melanie thinking?

Lucky doesn't answer the door. Of course. As Lucky's wife, Althea, answers the door, I notice that although she looks better than the last time I saw her, she doesn't appreciate my presence any more than before.

"You look like you fucked something up," she says, swaying her waist-length red dreadlocks out of her face and eyeing me with suspicion. I can hear Chiara squealing and running around inside. I miss my niece... but Lucky wants my head in better shape before I see her again.

"Melanie's missing."

Althea's warm face immediately twists into a completely disapproving expression. She closes the door. Fuck. She's getting my cousin. Lucky returns a few minutes later with a pistol in his pocket and his jacket on.

"Althea says you fucked up and lost the pregnant girl. Let's go get her."

"Aren't you going to invite me in for a cup of coffee..."

"I told John this was a bad idea," Lucky grumbles. "He never fucking listens to anyone."

I've been privy to John's similar complaints about his brother, but I bite my tongue. I need him now.

"Any idea where she's gone?"

I wish I had the answer Lucky wants, but I don't. I don't have the faintest fucking clue where she ended up or where she could have gone.

"No."

"What do you know about her then? We can figure it out."

"I know where her mother lives. That's about it."

"She wouldn't have gone to her mother?"

My chest tightens. No, she wouldn't have. Melanie probably goes through her life thinking no one in the world cares for her. She thinks I abandoned her.

"No. But her mother might know where she went."

"Where the fuck is your cell phone?" Lucky chides me. Unlike John, he doesn't have nicotine to smooth over his crude, Vicari temper.

"I don't know. I came back from the fucking appointment and it was gone."

"Fuck, Sammy..."

"I just need your help finding her. I can do the rest. I haven't lost my touch. I just..."

"You need to stop beating yourself up over screwing the pregnant girl," Lucky says. My cheeks burn. How the fuck does he know about that? Clearly I don't understand the extent to which he has John's ear.

"She's too young for me and I wasn't in my right mind when it happened."

Lucky smirks. "Are you ever in your right fucking mind anymore? I've seen the girl. She might be young, but she's a fucking fighter. Maybe she's what you need."

"You two have fucked up morals."

"Yeah. Maybe. Or maybe we know there's a way out of this mess and it ain't through killing, drugs, or a fucking shrink."

I DON'T KNOW exactly what my cousin Lucky's suggesting. Does he think I can hop into bed with an eighteen-year-old pregnant woman and forget my troubles? She's an adult, yes, but a very young one and even if she insists on getting into fights… she's still female. Fragile. She needs protecting, even if she would disagree with me and call me old-fashioned for suggesting such a thing.

She needs protection from the world and that includes me. I can't have her, especially when I'm not in my right mind. When Lucky and I arrive at her mother's house, I half-expect to see her appear in the doorway. Her mother notices when we approach and flings the door open with a disapproving look on her face. She doesn't like me or trust me, but the feeling is completely fucking mutual.

I have a touch of humility about me this time. Melanie's mother folds her arms and gives us a once over.

"She ain't here," she says. "And I'm busy, so you can run along now."

"Melanie left my house and I can't contact her. Can we at least use your phone so I can call her? Please. It's important."

Melanie's mother eyes me with shrewd distrust. I can't blame her considering my son knocked up her daughter. The men in my family can't be trusted, but her suspicions have more to do with her desire to profit from the situation than her care for Melanie. That's what pisses me off.

"You can use my phone if you pay to use my phone. My bill is $99 a month and you look like you can afford it. I just lost my job again because of this bitch at work, so I can't afford to have strangers making calls."

"Don't you have unlimited calls?" Lucky grumbles matter-of-factly. Ms. Stevens appears to only just notice him and she gives him a disinterested once-over before handing me her unlocked phone with no further mention of payment. I don't understand Lucky's way with people. Melanie doesn't answer when I call. Of course.

Her mother smirks when she notices. "See why I have nothing to do with that bitch? She won't pick up a call from her own mother."

"I'm not giving up on her," I growl while calling again. Melanie answers.

"Hello?" she says.

Yes. She's alive.

"Melanie? Where the fuck are you?"

"I CAN'T TELL YOU."

"Melanie, you tell me where the hell you are right this second or I swear, I'll spank you so hard, you'll end up in Pennsylvania."

* * *

Chapter 9
He Sounded Sexy...
Melanie

Sammy is out of his fucking mind and when he shows up here, I'm going to give him a piece of mine. Threatening to spank me is out of the question and I tell him as much, but he's also firm that he wants to know where we are. Shawnte and I are in a tiny studio apartment in Hartford, Connecticut. Shawnte is way too well-connected and has a cousin with a place out there who needs a housesitter. We have four days before we have to move out, which we thought would be plenty of time. I didn't expect Sammy to track us down this quickly.

"We should get pizza," Shawnte says. "Since you have a man coming out here... we might as well blow our money."

"Sammy's not a man. He's a crazy person."

"He sounded sexy," Shawnte says. "And he's had you up in his house pregnant and never looked at you? That doesn't sound realistic."

"Not all guys want to jump everything with a pulse."

Shawnte snickers. "You're not just something with a pulse, Melanie. You're thick. You're pretty. Guys at our school pick on you 'cause they know they couldn't handle you."

"That sounds like cope."

Shawnte laughs. "Okay, then. But I bet that guy has been looking at your ass every time he walks away."

"He hasn't looked at me at all. I wanted to run away. The dead rats were just the nail in the damned coffin."

"Who the fuck did that? You think he has enemies?"

"Yeah."

"Do you think it was Damzel's boyfriend?"

"It couldn't have been."

"Why? Do you believe the rumor that he's dead too?"

It's not a rumor. Sammy Zagarella killed Damzel's boyfriend and buried his body in the woods. I'm keeping his secret because... I don't know. I think it's because of the night we had and how he made me feel. Sammy protected me, even when his mind was frayed completely. I want to protect him now.

"He's dead," I tell Shawnte. "Don't ask me how I know."

Shawnte looks me over a little suspiciously, but then she nods. "I get it."

"Really?"

"You tell me everything. If you don't want to tell me something, I know you have a good reason."

"Thanks, girl."

"Damzel's saying she killed him."

"That's not true," I mutter. "But maybe she wishes she did."

"She wanted to kill *me* over him," Shawnte reminds me. "She was bamboozled by that man, so I doubt she would hurt him."

I guess it doesn't matter whether Damzel would have hurt her boyfriend. Sammy took care of that for her.

Shawnte and I order pizza and after we eat, we fall asleep watching TV and I don't wake up until the doorbell rings.

I sense it's him before I get off the couch. Shawnte yawns and curls up under the blanket we were sharing, unmoved by the doorbell. I want to see Sammy, even if I shouldn't. He came to get me. He drove all these hours to find me and there's a tiny piece of me that hopes Sammy did it because he remembers our night together and he wants me...

IT'S DUMB AND NAIVE, but why else did he want me back? He went to my mom's house to find me and when I heard his voice... I forgot about the stupid dead rats and I just wanted to be in his arms. I just wish he would return my love. I just wish he cared.

I OPEN the door and Sammy rushes in, approaching me and wrapping his arms around me, hugging me tightly in front of his brother. Finally, the sound of their boots entering the studio apartment awakens Shawnte from the couch.

"Hi, y'all," she calls out. "I'm Shawnte, Melanie's best friend. I'm tired as hell, so I'm going back to sleep."

She curls back up and falls asleep again. Seriously, Shawnte? All that pizza has her passed the hell out. She always gets like that when she eats pizza. I want to roll my eyes and turn to drag her off the couch, but Sammy doesn't let me go when I pull away from his hug.

"You should have *never* left New York," he growls.

I can't meet his gaze. I don't want him to give me that disapproving look when I've been hoping that he would come here because he cared about me, not because he wanted to lock me up.

"If you saw what I saw, what would you have done?"

"Called."

"I *did.*"

Lucky clears his throat and elbows Sammy. "I'll be in the car."

"I'm not leaving without Shawnte," I snap at Sammy. He glances over at the couch and then he looks at me. For the first time since he walked through the door, he actually *looks at* me. Sammy's green eyes fixate on mine. He scowls and then he presses his hand to my face

"I was worried about you," Sammy says. "I found the threat and I thought someone could have hurt you. Does Connecticut seem like the safest place on earth to you?"

"I'm fine. Shawnte and I had a plan."

"To run away?"

"Yes."

Sammy scowls and shakes his head. "No way, honey bun."

Now I'm properly looking at him.

"Honey bun?"

Sammy sighs. "I'm not letting you run away. Not only would that put you in unnecessary danger from my brother... I don't want to be without you."

"Shut up."

"I mean it, Melanie. I... enjoy your company."

"We haven't had each other's company since John locked us up in that house. You barely look me in the eye and you've made it clear that..."

I bite my lip and then I make the smart decision of looking over at the couch. Shawnte is sitting up, leaning over the back of the couch and staring at us.

"No, keep going," Shawnte says. "It's like a free Tyler Perry movie."

"It's not that I don't care about you," Sammy says, color rushing to his cheeks. Now that Shawnte's staring at us, he puts extra distance between us. He runs his hand over his chin and clears his throat. "I want you safe, Melanie and I want you with me. You were important to my son and now you're important to me."

Sammy's gaze fixes on me and even if he's trying to hold back, I see something in his eyes. *Something real.*

"I'm not giving you a choice," he says. "Your friend can stay, but you're coming with me and we're going to find out who sent you that message."

"It might have been Damzel," Shawnte says. "You know, the reason we got kicked out."

Technically, we were the reason we got kicked out. I was only trying to defend Shawnte, but we still got into a fight at school that maybe we could have avoided. *Maybe Sammy wouldn't have killed him if we hadn't been so quick to fight.*

Sammy bites his lip, considering her statement, his gaze never leaving me. I want to be strong enough to fight the pull towards Sammy Zagarella. I know what will happen if we're in close quarters. I'll want him so badly it hurts and I'll feel so guilty for wanting a man whose grandson I'm carrying in my womb.

"I'm not coming with you," I protest, folding my arms and getting ready to put my foot down. Shawnte and I ran away once, we can do it again.

SAMMY DRAGS me to the car. Shawnte walks. He doesn't understand why I'm "suddenly moody" and keeps muttering under his breath about pregnant women like I'm not right there. Shawnte and I sit in the back together, while Lucky and Sammy sit in the front. Sammy keeps his gaze fixed on me through the rearview mirror. Shawnte falls asleep immediately once the car starts and Lucky turns on Pink Floyd. I can't sleep and it's mainly because of Sammy's staring.

I hope his ass is on medication. And where is his cell phone?

"HEY," I whisper, leaning between their seats. Lucky glances at me disinterested and assumes I'm addressing Sammy, which I am.

"Yes?" Sammy asks impatiently.

"Where's your phone?"

"I don't know."

"Where's the last place you saw it?"

Sammy can't keep track of *anything*.

"I don't know," he says. "My therapist."

Lucky coughs. "The one who gave you the murder pills?"

"Can you shut up?" Sammy growls, glancing over his shoulder at Shawnte.

"Don't worry, she's my ride or die."

Lucky smirks. "She'd better be."

Sammy glares at his cousin. "Threaten her again and I'll cut your dick off."

"Jeez, Sammy. Chill out. I'm looking out for you and I'm telling you that this shit is no good. Drugs never solved anything."

"John needs me to heal."

"Try giving a fuck about someone other than yourself instead of doing fucking pills. How about that?"

"I care about plenty of people."

"Care harder," Lucky growls. "Care about the future you're leaving your grandchild and care about your lost cell phone and care that you aren't in control."

I slink into the backseat and try to disappear. I feel like I'm witnessing something I shouldn't. Sammy grunts and leans back, his eyes fluttering shut. He has a handsome face and I know he's forty, but he doesn't look like it. No fine lines, just smooth, olive Italian skin and a jawline that makes you want to lick his neck. *He's beautiful.* He might be a monster, but he's my beautiful monster and I wouldn't have him any other way.

Chapter 10
Emotion.
Sammy

Once we get back to the safe house, I show Shawnte to a room upstairs where she promptly falls asleep. I have weapons, Lucky went to John to ask for a couple guys to watch the house, and everything is back to normal. Except me. Except her. Losing her for this brief time…

I knock on Melanie's door. I still haven't found my cell phone. That's fucking important, so Lucky has three guys looking for it. I have my new prescription from my psych, but Lucky made some fucking sense in the car. John wants me to fix my head, but maybe he's wrong about how I should do it. Maybe there's something better than pills.

Maybe there's something that I actually want.

I KNOCK on the door to her bedroom. I can't help but imagine that she's in there, alone and naked.. *No, I shouldn't imagine that.* It doesn't matter that the memories come back to me whenever I close my eyes. It doesn't matter that the most primal part of me remembers how her body feels. It doesn't matter.

I don't have to touch her. I shouldn't. I just need to show her that I genuinely care – that I'm not a head case, and even if I am… there's someone good there deep down.

Melanie opens the door, her belly slightly protruding forward through a black sweater. *She's pregnant and she smells like an incredibly delicious pregnant woman. I never had the experience with Enrico's mother and she's… something else.*

"Yes?"

She always answers me with a little attitude and I fucking love it. She reminds me that I need to be kept on my toes.

"I don't want to take my medication."

"Great."

"I'd much rather spend the night with you…. Since we're stuck together and your friend is fast asleep."

Melanie rolls her eyes. "Shawnte took one look at that four poster bed and she's determined to sleep there all night."

There's a hint of a smile on her face that makes me want to tease out more of it. I want her to smile because of me, not despite me for once.

"You don't have to hang out with me out of pity. I have my cell phone."

"Maybe that's a problem. How did anyone know you were here?"

Melanie sighs. "I don't know, Sammy. I don't want a lecture. I just want you to promise that there won't be any more dead rats."

"I don't plan on letting you out of my sight."

My voice sounds more intense than I had intended, and Melanie's eyes flicker nervously up to mine.

"You don't mean that."

"Trust me, honey bun. I do."

I smile at her, but she doesn't return my smile. "It's not funny, Sammy. You're old enough to know not to play with my heart."

I adjust my stance in her doorway. Playing with Melanie's heart is the last thing on my mind. I don't want to hurt her at all.

"I'm sorry for what I did with or without that medication. There's no excuse. I'm quitting the pills. I'm quitting the psychiatrist. You might hate me now, but I can't help but feel that we have this...bond."

I can't stop myself from glancing down at her stomach and I hate that just the sight of her gets me instantly hard. It's like my brain doesn't register that she's carrying another man's baby. My dead son's baby. It's like my grief has twisted itself up into a fucked up mess and I don't know what to do.

I continue, "I care about my grandchild and I care about you. Perhaps I got confused about that in my... state. But you've been here. You've stayed with me despite all that. I owe you more than my silence."

Melanie folds her arms. "Yes. You do."

She won't budge and the challenge of winning her over spurs something in me that I thought long dead. I straighten my posture and clear my throat.

"I genuinely enjoy your company. Although I wish you would stop getting into fights, running away and otherwise engaging in mischief."

"I'm almost nineteen. I can't stop myself."

"I'd better find a way to stop you then."

Melanie rolls her eyes. "I'd like to see you try, tough guy."

"Tough guy?"

"Oh my bad, what do you and your buddies like to call yourselves? Wise guys?"

"We can't talk about that."

I'm partly serious, but I keep smiling at her because I can't help myself. I just want her to say yes.

"What do you want to do tonight to keep yourself away from the pills, Mr. Zagarella."

"Mr. Zagarella?"

"You obviously regret what happened and you're trying to start off on the right foot so... I'm being formal for once."

"I prefer Sammy. Seriously. Especially from you."

"Whatever."

"We should do something for the baby," I suggest. The suggestion comes from a warm ball of energy that seems to pulse suddenly and chaotically in my chest. I want her so fucking badly it *hurts*.

"Like what?"

"My cousin can't keep us here forever and I haven't exactly had kids around my place in a while... so maybe we could use a computer and... search for a place to live."

"Um... what?"

"You, me and the baby."

Melanie finally leaves her bedroom and shuts the door behind her, but she seems to only leave the room to lecture me.

"Sammy, what the hell do you mean? We aren't..."

"You're carrying my grandchild and you can't exactly go back to your mother's house..."

Melanie frowns and I wonder if I've gone too far. She shakes her head. "If you let me get a job, I can stand on my own two feet and get out of here. On my own.

"That's not what I want."

"What do you want then?"

Her gaze flickers up to mine and I don't know how to express what I want with words. They seem insufficient and I always seem to say the wrong thing anyway.

"To be a good person. To be a bad person. To be there for you."

"I never understand a fucking word that comes out of your mouth."

"I'll never understand when women started swearing so much," I murmur. "But I like it."

"That's right," Melanie smirks. "Screw house hunting, Sammy. Can we watch a movie instead? My feet hurt and I think the baby's giving me a newfound awareness of my pancreas."

"Is that why you're scowling at me?"

"No. I'm just scowling at you."

"Great."

"You can make it up to me though," Melanie sighs. "Hot tea. Movies. Foot rubs."

"I don't do foot rubs," I grumble. Melanie raises a skeptical and very judgmental eyebrow.

"Is that so?" she challenges. "It might be in your best interests to get with the program."

"Is that so?" I push back, smiling and getting close enough to touch her. *I can't. I desperately want to hold her, but I can't. Still, this feels better than drugs and for once in my fucking life, my head is clear. I don't want the pills, I don't need the psychiatry. I just want her.*

"Yes."

"I'll do my very best with the foot rubs."

"Didn't you go through this before?"

I guide Melanie down the hallway. I want to be on my ass with a beer before I tell Melanie about my first time going through this... twenty years ago? Fuck, I was just a kid and Enrico's mom... her people didn't want anything to do with me. Alfonso Vicari paid them off to leave Long Island and

Enrico's mother never wanted the kid. They were Catholics and wanted me to marry her. Neither of us wanted it.

The whole situation was a fucking mess.

"I don't remember all the details," I whisper. "But this is my second chance, so I'd like to do it a lot better."

"Add ice-cream to the foot rubs. That would give you extra points."

She reminds me of the girls I would have liked. She's not white, and that's very different, but now that I'm older... I don't mind. I don't care anymore. Lose your son and you lose your attachment to unimportant things like skin color.

Melanie plops down on the living room couch and I sit across from her.

"Give me those feet and then I'll go get some tea." I say, patting my lap.

"I was joking about the foot rubs," Melanie says.

"Do they hurt?"

"What part of me *doesn't* hurt?" She throws her head back, exposing her neck. The soft brown skin on her neck looks especially kissable and I feel like a fucking pervert for looking at her. I remind myself that even if she was joking, I still owe her some foot rubs. Melanie flicks on the television and heads straight for *Netflix*. I don't get her obsession with all those theatrical shows with women crying and screaming about their boyfriends.

"We're watching *Scandal*. Don't care what you say."

"Whatever..."

"I don't need the volume on. I just like to watch Kerry do her thing."

See? I'll never understand her. "Give me one of those feet then."

"Sammy..."

"You're pregnant. I'm your child's grandfather. A very *young* grandfather, but it's my job to take care of you now."

"I'm not a *job*."

"I didn't mean it like that," I tell her. "I mean... I want to take care of you."

"I have to take care of myself. It's always been like that."

Her feet must really hurt because Melanie reluctantly puts her feet on my lap. The second her foot touches my thighs, my cock jumps in my pants. I move one of the throw pillows over my lap and clear my throat, setting up Melanie's foot on the pillow. I touch the bottom of her feet and Melanie moans. *Jesus Christ.* My cock nearly jerks the pillow. Melanie gasps, seemingly embarrassed.

"That felt too good. You need to chill."

"Are your feet that sore?" I grumble, touching the bottom of her feet more gently and slowly massaging the tightness in her muscles. She holds a lot of tension in her feet and I bet she holds more in her legs. I wouldn't mind massaging her legs. I don't remember what those felt like and I'm still male – there's still a part of me that wonders what those pretty brown thighs look like wrapped around my face and what she tastes like between those thick, delicious pussy lips. I have impulse control. I don't need to sleep with her. I can resist her...

Melanie makes a more subdued moaning sound and leans back, her hair cascading down her shoulders. She takes very good care of her hair and she's always very shiny. She smells like nutmeg and as I press my fingers into the balls of her feet, the sweet nutmeg smell becomes almost overpowering. My dick jumps again and this time, I swear she feels it.

Melanie only reacts to my massage and occasionally glances at the dramatic scene on the screen with a very fancy looking black lady and an old white guy. *Hm.* It's the type of show that could give a man ideas, I suppose.

"Other foot," I grunt, hoping to cut through the building

tension between us. Melanie switches out her feet and then she shakes her head.

"That feels too good," she says. "I can't remember the last time I felt this good."

She bites her lip and then shakes her head. "Never mind. I can. But I shouldn't bring it up. Your massage is getting to my head."

I continue massaging the balls of her other foot. I want to get to her head. I want her to unload all her troubles for once. I want something that isn't just about me. Melanie groans and moves her foot away.

"I can't take it."

No. I don't want her to move away from me. I foolishly and impulsively reach for Melanie's hand despite my promise to myself that I wouldn't. She doesn't pull her hand away, but she looks at me.

"Sammy?"

"I just want... to hold you."

"A massage is good enough."

"No," I insist. "I want... Could you..."

"Are you asking me to cuddle?"

"Don't say it so loud..."

"There isn't anyone to hear you, stupid," Melanie whispers. "And I'm pregnant. I obviously want to cuddle."

"Then come here and let's watch your strange show."

I pull her body against mine and Melanie curls up against me, her head resting on my chest. She falls asleep for a few minutes, ignoring her show and pressing more of her weight against me. I throw my arm around Melanie and allow myself to *feel*.

Chapter 11
Thug Kisses
Melanie

I wake up to a soft kiss on the top of my forehead and Sammy shifts his position on the couch. I don't even care about *Scandal* anymore. His lips on my forehead feel amazing and it's easy to lean into Sammy, even if there's a part of me that knows I shouldn't indulge in his lips or his warm biceps wrapped around me. I murmur something half-heartedly and then I nuzzle deeper into Sammy's arms.

He kisses my cheek and I move again. Sammy pulls my body atop his, still so relaxed and comfortable that my eyes are half closed. He wraps his arms about my waist and then drags me up against him so that my head is in the crook of his neck. Sammy shifts slightly, and when I first feel Sammy's lips against mine, I want more.

I move my body more on top of him, allowing the motion to wake me up more before I lean down to kiss him.. Sammy lets out a small moan at my kiss, and my tongue slips out of my mouth as I try to push into his.

Sammy makes a frustrated grunting sound and then sucks on my tongue gently as he kisses me. My thighs squeeze together against my will and my hands press against

Sammy's chest. It's firm. He kisses me more deeply and a rush of feeling swirls straight to my tightness.

"You're very soft," Sammy murmurs.

"Did you take that medication?"

"No," Sammy growls. "I just... regret pushing you away."

"Technically, I ran."

"Only because I pushed you."

I try to wriggle away from him, but Sammy clamps his hands around my waist, hard.

"I don't want you to go," he murmurs. "And I'm sorry for being a coward. I want to get better. No pills. Just you and... the baby. Our baby."

"This is *not* our baby," I protest, speeding up my squirming. One of Sammy's hands moves up to my back, helping to keep me on top of him. "We are the two people in the world this baby has." Sammy says. "Unless you're willing to nominate your mother."

I give up on trying to squirm free, and instead drive my toes into Sammy's shin. He should know that my mother is the last person I want to talk to about. Despite my obvious annoyance at the mention of my mother, Sammy moves his hand up to my face to gently tilt my head before kissing me. He drags my lower lip between his teeth and sighs as he lets go of me, sucking slowly on my flesh as he drags his hands down my body to squeeze my ass.

"What if I don't want to share? I can feel him or her or whoever growing inside me and... I guess a part of me ran because I feel like I want this kid all to myself."

"I never intended to take your child, Melanie. Clearly, I'm not a fit parent."

"What happened to Enrico wasn't your fault."

Great, now I've mentioned someone between us. Sammy's hand falls away from my ass and back to my hips. I push up against him, guilt pulsing through me as Sammy continues to hold me despite what I've said.

"Maybe not," he whispers. "But I won't screw up with your kid. I won't screw up again. You aren't here under any obligation, Melanie Stevens. You're here because... you're my family."

"That is... so fucking weird."

Sammy grins. "I like women who swear. Naughty, bad, dangerous women. Is that weird too?"

I kiss him again, because it's weird, but I fucking like it. I know I shouldn't want Sammy, but it's hard not to fall for someone who genuinely cares for you – for real. I never got this from my family or even from Enrico. He was always just out of reach...

"Yes," I whisper. "Very weird."

Sammy flips me onto my back, positioning his body on mine. "Good. Maybe I need to be weird... for tonight."

"You're going to regret this in the morning again," I whisper, trying not to moan as Sammy presses his nose to my neck as he kisses me there. I love neck kisses and Sammy knows the exact spots on my neck to tease with his lips.

"No," he growls. "I won't. Not this time."

"What's the difference?"

"I'm in my right mind. I know you want this. I'm not... hurting you."

He kisses my cheek gently and then pulls away to gaze deeply into my eyes. He doesn't look like he wants anything from me, he just wants to *look* at me and that bothers me even more.

"I... I care about you, Melanie. I don't want you to feel alone and... I'm selfish. I don't want to feel alone either."

"You're not selfish. I lost someone too, Sammy. I get it. Maybe that's why we were drawn to each other, you know?"

"Hm," Sammy grunts. "Maybe."

He pushes me deeper into the soft couch cushions and kisses me again. I rake my fingers through Sammy's thick, long hair. His messy, tangled hair resists my fingers raking through it. I tug a little and the slightest pain causes Sammy to push his hips forward into me. As his body rests against mine, I feel his thick hardness pressing against my thigh. My stomach lurches from the memory of that gigantic thing pressing into me.

He's too big to fit inside me, so why do I get so horny with Sammy rubbing up on me? Being responsible isn't just his job because he's older. I'm pregnant, I'm going to be a mom soon... and every cell in my body is telling me to draw Sammy closer. To have him. *He's so protective and fatherly, I can't resist it and I don't want to.*

Sammy eases his hand into my sweatpants. I bite my lower lip because there are only a few moments before Sammy discovers just how wet all this kissing has made me. His hands slide into my underwear and I squeeze my thighs together in a failed attempt to stop him from reaching down there. Sammy thrusts my thighs apart easily and presses his fingers between my legs.

"Fuck," he grunts enthusiastically. "You're so wet, honey bun."

I don't know why I let that nickname stick. Sammy's fingers spread my lower lips and a rush of pleasure excites me to push my hips against his hands. I cry out as Sammy's fingers find my clit. My body is either desperate to be touched, or Sammy really knows what he's doing. I would say it's some mixture of both. I bite my lower lip and moan as Sammy finds just the right spot on my clit and rubs me in slow, smooth circles. His cock stiffens even further against my thigh as Sammy finds a pleasurable spot between my legs and rubs me there until I moan and buck my hips against him.

An orgasm builds in my core and as I get closer, I press my body against Sammy who keeps kissing me and rubbing me slowly until I finally explode. *Holy fuck, he's amazing.* I cum hard against Sammy's fingers and as I cum hard, Sammy takes two fingers and slides them inside my tightness. I moan loudly as I cum, and Sammy kisses me to shut me up as he pushes his fingers deeper.

"Quiet," he murmurs. "You don't want to wake Shawnte..."

Sammy makes me cum again, waiting to remove his fingers until the last ripples of pleasure have passed. As he pulls his hand out of my pants, he grabs the hem and slowly eases my pants off while leisurely moving down the length of my body. He stops to kiss my stomach, focusing his attention on my navel and then running his palm over my bared, protruding stomach before he starts pushing up my shirt.

He's a lot quieter sober – and a lot rougher in some ways. He coaxes my legs apart as he finally gets down to my hips, and then flattens his tongue before rubbing it over my clit in smooth, flattened strokes. I moan as Sammy's soft tongue touches my extremely sensitive clit. I cry out as he touches me, and moan even louder when Sammy's tongue begins its slow, smooth circles around my sensitive nub.

"Yes..." I whimper.

Sammy presses his hand against the top of my mound and licks around my outer lips before diving between my legs again and focusing his attention on my clit until I climax.

When I cum again, my thighs tremble with arousal and Sammy kisses my inner thighs as he slowly pulls his face away from between my legs.

Sammy sighs as he kisses my outer lips and then the tops of my thighs. He kneels between my legs, gazing at me, his lips pink and engorged from his efforts between my legs. I didn't find white guys sexy until Enrico. I didn't *know* any white guys in my neighborhood so I never had any occasion to look at one with romantic intentions. Spanish guys might have silky black hair and pale skin too, but there's something different about a Long Island Italian man.

"What are you waiting for?" I whisper. I don't want Sammy to break out of this moment yet. I don't want him to give up on me.

"A lightning bolt to strike me down," He growls. "Or something."

"That's not going to happen."

"Then why do I feel like I'm fucking up?"

"Because you're scared," I tell him. "Because we both lost someone and this feels like betrayal. But what about us? What about our loyalty to ourselves?"

Sammy leans forward and I grab his shirt, if for no other reason than to make sure he doesn't squirrel away from me again. Sammy smirks as I hold onto him.

"You... you are trouble."

"I'm not. I'm making sense and for some reason, you hate that."

"Yeah," he whispers. "I do. Because you shouldn't make sense, Melanie. You're too young. You're too pregnant. And I care about you way too much."

Sammy kisses me again and I use my opportunity to wrap my thighs around him and draw him against me. Sammy's cock moves against my leg and I use his shirt to drag him against me. I don't want him to disappear tonight.

"Don't leave me."

"I won't," Sammy breathes, tensing as my hands slide between his legs so I can grab his cock. "I promise..."

Chapter 12
Honey Bun.
Sammy

Melanie wraps her hand around my cock through my trousers. I grunt and shift my hips forward more forcefully than I intended. My dick has a mind of its own, and it's like a missile fixated with desire for the dripping apex of Melanie's thighs. I know men are dogs, but man it fucking sucks how badly I want her. I should know better. I *do* know better – but I *love her*. I can't stop myself from how much I want her.

I grunt as she touches me and Melanie gazes up at me with an eager expression on her youthful face. Desire quickly suppresses the flicker of guilt that surges through me as Melanie touches me. *Yes, she's so fucking beautiful.*

I kneel between Melanie's legs, briefly pulling my dick away from her eager hands. It hurts to be this far apart from her. Our bodies so badly need to join together and I can't resist her any longer. I undo my belt buckle and hurry my pants over my hips. Melanie makes me so rock hard that it *hurts.*

Once my cock springs from my pants, Melanie shakes her head.

"No way. It got bigger."

My cock lurches with the reminder that I've had her before. The memories don't exactly rush back to me. They come in bits and pieces, but my body remembers exactly how good it felt to bury my shaft between Melanie's perfect legs.

She sits up and grabs my dick, gazing up at me as she wraps her hand around the entire girth of my dick. Her hand barely fits around my cock all the way. She squeezes and pumps my dick, forcing a moan from my mouth.

"Fuck, that's good."

"You are way quieter when you aren't drugged up," she says. "Let's change that..."

Oh God... I don't want to let her pleasure me when tonight ought to be about her, but I can't help my response to her. Her hands pump up and down over the shaft of my dick. I don't have any self-control around her and it fucking hurts.

I groan as Melanie plays with my dick. I can't take this anymore.

"No more, honey bun."

I gently smack her forearm to push her hand away from me. Melanie pulls her hand away with a sassy look on her face.

"Rude."

"I want to fuck you now. Is that rude?"

"Very," Melanie says, wrapping her arms around my neck and pulling me on top of her. I lose all sense of reason then. With no hesitation, we tear what's left of each other's clothes off. Melanie reaches between my legs for my dick and then presses it against her entrance.

"You have to go slow," she says.

"Hm," I grunt and attempt to push my dick into her slowly. My hips thrust forward too quickly and I spear Melanie with one unintentional thrust between her legs. Her pussy spreads to accept my cock, but she's unusually tight and she cries out in absolute pain as I push the full length of my shaft between her legs.

Melanie's weight presses into the couch and my body leans against hers. We're together. Her body is so deliciously soft and I love touching her smooth, brown skin as I adjust to how fucking tight her pussy is. *I want to cum inside this soft, warm woman immediately.* Her stomach protrudes into my abdomen. I feel the movement of Melanie's chest as she breathes and her pregnant stomach gets me harder between her legs.

"It hurts," she gasps, tilting her head back and exposing her pretty neck. If I kiss her neck, she'll relax enough to let me inside her. I press my lips to her neck and take some of her between my teeth. I bite Melanie's neck possessively as I withdraw my hips slightly and plunge my erection between her legs.

Fuck yes…

She cries out in a mixture of pain and pleasure as I push my cock to its hilt while continuing to bite her neck. Melanie has a gorgeous neck. I take her hands and pin them above her head. This will feel much better if she doesn't fight my efforts to get her adjusted to my cock. She squirms as I take her hands and raise them over her head, pinning those trouble-some hands to the arm of the couch as I move my hips between her legs again.

Melanie squirms and fights against my hold.

"Trust me, honey bun," I growl and move my hips again. She spreads her thighs wider and I pin her tighter to the couch as I thrust deeper.

"Sammy…" she moans excitedly. Melanie moaning my name turns me on and makes me thrust into her harder. Her juices gush around my dick and her delicious tightness grips my cock perfectly. I growl and bite her neck again as I pin her to the couch and make love to her.

Melanie's arousal begins slowly at first. Her whimpers turn to moans and then her pussy gets completely soaked. Melanie bites down on her lower lip every time she gets close to orgasm and when she bites down this time, I want to pump into her deeper and fill her with my cum. With my teeth sinking into her neck again, I thrust deeper into Melanie and she cums hard as I touch the deepest parts of her.

Her body heaves with arousal and moves towards me as she thrusts back against my dick and enjoys the throbbing climax overwhelming her. I release her hands and pull her towards me, cupping Melanie's perfect ass as I draw her close.

"Cum for me, honey bun. Cum all over my dick…"

She whimpers and wraps her arms around my neck gently as she climaxes and her thighs wrap around me as she moves her hips against me.

"Cum inside me," she gasps as she continues to ride the wave of her climax. "Cum inside me, Sammy."

Cum erupts from my dick and Melanie whimpers and moans again as thick spurts of my seed pulse between her legs. My body tightens as euphoria unlike anything I've known forces me to lose control. I feel myself starting to go weak as the waves of pleasure from my orgasm keep me shooting ropes of my seed between Melanie's legs. She gasps and moves against me as I fill her with my cum and when we're both finished, neither of us want to pull away from the sticky mess we just created on the couch.

"Don't move," Melanie whispers. "Don't move."

"I'll get hard again if I don't move," I whisper.

"Aren't you too old for a second round so soon?" Melanie whines.

Brat... The comment hurts, but that's what you do when you're young – you speak earnestly without the inhibitions you develop over your thoughts and feelings as you age. She's completely raw and it's not just her youth. Even now, Melanie's pretty face is still healing from the bruises she got. She's a fucking fighter. I've never met a woman like her – it doesn't matter her age.

"I'm not too old to cum inside you again," I whisper. "Don't test me, woman."

She wriggles her hips against me, doing an excellent job of teasing me to arousal again.

"Woman? What happened to calling me honey bun?"

"Good girls are honey buns," I whisper. "And calling me old? Hm... that makes you very bad..."

I want her again and I want her badly enough to make a fool of myself. I know it's fucking irresponsible, but I can't resist her. I want her so badly. I kiss her cheek and brush my finger against her bruising.

"Look at all those bruises. What kind of woman gets into so many fights?"

"A woman who doesn't take any shit," she teases, her toes wiggling along the length of my thighs. I smile down at her and pull her in closer, realizing that trying to hold her at arm's length was always going to be impossible when this is what I get holding her to me. Even with John's approval, she still feels so wrong... I remember the days when walking around with a girl of her skin color would provoke outrage in everyone.

I'm free to touch her, to inhale the scent of her sweet, soft skin and draw Melanie against my chest like she's precious. I want her again.

"A woman who gets into so much trouble needs to be tied up and spanked thoroughly."

"Spanked?" she teases. "Who do you think you are, Sammy"

"Crazy fucking Sammy, the guy who's gonna spank your ass so hard you scream."

"You can't do that in the living room."

"You're right," I whisper as I quickly withdraw my already hard cock from her. Melanie lets out a sharp gasp at my quick motion that does nothing to stop my desires to fuck her again. I scoop Melanie off the couch and hold her body against me. "I'm taking you to the bedroom for the rest of the fucking night and I'm not letting you out until you cum."

Melanie's sweaty skin presses against mine and she looks like a beautiful, pregnant vision. Her breasts swell from her chest and move with each strained breath. We both struggle hard against our desire for each other. It physically hurts me how much I want her.

Melanie kisses me and I stumble a few steps forward, clasping her against me so I won't let go. Kissing distracts me from moving smoothly across the room and I take several risky minutes to enter the bedroom with Melanie in my arms. I want to spread her dripping thighs again and enjoy her. I don't even care about her age or anything else.

I'm just a man, loving a pregnant woman, wanting her to be his family. It won't be this that sends me to hell considering how many men I've killed. I need to make love to her. I need to make love to her the way I need to breathe. I push Melanie onto the bed and flip her on her stomach. She gasps and arches her back, her voluptuous buttocks spread for me and juices from her thighs spread out in a sticky pattern over her gorgeous dark brown skin.

Her body drives me wild. Her body ain't the only thing. She has a sharp tongue, a quick mind and she's so damned independent for her age. I throw my weight on hers and kiss every inch of Melanie from the back of her neck all the way down her spine until I get to the soft, plump curve of her ass.

Melanie whimpers as my tongue slips between her butt cheeks and I taste more of her soft flesh as I work my way towards her wetness. She already drips with my seed, but I want more. I never want to let her go. The closer we get and the more our bodies intertwine in bed together, the harder it is for me to imagine healing without Melanie.

"You're perfect," I murmur, slowly spreading her lower lips and sliding two fingers inside her. Melanie bites down on her lower lip and moans. Her moans sound perfect. I press my nose into her skin and inhale her scent as deeply as I can. I run my hand over Melanie's soft bottom and she makes an eager moaning sound.

I haven't forgotten my promise to punish her. As I rub my hands over Melanie's smooth globes, I plan the exact part of her ass I'm going to spank. She nuzzles into my grasp, blissfully unaware or perhaps hopeful that I've changed my mind. I tighten my resolve and raise my palm to Melanie's ass, swatting her voluptuous butt.

Melanie cries out in pain and surprise. She attempts to wriggle away from me, but I'm not done. I swat her again. She cries out and kicks out against me. I chuckle at her resolve to get away from me. *You aren't going anywhere, honey bun.* I don't want to hurt her too badly, just give her enough pain to get her excited. After a third smack, I release Melanie from my grasp and she hurriedly rolls onto her back, pushing an angry foot against my bare thigh.

"Monster," she grumbles. "That *hurt.*"

"Not enough if you can lie on your ass," I grunt, resting my body against hers and taking her lips against mine. She tastes fucking delicious and I want to stroke her ass more and kiss away the soreness I just caused.

Melanie scowls and pushes against me.

Sammy

"You really *spanked* me. Crazy ass man."

"Hm. I think you deserved it."

I hold her against me and kiss her softly. "It's a little reminder that you're mine and I don't want you running away from me anymore."

"If you stop all future dead rat deliveries, that will be a lot easier."

She's right. But right now that is the furthest thought from my mind as I stare down at her, knowing how badly I need her one more time. Later, I think to myself. We'll talk about that later, after I've made her cum again.

* * *

Life With Crazy Sammy
Melanie

I tried to tell Sammy that dragging a pregnant woman out on a run was a bad idea, but since we got back to Westhampton and John hired security guards to watch both of us, he's been obsessive about exercise and staying away from his psychiatrist so he can heal naturally. *Whatever.*

Sammy finishes the last few ounces of his protein shake, ignoring the disgusted look on my face.

"I can't believe you drank a raw egg," I say to Sammy with a grimace. We've been back here for one week, we're no closer to learning who sent the dead rats, and Sammy's health kick has been driving me crazy.

Sammy flashes me an annoying grin. "Protein. It's good for you."

"It's a dead chicken. It's nasty."

"You had me order Chick-Fil-A last night from the location in Queens and the delivery fee was $30. I don't want to hear it about *my* dead chicken."

"Everyone knows the one on 82nd has roaches."

Sammy's brow knits together. I can't tell if he hates me, or if his outward frustration hides his inner feelings.

"Hm," he says. "You can set the pace today."

"So we can sit on the couch?"

"I'll make you a spinach shake as motivation."

"I'm good," Melanie responds, wrinkling her nose and making a fake gagging noise. I don't know how she's made it this far without regular vegetable consumption.

"Spinach isn't evil, Melanie."

She snorts with obvious skepticism.

"That bad taste is the vegetable screaming in pain," Melanie says. "Simple as that."

Sigh.

"Let's start this run before I chase you upstairs…" Sammy growls as he heads towards the door. I roll my eyes at the back of his head, reluctantly following him to the door.

At least he's honest about allowing me to set the pace. I'm no runner by nature, but the past few days with Sammy, running hasn't been the most horrible thing on the planet. We run slowly enough that I can talk and Sammy gets really patient when I need to stop and rest.

"The doctor says you aren't healthy enough," he says.

Yeah, John sent a doctor and he has all these ideas about how I need to handle my pregnancy. I'm 16 or so weeks along, and in my opinion, far too heavy and sore to move my body, but apparently I'm at risk for gestational diabetes and now John thinks it's his personal mission to turn my body into a *Four Seasons* for my unborn child who has been getting along just fine. Well, for the most part.

After a few minutes of running, a flood of unexpected endorphins numb my desire to throttle Sammy for dragging me out of the house. Once I reach the point of feeling like I'm going to pass out, I slowly come to a stop and put my hands on my knees. As I try to catch my breath, I look up at Sammy to judge how his breathing is, only to see a bright smile on his face like this painful ass run was only a light jog.

"How do you feel?"

"How do I look?" I gasp, sputtering and coughing into my elbow, willing myself not to spit in front of Sammy. He's too hot to spit in front of... I cover my mouth and swallow the gross mucus in the back of my throat.

"Sexy as fuck," Sammy says without hesitation, as the long string of spit I was trying to swallow hangs from my mouth. I quickly wipe it off and push my sweaty hair out of my face. My edges are growing out a little and I'll need a hairdresser soon to fix my hair. It doesn't help that Sammy and I sweat them out a little more each night.

"I'm the furthest thing from sexy," I choke out, coughing again as I gasp for more air.

Sammy chuckles. "You're sweaty, you smell good... and most importantly..."

He drags me against him, teasing out the 'most important' part of his sentence until my body presses against his. Sammy touches the base of my chin and draws my face up to his. Kissing him sends a rush through me and I want to pull away from Sammy because my sweaty body presses against his and my skin feels so sticky and gross. He can't possibly want to touch me...

As I try to push away from him, Sammy grabs my hips and pulls me against him for a deep, long kiss. I lean into his embrace and kiss him back, but I pull away quicker than he does.

"We're in a public park," I remind him. "What will people think?"

"That I'm *way* too old for you," he says. "But I don't care. I just... I love you Melanie. I know I... I know I shouldn't. But I want to be with you. I want to look after my grandchild and keep you close and keep you out of trouble."

"I can get out of trouble on my own," I tell him. "As long as you know that."

Sammy smirks. "Yes. I know. But you're still young. You don't know what kind of trouble you'll have up ahead."

"I'm pregnant. That'll make things complicated pretty soon."

"You'll have me, Melanie. No matter what happens, I'll be there."

I don't want my face to fall. I don't want to doubt Sammy right now, when he's spilling his heart out to me. When there's a crack in Sammy's harsh, strong exterior, it scares me. Guys like him don't show vulnerability and when you see it, the sheer force of their emotions can be scary.

I press my hand against Sammy's chest. His heartbeat makes this more real. It's racing.

"I love you, Sammy Zagarella. But… What happens if you go to prison? What happens if someone finds out about what you did or if you do something in the future? What about me?"

"I will *always* find a way to take care of you," Sammy reassures me.

"That's not what I mean. I'm a high school drop out. I appreciate you offering to take care of me, but I need you to help me find a way to take care of myself, so if anything happens to you, I can look after *our* family."

Sammy scowls and then shakes his head. "Looking after our family is my responsibility. Not yours."

He runs his finger over my lip and it's very tempting to give into Sammy's view of the world, much better suited to a different time. I want to let him wrap his arms around me and promise me everything, but I can't put that weight on him. I have to grow up too.

"One thing you need to learn about women of my generation, Sammy Zagarella, is that we're very independent. I won't sit around and let you take care of me."

Sammy smiles and nods, kissing the top of my forehead.

"You are so... fierce for your age and I would love to support your independence, but there's still someone out there who threatened you and you aren't safe until we learn who that person is."

A part of me knows he's right. The more obvious my pregnancy becomes, the less I can pretend that there isn't someone else I need to be looking out for. Sammy glances down at my stomach and then sighs.

"I'd better take you home," he says.

"I told you, no more running away."

"Good," Sammy says, slipping his hand into mine. "I don't want you going anywhere, Melanie."

SAMMY LEAVES early for work and it's his first week back since he's been in a clear enough mental headspace to head out to the work sites out in Long Island City. We finally have custody of Big Tex again, since John trusts that Sammy won't lose his shit and somehow hurt the dog, and he finally seems to be adjusting to my presence. Sort of.

I walk into the kitchen and I hear Big Tex's nails clicking across the tiles as he wags his tail and hangs his tongue out. Since he's a retired racing dog, Sammy has to be strict about his diet, which means no snacking on the scraps from my cooking.

"Big Tex, sit."

He's too old to go on runs now, but he loves his food and he still has a lot of energy even with his hip pain and other health problems. Big Tex points his long downward, giving me the sweetest puppy eyes. *And* he's listening to me? We're making progress.

Big Tex sits for about forty-five more seconds before contenting himself to follow me around the kitchen. I'm extra careful as I chop up the onions, peppers, beef strips and other ingredients for my little stir fry. Big Tex keeps wagging his tail and acting like he's gonna get some of my food. *He's growing on me, just like Sammy.*

Pregnancy sends me down the path of following all my urges and I'm especially weak when it comes to stir fry and anything that reminds me of delicious, spicy, Chinese food. I prefer making my own food at home and soaking up all the smells. So does Big Tex, who keeps wagging his tail and licking his lips hungrily. *Is Sammy sure I can't give him a little piece of beef?*

I contemplate sending Sammy a text pleading on Big Tex's behalf, when Sammy's landline rings. I didn't even know people had landlines anymore, and as I search all over the kitchen for the phone I've never noticed, I make a mental note to tell Sammy that we can get rid of his boomer phone.

I answer, just in case Sammy's the one calling.

"Hello?"

There's nothing on the other end for a few seconds.

"Hello?" I ask again and I hear what sounds like shuffling papers and a deep bark in the background.

There's nothing after the shuffling and the bark, so I hang up. *Weird.* I text Sammy and suggest that he gets rid of the landline, but he's at work, so I don't expect him to respond. Big Tex remains unsuccessful in his quest for a piece of beef, but I give him one of his permitted bacon treats after lunch since he was such a good boy.

We curl up on the couch together and I wonder how the heck I ever could have thought Big Tex was annoying or out of control. He's just a sweet old dog and when Sammy isn't here, he makes me feel a little bit safer, even if he isn't exactly a pit bull or anything. I pat Big Tex's head and close my eyes for a few hours.

I feel safe here and I haven't felt that way my whole life. I don't want to lose Sammy and I don't want to lose this.

. . .

I CAN'T HELP but worry that it will all slip away. When you grow up with a mom like mine, you learn that the good times don't last. She always picks up drinking again, or gets a new man who brings out the worst in her, and some days she just wants to go crazy and let all her pain out on me.

I never knew what waking up to someone who actually wanted to be with me was like until Sammy. I know he's done some fucked up things and I don't know if the world could forgive him, but I can. I see the good behind Sammy Zagarella, but I'm terrified that the good won't last and that he'll lose himself again.

Big Tex whines and nuzzles me deeper, willing me not to freak out and just appreciate what I have – *Love. Family. Peace.*

* * *

Chapter 14
The Mother-In-Law
Sammy

Alexis rolls her eyes when I show up at John's front door, planning for us to get our shit together today. I told Melanie I was working, but that wasn't exactly the truth. I have a surprise for her and John for helping me out. Unfortunately, I haven't exactly patched things up with the boss's wife over the kidnapping incident last year. I can't show up at Alexis' front door without her eyeing me with unforgiving suspicion.

"John, your cousin is here," she calls out to him, returning her fierce gaze to me.

"Hello, Alexis. You look… um… very nice today."

"Whatever, Sammy. JOHN! I don't want to stand here talking to Sammy, I have to study for the MCAT!"

"MCAT? What's that about?"

"Med school," Alexis says. "I'm going to med school. John, seriously?! How long do you need in the damn shower!"

She has a little baby bump. Baby bumps and med school. That ought to be a good combination for my cousin. I swear, he enjoys the stress of having a high strung, younger wife. I suppose Alexis might be a little less high strung if I hadn't kidnapped her.

"I'm much better," I blurt out, in an attempt to reassure her. "I'm off the drugs and sticking to natural healing methods."

Alexis rolls her eyes. "Yeah, John told me his little plan. She is way too young for you."

"What little plan?"

The boss appears at just the wrong time. Alexis rolls her eyes and eagerly disappears without answering my question. John, unperturbed by his own lateness, lights a cigarette and walks out the door, shutting it behind him.

"Fuck," he says after taking the first puff. "She's gonna kill me before she finishes med school. I swear."

"Moody?"

"SHHH!!" John hisses. "Are you fucking stupid? She could've heard you."

"Relax. She's not a bat."

"She's worse," John mutters. "I love her, but pregnancy has turned her into an entirely different person. How's Melanie?"

"Great. Great. We went for another run this morning. She hated it."

"Any closer to finding the rat fucks?"

"Maybe you can call them something else… and we don't know if it's more than one person."

"I suppose you don't need more than one person. But who is it? Someone who wants to fuck with her ought to be easy to track down. The girl threw more punches than the average teenage boy."

"She's nothing like a boy," I grumble defensively. Despite Melanie's willingness to fling herself into the middle of trouble, she's gentle with her walls down. She might stiffen her lower lip and curl her hands into fists when she feels threatened, but I've seen her cry and felt just how vulnerable the girl can be beneath that outer strength.

With a mother like the one she had, it's no wonder she had to toughen up. There was no softness in her world, just like there was no softness in mine. Maybe that's why we're good for each other. She brings tenderness out of me that reminds me I'm still human and I can give her a place where she'll always be safe.

"Never said she was," John said. "She's got enemies, that's all."

"Teenagers don't strike me as the type to cut up dead rats into pieces."

"What about that Damzel character?" John says. "Think we should pay her a visit?"

"She's a teenager," I grumble. "I recently killed a teenager and I probably shouldn't do anything else to risk my time on the outside."

"I took care of your fucking mistake," John says. "Listen, Melanie's pregnant and she's a flight risk. The sooner we find whoever's responsible for fucking with her, the better."

"I don't have any suspects outside of Damzel and maybe her mother."

"Her mother?"

"She's a crazy fucked up woman."

"Sounds exactly like the type of person who could fuck up a bunch of rats. How 'bout we check out the kid and then we'll go to her mom's place."

John sounds like he's asking a question, but he's the boss, so pretty much whatever he says goes. My younger cousin was born for Alfonso Vicari's role. He was always the more serious one out of all of us kids growing up. He was born for this. I don't know what I was born for. It feels like I was born to lose people, at least that's what it felt like until I met Melanie. Until I kissed her. She's special and I want to stop whoever's hurting her and make all this shit disappear.

"Once we're done, I've got everything you asked for at the hotel downtown. Fancy dinner. Roses. Violin. You can do something special for Melanie."

"I don't know if she likes that romantic crap."

"Every woman likes that romantic crap," John says. "It'll be even more romantic when you tell her you solved her problem. Women love when we solve their problems without being asked."

John makes a fair point and if he can keep a woman like Alexis happy, he must understand something about women that I don't.

We drive to Damzel's neighborhood and leave the car a few blocks away from her place. The high school seniors are out of school for a couple days. They have a "reading day" to study for regents, but I'm pretty sure most of the kids in Melanie's class are getting drunk or high.

John did all the research ahead of time, so all we have to do is wait for Damzel to take the route she normally does to the bus stop so she can get to Harlem – the place where all the cool parties are. Social media makes it easy to pick out which party Damzel is most likely to go to and when it starts.

John notices her two blocks away from the bus stop, right on time, bobbing her head with headphones in and completely oblivious to us watching her. Once Damzel walks past us, John and I follow her a couple blocks. We know she's heading home, and she still doesn't know we're following her. Once we're away from foot traffic, John lets out a high-pitch whistle and we both move on her.

Grabbing each of Damzel's arms, we drag her away from the main road and down an alley between a Jamaican patty joint and a cell phone store. Damzel screams and shoves her elbows into us.

"If I let go, you don't move. You move, you run, I put a bullet in your head, kid," John growls.

I think he's afraid to let me do the dirty work. I've been hit in the head one too many fucking times and I have too many screws loose for John to let me be the bad cop again. Damzel, to her credit, doesn't back down and she doesn't look scared. She must be scared, because she's a teenage girl, but she does a good job of hiding it.

"What do you want? I don't have nothing for you to steal. These headphones are old as hell."

She has a heavy Queens accent and the fight in her voice tells me that she might've been robbed before.

"We don't want your headphones," John says. "We want to know why you threatened Melanie Stevens."

"How the fuck do you know Melanie Stevens? What are you, her pimps?"

I don't completely understand her vitriol towards Melanie. They don't seem so different. They're both tough, harsh on the outside, but if Damzel has any of Melanie's gentleness, she doesn't immediately show it.

"No."

"I thought her pimps killed my man. I knew what he was. I would've done something about it if I had evidence. Alex told me what happened and I figured... Well, I figured she was doing hoe shit and her pimp must've killed him."

It's not a bad assessment of the situation. Unfortunately, in Damzel's world, it's not too uncommon for high school girls to occasionally fall into sex work. I don't remember anyone named Alex being in that alley, or much of anything that happened in the alley, but Damzel's practical assessment of the situation makes me deeply uneasy.

She's too cool and collected about losing someone for a girl her age. Even John notices.

"We aren't her pimps. We're her family," John says. "You say you didn't threaten her, I want proof."

"Why would I threaten her? We all got in trouble for that damn fight, which wouldn't have happened if me and Shawnte weren't fighting over a loser. I'm not stupid. I don't blame Melanie for what happened."

"I didn't think you were stupid," I offer somewhat apologetically. My tone doesn't seem to impress Damzel who keeps her arms tightly folded and glances with equally disapproving looks between me and John.

"Whatever," she says. "Whoever the hell you are, I didn't hurt Melanie. I just want that bitch to stay far away from me. Got it?"

"Calm down, kid," John says. "We got it. Sammy, come on."

John's right to get us out of there. The kid doesn't know anything. We walk back to the car and I grow more unsettled as we approach. I don't want to see Melanie's mother again. I don't know if I can keep my calm around her, especially considering how she's treated her daughter. Melanie doesn't even want to see her. I've offered.

The last time I encountered the woman, we didn't exactly meet on pleasant terms. It's not that I don't like her. Well, I don't... but that's not what's so infuriating. I hate a lot of people.

What upsets me the most is that she's... inadequate. Melanie deserved a better parent. She's smart and she's quick on her feet. Her impulsive behavior gets her into trouble but... Fuck.

I catch myself thinking like her father and I feel even guiltier than I normally do about our relationship. I love her... and the sex part crept up on me at my weakest state of mind. I can't deny how much I enjoy the sex. She has all the energy for it that a man my age could possibly hope for.

When it's over, the guilt settles in and I wonder if she'll grow up and regret falling into bed with an old man like me.

One day, one day that will be far too soon, I'll leave her behind and all I can hope for is that Melanie Stevens doesn't regret giving her time to an old man.

"Nervous about seeing your mother in law?" John teases as he starts the car. John has the luck of in-laws who live in the Midwest who seem utterly taken with their daughter's Long Island fiancé. I don't have that much luck.

"I don't see the point in visiting her. She doesn't care about Melanie and I doubt she's the one who did this."

"Do we have any other options?"

"No. Not obvious ones."

"It's just how the job goes," John says, in an effort to calm me down. "We rule out the obvious options, then we think outside the box."

"As long as we get this shit done before tonight."

"Relax, buddy. We've got this shit under control."

I don't share John's blind confidence in our control of the situation. Like before, we park a couple blocks away and walk. John mocks my tension again, but he doesn't understand how hard it is to watch someone speak so dismissively about someone you care for. I might not have been the best parent, but I loved my son all the ways I could. I would have done anything for him. Melanie deserves better than this.

"That the house?" John asks as we approach. For a man who claims he isn't nervous, he's burned through three cigarettes, which doesn't exactly make him seem like the calmest guy on the fucking planet.

"Yeah. That's the one."

"She normally leave the front door open?"

Nobody in this neighborhood leaves their front door open. It's not like it's a particularly bad neighborhood, but there are lots of troublesome kids and teenagers who steal just because they can. Law of the jungle.

"No. She's paranoid, but she could also be on drugs. I could never tell."

"Didn't you spend half of Lucky's junkie years looking after him? What do you mean you couldn't tell?"

"You have to have your wits about you dealing with that woman," I remind John. "You can't sit around observing her."

He won't heed my concerns about Melanie's mother, but that woman is trouble to deal with. The open door should be all the required evidence.

"She ought to have her wits about her," John says. "I can walk right through the fucking door. Come on, stop being a baby. Load the pistol if you're scared."

"I'm not scared of her."

John misunderstands my concerns. She's the sort of woman who could piss anyone off, so it might not be a long shot to assume that some of the people she could've pissed off are batshit crazy.

"If what you say about her is true, she's probably passed out drunk somewhere and you have nothing to worry about."

"Except for the fact that she's drunk enough to pass out with the door open. What kind of grandparent is that child going to have?"

John smirks. "Do you really want me to answer that question?"

"Shut up."

John laughs, which does plenty to diffuse the tension as I walk up to the house with him. He calls through the front door, just to make sure we aren't going to be in big fucking trouble walking through that front door. After waiting half a minute, there's still no response. Great.

I don't want to enter her house without permission. She

seems like the sort of woman who would be armed and shoot first, ask questions later. We walk through the front door and John wrinkles his nose.

"Christ, doesn't she clean up around here."

"Not since Melanie left."

Melanie's account of her living situation appears to have been true. She told me that she cleaned up after her mother, kept the bills paid, and made sure that her mother didn't have to worry about anything. The place appears to have fallen to disrepair since Melanie's departure.

There are dishes stacked high in the sink, two mouse traps on the kitchen counter which are mercifully empty, but draw John's attention. A calm, yet purposeful cockroach ambles over the sponge soaked with a red sauce.

The smell of old food and mold fills the room. I wish John would start smoking again to kill the scent of rotting. The cockroach continues its journey over to a banana peel on the other side of the counter.

Melanie doesn't belong here.

"It doesn't look like anyone's home," John whispers, keeping his voice quiet just in case, I suppose. "But it looks like we have a case for where she might've gotten some mice."

"They were rats, not mice."

"You catch them both in a trap, don't you?"

I want to tell John that it's besides the point, but we both hear a loud groaning sound coming from upstairs.

"Did you hear that?" I whisper.

John presses his fingers to his lips and nods. I approach the stairs and let John take the lead. From his waistband he pulls out a glock, already loaded, and racks the slide. The groaning sound can only be coming from one person and the hairs on the back of my neck stand up. There's trouble here and I don't know the extent of it.

"Hello?" I call up the stairs. The faint groaning sounds discernibly louder this time. John takes the stairs two at a time with me right at his heels. Once I get to the top of the stairs, I call again. All three bedroom doors are pulled shut. John and I listen at the top of the stairs, saying nothing and hoping that we haven't just stumbled into a trap.

John calls out this time. "Hello? Are you up here? I'm here to help you, ma'am."

The loud groaning comes from behind the first door and John instinctively slams his body into the door while turning the handle. The door isn't locked, but it's clear once we enter the bedroom that Melanie's mother couldn't have shut it.

"Holy fuck," John grunts. This is a mess. A big fucking mess. At just the wrong time, my phone rings.

"Seriously, Sammy?"

"I gotta get this."

Melanie's mother groans on the bed. Blood soaks through her sheets and she has an injury that has her pinned in place by all appearances. Her flesh is ripped open with blood pouring from her arm and there are two deep puncture marks near the rip. *An animal bite?* My instincts don't match up with what I know about Ms. Stevens. She never had any pets and that didn't change when Melanie left – there are no signs of a dog bed or dog food, or even a leash near the door. *But something bit her.*

She groans again and her fingers move slightly. She's alive, but there's enough blood soaking through the sheets that she might not be alive for long. I'm unsettled by the amount of blood and by the strain in her voice. *She's lost a lot of fucking blood.*

John glares at me and approaches the bed as I answer the phone. He doesn't find himself as turned off by grisly scenes as I might imagine. I click the option to answer the call.

"Sammy, you missed our last appointment."

Shit. I didn't just miss our last appointment. I canceled it.

"Dr. Gabriel, I canceled the last appointment. I spoke with the front desk girl."

I can't remember her name, but I was sure I spoke to someone.

"Sammy, the medication I gave you can't be stopped without medical oversight. By missing this appointment, you're putting yourself and others at great personal risk. I need you to come down to my office immediately."

Surely she can't mean that I visit her immediately.

"Immediately," she insists.

"Dr. Gabriel, I'm in the middle of something serious."

"Sammy, I'm speaking to you as a medical professional. The drugs I gave you are dangerous to your health and safety if you stop them without medical oversight. You need to come down here. *Now.*"

"I'll be there."

I don't know what possesses me to make such an insane promise considering the situation. I hang up and John gives me a *look.* Yeah, I know I fucked up.

"Where the fuck do you think you're going?"

"I have a medical emergency."

"Aside from this one? It looks like she has three or four animal bites. What the fuck is going on here? Ma'am? Ma'am?"

Melanie's mother remains unresponsive aside from the groaning. John's right that there can't be a bigger priority than this one, but...

"We should call an ambulance or at least get her to a doctor," I concede. "But then I have to leave."

"What about your plans?"

"John, trust me. I need to take care of this."

John's disapproving look doesn't inspire my confidence in his trust in me. We move Melanie's mother together and get her downstairs. There's a lot of blood on the bed, but the bleeding appears to have stopped. She's weak. She needs bandages and she probably needs hydration. John has me get my step-sister on the phone. Dr. Gianna Zagarella rarely wants anything to do with us, but when we need her, she pulls through.

Before she gets there, I tell John I need to leave.

"I'm keeping the car. Where the fuck are you going, Sammy?"

"Doctor."

"Why?"

"Something's wrong with my meds," I answer him gruffly. I don't relish having this type of conversation with John. It's bad enough he witnessed and forgave my first fall from grace. I can't give him another opportunity to feel slighted by me.

John's face reddens. "You seem fine to me."

"I can't lose myself again, John. It's not about me. It's about Melanie."

"How the fuck do you think she'll feel when she finds out about this?" He says, gesturing behind him to Melanie's mom laying on the couch.

He's right. I grit my teeth as a look that's a bit too close to pity for my comfort crosses John's face.

"You know what, I'll get Melanie sorted out. You get your meds sorted out. Clearly, you need a break."

"Thanks."

John pats me on the back. "Gimme her number and get the fuck outta here."

* * *

Chapter 15
The Big Lie
Melanie

My phone doesn't wake me up, Big Tex does. He barks as I turn to reach for my phone, groaning as it continues to ring. As I look at the screen, I notice several missed phone calls, all from the number that just finally stopped calling me. I don't recognize it, but Sammy gave me this phone so it must be his office phone or something like that. I call back, but the voice on the other end is John's, not Sammy's.

"Thank fuck, you're okay," John Vicari snarls into the phone like I hurt him or something. I swing my legs over onto the floor and try to wipe the sleep out of my eyes. Why the hell does he sound so pissed off?

"Is everything okay with Sammy?" I reply, trying not to sound as tired as I am.

"I'm at your mother's house. Sammy's gone. Your mom's in trouble. I got her to a hospital with my cousin, avoided the ambulance, but I need you to get down here and do so without getting into trouble. Can you handle that?"

"You're at my mom's house? What are you doing there?"

Melanie

"Melanie," John says through gritted teeth. "It's urgent that you listen to every word I say. Take the keys in the cookie jar, there's a black Toyota Camry in the garage. Drive it to your mother's house and don't stop for anyone or anything."

"What about Big Tex?"

"What about him? Leave him in peace and get down here. It's urgent."

It's urgent. Sammy isn't calling me. John is. Putting the pieces together, my stomach lurches with the next words out of my mouth.

"Is she dead?"

John pauses a beat too long. I can feel myself starting to become light-headed as the severity of the situation takes hold

"No," he says. "But this is serious, Melanie. Get here now."

He hangs up before I can ask anything else and once he hangs up, I have no choice but to move. I know enough from Sammy that John is the boss and listening to him means everything to him. *Where the hell is Sammy?* As I search for the hidden car keys, I call Sammy, but he doesn't answer me. Big Tex stays curled up on the couch, so I guess I don't have to do anything about him for now.

I find the keys and start to get dressed. As I'm changing, all I can think about is that I don't know what the hell happened to my mom. I picture a million horrific scenarios and it just bothers me that she could die, she could really be gone and our relationship will have ended the way it did. I don't regret walking out on her or anything – I regret not telling her that I wouldn't let her bring me down. I regret not telling her that no matter what she said about me, I could make my life better.

I don't know how I'll make my life better yet, but I know

I'll love my kid enough to get my life together. But first, I have to get down to my mother's house and face John Vicari's bad mood and whatever's causing it. I start the Toyota Camry in the garage. It's been a long time since I've driven a car, but I delivered pizza for Domino's when I was sixteen for a couple months before Shawnte got us both fired. (She was caught on camera stealing too much garlic bread while I stood watch by her request).

I struggle getting out of Westhampton, but once I'm in more familiar territory, I whip around the less crowded side streets until I get to my mom's place. I park across the street and run over. John left the front door open and I can see the light from the street. All the other houses are dark, and there are no cops or ambulances around. There's also no sign of Sammy as I approach the house. If he were here, he would be outside, making sure I crossed the street safely.

I hurry up the front step and through the front door, walking straight into a cloud of John Vicari's cigarette smoke.

"Sorry," John says as I cough. "Didn't think you'd get down here that fast."

"Where's my mom? What's going on?"

"Doctor has your mom. You can't see her, kid."

"Why not?"

"Because some animal attacked her, and I don't know who the fuck did it. It looked like dog bites, but I'm no fucking forensic specialist.. Sammy fucked off and… I'm not sure I understand what the hell is going on. I need your insight."

"What insight could I possibly have?"

My stomach flutters with nerves. It's impossible not to feel nervous around the visibly shaken up John Vicari. The cigarettes, big gold rings and wicked blue stare don't help. He puts out his cigarette in my mom's full ashtray and gestures towards the stairs.

"We found your mother upstairs. There's a lot of blood…

wounds all over her arms. It's a mess up there, but I need to know if you or your mother have enemies who might have mob ties."

I want to ask where Sammy is, but John doesn't give the impression that he's in the mood for questions.

"I don't have enemies," I reply. Is John really asking *me* about enemies when he's the one in the mob?

John reddens slightly before pressing me, "Are you sure?"

"Yes."

"What about Sammy? Has he been talking to himself? Has he been acting funny lately?"

"No. I swear."

"Good," John says. "I know he wants to get better for you and his grandkid. I know he wants to be a good guy but... what if he sent the rats? What if he's lost it?"

He watches how I respond to his theory. I try to keep my face neutral. If John has anything in common with his cousin, he's great at reading people. I can't hide anything from Sammy and even making my best efforts, I might not be able to hide anything from John.

"I don't think so."

John's shoulders relax. "Okay."

"That's it?"

"If he were acting weird, you would tell me. That doesn't explain why the fuck he left but... if he didn't send the threat, someone else did."

"Doesn't your family have enemies?"

John smirks. "We used to. We cleared up all the bad blood, or so I thought."

"If it's not business, then it's personal. Isn't that how the mob works?"

John chuckles. "The mob. You're a smart girl. We shouldn't be talking about the mob in public."

. . .

"We're in my mom's house. This isn't public. Plus, you were the one who brought it up," I say, crossing my arms.

John doesn't seem to mind my sass, thankfully. He shifts his weight and shrugs.

"Listen, my gut tells me whoever hurt your mom sent the rats and maybe if this isn't about Sammy, it's about you. We found all your enemies, so I need to hear your theories, kid."

"My gut tells me to ask you where Sammy is."

John smirks and tilts his head to the side. "We can work this out without my idiot cousin."

"Answer the question, John."

John raises a curious eyebrow. "Doctor's emergency."

"What kind of emergency?"

"Those head pills he told me he stopped taking."

"He *did* stop taking them," I tell John. "What was the emergency? I don't get it."

"Listen, I don't get it either. But someone and or something attacked your mother. It's more urgent."

"You told me to listen to my gut and my gut tells me that if my mom is with a doctor, we have time to find Sammy."

"I know where he is," John says. "I know the shrink. Let's go find Sammy, and then when we're done I'll take you to your mom. She's probably in surgery right now, but she'll probably want to see you once she's out.

She probably won't want to see me, but I appreciate John's faith in her humanity.

"She won't want to see me but… I want to see her. I want to make sure she's okay."

"You don't have the best relationship?"

"What clued you in?" I grumble.

John nods. "I get it. I didn't have the greatest relationship with my dad. It was complicated. We have a fucked up family, Melanie. I dunno why you want to belong to it."

"I don't have a choice. Enrico's gone… Sammy needs someone… and I need someone too."

"We protect our people," John says. "So if you stick by him… if you treat Sammy like family, you'll have me as a family too. I'll see what I can do about your mother once we find my idiot cousin."

"Let's go," I reply, almost anxiously. I don't trust this Sammy situation and I don't know what happened to my mom, but my instincts are guiding me this way.

"OKAY, kid. You make the rules tonight. You know how to lock this place up?"

"Yup."

WHEN I WALK out the front door, I wonder if it will be my last time coming here. It doesn't even feel like my home anymore. *I have a new family now.* I lock the front door and walk over to John's car. As I sit down in the passenger seat, I can smell Sammy from when he sat here on the ride over.

"I wanted him to get help," John mutters. "That's all."

He doesn't say anything for the rest of the drive to a small brick office building on the other side of Queens. I've never been to Sammy's psychiatrist and I'm surprised John knows where it is.

"I don't know if the shrink was a good idea," John mutters. "Some people do better healing on their own, you know?"

"I don't know. Sammy seemed like he needed therapy to me…"

"Hm. Come on, kid."

• • •

I WANT to tell John that I'm not a kid, but he doesn't seem like he'll respond well to it. I freak out when he starts loading his pistol.

"We're going to a doctor's office. Why are you loading the gun?"

"Do you trust that doctor?"

"I don't know his doctor. So no."

"Smart cookie," John says, throwing open his car door and exposing both of us to the elements. He's concerned enough to bring a gun, but he clearly doesn't think we're in real danger, or I doubt he would let me out of the car.

"Are you sure this is a good idea? He's probably crying about his fucked up childhood and we're making a big deal out of nothing."

I want that to be true, but a part of me knows it isn't. My gut drew me here for a reason. I want to worry about my mom first, but it's not like she ever put me first. John says he got her help, I'll have to trust him. *Sammy needs me more... and I need him more.*

John knocks on the door, but there's no answer. He pushes the glass door open and we walk into the place he claims is the psychiatrist's office.

"JOHN... IT'S EMPTY."

AND I MEAN EMPTY. No chairs. No furniture. The walls are blank, the doors are all open and there's not a single human being in sight. It doesn't look like any building in particular.

"What the fuck?" John says. "I'm calling my idiot cousin."

"I tried calling him before I drove over. He didn't answer."

Melanie

John whips out his phone anyway. Sammy won't answer. There's something fishy going on here, and I don't know what. John senses it too. Sammy's in trouble.

Chapter 16
Mobster's Mistake
Sammy

My head hurts. I don't remember what happened after I walked through the doors of Dr. Gabriel's office, but I suspect someone in there has something to do with the pain I feel now. I try to open my eyes, but I'm blind folded. I feel my lashes press up against the fabric bound tightly across my face. *Fuck*. How the hell did I lose consciousness? I realize that I'm lying down on a bed, with my arms tied underneath me. I try to wrestle my wrists out of the tight rope binds, but nothing works. How the hell did I lose control again?

I promised Melanie this would never happen. I promised that I would stay in control and... I don't even know where the fuck I am.

Think, Sammy. I got the call. I left the Stevens' residence. Next thing I knew...

It has to be her, doesn't it? Only, it doesn't make sense. There's no reason for a psychiatrist to want to hurt me. I haven't... Fuck. I'm trapped and wherever I am has no distinct scent, nothing I can sense that can place me. I can hear my own breathing, but no other noise.

. . .

THE SILENCE DOESN'T LAST. I hear a low whining sound and then an animal growling. I recognize the growl from my sessions with Dr. Gabriel. Still, there's no explanation for any of this... If I want my freedom, it won't come easily.

"Hello?" I call into the dark room. I don't fear the dog, or what she'll do to me. I've been in deeper shit before. Survival in situations like this requires one thing – you keep in mind a reason to get the fuck out of there. For most of my life, I kept my shit straight for my son. Right now, he isn't here, but that doesn't mean I have to let my world fall apart.

I can fight for my grandchild. I can fight for Melanie. I can fight for my family.

There's still no response.

"Don't be a coward," I growl into the darkness. "I'm talking to you. You went through all this effort to get me here. The least we could do is talk."

My heart pulses nervously as I await a response. The dog stops growling. Animals have sharper senses than we do. The cessation of growling probably resulted from his owner returning to a calm state. Good. I need her calm. She'll be much easier to manipulate if she thinks she's in control.

I have to fight the urge to learn why she's doing this. I just need my freedom, not my satisfied curiosity.

"What are you afraid of? You're not the one tied up or blindfolded."

"Hello, Sammy."

It's the clear voice I expected. I hear the dog's nails clicking across the floor and assume her owner follows. I don't bother holding my breath.

"If there's something that you want from me, ask for it. I would rather not waste any time. If you're going to kill me, make it quick but allow me a minute to say the Lord's prayer. I've always known someone would come and kill me."

"We aren't in a session, Sammy."

"I gathered that."

"I'm sorry for the way I lured you to my office. It genuinely bothers me that I had to deceive you. We've always been open and honest with each other. You've always confessed your darkest secrets to me."

She exhales a slow, purposeful sigh afterwards. I wait for her to continue. I want information, not to genuinely engage with her right now. I might have to put my pride aside... but haven't I done that enough?

"I told you the medication would help you and it *was* helping you. You did things that you never would have done. You were becoming a better person."

No. That's not what happened. I lost my mind. I killed someone. I disappeared far away from the city with the woman pregnant with my grandchild and I made love to her until we both hurt from it.

"That's an opinion," I grunt. "I don't want to talk, doctor. I want to give you whatever you want."

"I want you to finish your course of medication."

"That's never gonna happen."

"You don't understand, Sammy. I *need* you to finish the course of medication."

"You'd better kill me then. If you can knock me out and tie me up, you can kill me just as easily."

"I know exactly who you are, Sammy Zagarella. I know you fell for that stupid teenage girl. I know you don't want me to hurt her. I know you want to get out of here... and most importantly, I know all your dirty little secrets."

"So what? You'll go to the cops? You'll die before you make it to the station."

I'm not alone. I have John. I have Lucky. I have a family and

Melanie. They are worth fighting for. They're all worth getting out of this shit situation for.

"I have nothing to do with the cops," she answers indignantly.

I can't celebrate Dr. Gabriel losing her cool too early, but at least now I know she doesn't work for the police or FBI. This isn't how they operate anyway. Cops and feds don't get you for the crimes, they get you for the money. Keep your books squeaky clean on the outside, pay your fucking taxes, and you're all good.

Dr. Gabriel sighs. "I've worked with several people in your family before, Sammy. People trust me. Alfonso Vicari trusted me."

I don't know why she's bringing up Alfonso. He's been dead for months. John and Lucky buried him. All I know is that he's dead and this woman might've known Alfonso, but I don't know what the fuck that has to do with right here, right now.

She approaches me and touches my face. "You're so much like him. So emotionally vulnerable... but terrified of your own feelings. I didn't expect..."

"What didn't you expect?" I grunt out impatiently. If it weren't for Melanie at the other end of this, I would have begged for her to quit talking and just kill me.

"I didn't expect to fall in love with one of my patients."

My throat knots uncomfortably. Love.

"You aren't in love with me," I throw back thoughtlessly, instantly regretting my words as Dr. Gabriel slaps me hard across the face, her acrylic nails cutting tiny scratches into my cheek as she hits me with all her force. My ears ring and saliva pools in my mouth as I struggle to contain my nausea.

Holy fuck, that hurt. There might be blood in my mouth, but I have to stay focused on getting out of here. Love? We can make progress with that.

"You don't tell me how to feel," she says. "I didn't expect to fall for you, Sammy, but I did. When you took that medication, when you finally let yourself be the man you wanted to be... you were beautiful."

I was sick. I hurt Melanie. I killed someone. I could have hurt more people. I *wanted* to hurt more people. Sex and killing controlled my thoughts. John was right — the medication hurt more than it helped. I don't even know what she prescribed me. I'm no fucking doctor, but I doubt this wackjob gave her best professional shot at fixing my head.

"I hurt people. You're a doctor, right? You gotta understand that's wrong. I wanted to be better. I don't want to indulge the sickest parts of my mind."

"You aren't sick, Sammy. You're strong. You're a Zagarella. I... I've always wanted to get closer to your family. You grow up around here hearing about the Vicari brothers or the famous Zagarella arrests in the nineties and... you just want to know more."

"My life isn't your entertainment."

"Not anymore," she says. "You had to ruin it by falling in love with that girl... you should have followed your instincts. Hurt her. Killed her. Abandoned her. Instead, you fell for her."

"Melanie and I..."

She's not listening. "You fell for her instead of me," she says. "After I gave you my soul. Hours of my time..."

"You billed me for those hours."

Dr. Gabriel touches my face again. I wince. Her fingernails must have cut me deeper than I realized.

"I never wanted to hurt you, Sammy. But you can't choose her. You can't choose a slutty, delinquent teenager who looks like a fucking cockroach over me. I won't let you."

"This isn't how love works, Dr. Gabriel. You can't force it."

Sammy

I'm forty years old. If this woman wants to kill me, I'll die with dignity, not begging her for my life. I'd rather beg for Melanie's than mine. She's the one I'm worried about.

I REALIZE that I have the woman who sent the rats. Well, technically, she has me. That problem I'll solve shortly. I understand her better now. Well, not completely, since she seems more fucked in the head than I was. John always said the only people who become shrinks are the ones who need them the most.

"You're very smart, Sammy. You know that I can't force you to love me, but I can force you to take your medication. . You'll come with me and I'll be… well, the dose I'll have you on, I'll be enough."

"What do you mean, enough?"

"I'll get to study you up close and you'll have me. My body. My heart. My womb."

My throat catches and my urgency to remove my binds deepens. I wonder if this itself is a hallucination. Is this really fucked up enough to happen?

"What about Melanie? You encouraged me to get close to her. You encouraged… She's still carrying my grandchild."

"I didn't think you would fall for her," she says. "She's half your fucking age, Sammy. Get a grip. I'm still young enough to do what you need. I'm young enough to give you the second chance you want…"

"You don't know what I want."

"I'm your psychiatrist," she says. "I know everything about you. I know you want another son. You want a second chance… Melanie can't give that to you and she won't want to when she finds out you're the reason her mother's dead…"

My throat catches and I thrash again.

"How much money do you want from me? Give me a number and I'll give you what you want," I growl.

"Are you listening, Sammy? I don't want money."

Right. She wants me. She wants me to give up on my grandchild and on a girl I promised to take care of so she can mess with my fucking head. I hate feeling this powerless. I'm just as stuck here as I was the night Enrico died.

I failed him... I can't fail his child and I can't fail Melanie, a woman we both loved. I'm sure a part of Enrico loved her. How could anyone spend time with Melanie Stevens and not fall madly, deeply and entirely in love with her?

"You want me."

"Yes."

"Where do you want me to go? My brothers will notice if I disappear from New York. People will look for me."

"You sound like you're coming around," she says suspiciously. "But... nothing's changed. So you can't have changed your mind."

"I'm asking you to think this through. I never said I changed my mind."

"I have thought it through," she says. "My office is completely empty. I'm gone without a trace. My sweet puppy helped take care of that bitch and her mother... We won't be here long. You're mine, Sammy. Once you get used to it, we'll discuss our future together."

"I'd rather discuss it now. I'd rather have a say in this future."

SHE SIGHS. "You want to have a say in how we have our baby?"

"That's not at all what I meant."

"Once you're medicated, you'll want me. You'll want

anyone with a pulse. That's why you fell for that little high school tramp."

"Don't talk about Melanie that way. Your *experiment* has nothing to do with why I fell for her."

"This is boring, Sammy. You need more time to adjust to your circumstances. The next time I come down here… we'll get to work on the baby situation."

I don't ask what baby situation, but Dr. Gabriel doesn't need my participation in any of this. She reaches her hand over my crotch and cups it around my flaccid cock. I grunt and tense up miserably. *No.* I fight against my binds, but I can't move.

"I have a drug for that too," she says. "I promised you a second chance and you'll get it Sammy. Don't worry."

She gives my cock a slight, threatening squeeze. I don't exhale until Dr. Gabriel lets go.

I WISH she would just kill me and be done with this. At least John would know I was fucked and he could do something about Melanie. I don't even care what happens to me. I just want that girl safe.

*** * ***

Chapter 17
Ride Or Die
Melanie

I thought Sammy was the most arrogant, impossible and completely annoying person on the planet... until I met his brother. John scowls at me as he bars the door to the house I've shared with Sammy in Westhampton the past few weeks. He *literally* dragged me in here without my consent and made me scream so loud that I could have shattered the baby's eardrums, and I told him as much.

"That's not how baby's work, Melanie," John says, his enormous frame leaving me absolutely no room for escape.

"I don't need you to mansplain motherhood to me," I snap back at him fiercely. The word *mansplain* sends John into three different shades of reddish-purple.

"Melanie, you aren't coming to find him and that's the end of the fucking story, cupcake. I have Lucky coming over with Vinnie, and Peter and a couple other guys are going to stand watch outside. You're pregnant. I can't drag a pregnant woman around New York and Jersey to find my idiot cousin who can't keep his ass out of trouble even if he's forty fucking years old."

"That woman kidnapped him!" I shriek at John, hoping

that raising my voice will scare him, or make him uncomfortable enough to do what I say. "She drugged him from the start and she obviously wants to kill him."

"You don't know what she wants and it ain't your job to take off running after Sammy."

"Who else is going to do it?"

"I am," John snarls. "And you're going to do what women ought to do – stay home and fucking listen."

"Are you serious right now?" I yell at him.

John scowls. "Like a fucking heart attack. I don't wanna fight you kid, but I'll tie you up if I have to. I've fucked up a lot with Sammy Zagarella over the years, but I won't fuck up this. I can't let anything happen to you."

"I'm not a prized possession."

"You're more than that," John says. "You're his family and by extension, that makes you our family. We protect the women in our family. That's the way it's always been. That doesn't change now."

"That's so fucking stupid."

John's reaction surprises me. He smiles and then he chuckles. "No, it isn't. I saw the way you grew up, kid. You gotta learn that's not the way the world works. There are people out there who will love you and protect you and fight for you no matter what."

"I'm that person for myself," I throw back at him.

"Not when you're in love with an Italian man," John says. "We love hard, especially when we love the wrong woman. That's when we love the hardest."

"The wrong woman?"

"A girl too young for us. That sorta thing. I get it. You care about Sammy... but you have to let me do my job and you do yours. Rest. Keep his grandchild safe."

"Fine," I tell him. "I'll stay here."

"Good," John says. "I'll wait for Lucky to get here before I leave."

JOHN MAKES good on his promise. Lucky arrives with the rest of my so-called bodyguards and I disappear upstairs in the bedroom I shared with Sammy. Once I shut the door, I pull my cell phone out and text Shawnte.

Me: SOS. Need escape from Westhampton

EVERY SECOND I wait for a text back from my best friend is complete agony. I pace around the bedroom, struggling to work out an escape plan for myself as I wait for Shawnte's response. For all I know, she'll text me back tomorrow and by then, John will be too far away. If he's searching for Sammy, he's probably heading back to the emptied psychiatrist's office to search for clues.

But that's John. He's old school... There are better ways to find information in this day and age.

I type Sammy's psychiatrist's name into a search engine and wait for the results to slowly populate the page. *Why is the internet always so damned slow when you need it the most?* Before the page populates, Shawnte texts me back.

Shawnte: U need my uncle and his friends to jump Sammy?
Me: NO!! Sammy's missing. John trapped me. Armed bodyguards though. Not sure if you could sneak in.
Shawnte: LOL. Give me time.

.   .   .

THAT'S IT? That's her entire reaction to Sammy missing. I guess that's Shawnte.

Shawnte: Where'd he go?

THERE'S the follow up I expected.

Me: IDK. Maybe mob shit. How much time u need??
Shawnte: I'll be there. Watch a movie.

A PART of me wonders if Shawnte's playing with me. Maybe she really needs ninety minutes, although my gut instinct tells me it would take more time to get past four or five mobsters armed with semi-automatic weapons scattered across the compound.

I can't watch a movie, anyway. I have to research Dr. Gabriel and see if there's anything on the internet that could lead us to Sammy. If we can figure out where Sammy is before John does, we can get out of here and rescue him. I just have to figure out how to get past the bodyguards...

I had scrapes and bruises all up and down my body when Sammy met me. Just because I'm in love and slightly-very pregnant doesn't mean I'm going to sit around and let him make all the rules. Hell fucking no.

If John were here, or if he'd given me a chance to participate in his little investigation, I would have asked him how

Dr. Gabriel and Sammy started working together, where she went to university, and how she got herself tied up with the mob. Weird...

My brain goes crazy with all sorts of theories I have no evidence of. I refresh the page and populate the search results again. There's a LinkedIn profile, a Facebook page, the typical stuff you would expect to find.

It's boring and even if I skim through all the pages, I won't find anything specific that would point to a motive, or even a place where Dr. Gabriel could've taken Sammy. It's frustrating being trapped here and not allowed to help. I feel like an utter failure just sitting here doing nothing. I didn't even bother seeing my mom in the hospital, which looking back could have provided my only opportunity at escape.

I give up on research after reading a couple more boring articles featuring quotes from Dr. Gabriel, and follow Shawnte's instructions to watch a movie. At least a movie will keep me busy until Shawnte's arrival. I watch my favorite feel-good movie, *The Nightmare Before Christmas*, on the little TV in the bedroom. Sammy hates when I watch TV to fall asleep, but I think he's slowly getting used to my need for constant background noise.

Kids movies always make me forget about my problems and remember a time when my mom spent more time passed out drunk than yelling at me. She was easier to get along with when she had less energy to pick on me. It sounds fucked up, but that's the way it was. I can't imagine treating my kid that way and the closer I get to popping out this baby, the angrier I get with her.

How could she treat me the way she did? How could she insult me and belittle me every chance she got?

John seemed surprised at my callousness towards her, but I don't know how anyone expects me to be different. She was the first person to break my heart.

Just when Jack Skellington returns with his news of the Santy Claws, I hear Lucky Vicari's voice booming up the stairs.

"Melanie Stevens. Get down here immediately."

Fuck... what happened now? My heart drops into my butt. It's Shawnte, isn't it. They caught her and possibly killed her. Shit...

I sprint out of the bedroom and race downstairs to find out that I'm half correct. My best friend stands in the kitchen with an overnight bag, surrounded by four mobsters who eye her with complete suspicion.

"What is the meaning of this?" Lucky growls at me, glancing between me and Shawnte like we planned this. I try my best to look innocent.

Shawnte chimes in eagerly. "I already told you. I'm under the strictest of orders from your boss John Vicari to come over here and spend time with Melanie. I'm on your side. You've met John. You know I have to listen to him."

She's making this up on the spot but damn, she sounds good. Even I would believe the bullshit she's spouting right now. Lucky seems annoyed, but he doesn't doubt Shawnte's story.

"Is he serious?" Lucky grumbles. "You could have been killed coming here. Did he send someone with you?"

"I live close by."

Another lie. We wait to see if Lucky buys it. He does.

"Okay... I don't see the harm in a couple teenage girls hanging out in their bedroom together. Go upstairs and no more funny business. You're very important to Sammy, Melanie. I hope you realize that."

"Yes, Lucky. We're just going to do normal high school sleepover stuff. I swear."

"You're pregnant," Lucky snorts. "So I don't know what you consider normal high school sleepover stuff."

Ouch. I guess John promised me a bodyguard – he didn't promise me the bodyguard would be sensitive.

"Well *I* can't get her pregnant," Shawnte says. "And I don't swing that way. So can you chill?"

"Just stay out of trouble," Lucky grumbles. "I'm missing Chiara's playoff game to be here. So don't make this any worse."

If I recall correctly, Chiara's his daughter. I've never met her because Lucky's too protective over her to bring her around Sammy.

"Yes, sir," Shawnte says.

We scramble upstairs together quickly. I know my best friend and neither of us plan to listen to Sammy or John or anyone else. We have work to do. Shawnte preemptively locks the bedroom door behind us.

"So bitch," she says. "What the hell is going on?"

I SUMMARIZE for Shawnte in whispered tones, just in case Lucky's suspicious and paranoid enough to listen at the door. Sammy would've been. I try to stick to the most important details and get the story out quickly, but Shawnte wants details. She asks follow up questions. Our gossip session costs us over half an hour.

"Fuck," Shawnte says. "So you found nothing about that psychiatrist bitch?"

"Nothing mainstream. Nothing she wants people to find."

"What about her dog?"

"Huh? What about her dog?"

"Didn't you mention a dog?"

"No. I said I didn't hear who was on the phone and then I heard breathing that sounded *like* a dog."

"What if it was her and she has a dog?" Shawnte says.

"So what if she has a dog?"

Shawnte is starting to get on my nerves. What's her obsession with the freaking dog?

"If she has a dog, you can track her that way. Maybe the dog has a social media page."

"Are you freaking serious, Shawnte?"

"Yes, I'm serious."

"Well, I don't know anything about the dog, so it's a dead end." I say as I lay back on the bed, exasperated.

As I lay there, a thought comes to my mind. John said that he thought maybe a dog had attacked my mom... What if it was her dog?

"We can call John and find out," Shawnte says.

"Are you serious? He'll get suspicious."

"Or, he'll think you're trying to help him. Call him. Put me on the phone, I'll handle it."

I don't like the idea of putting Shawnte in John's potential warpath. If anyone has to face John Vicari when he's angry, it should be me. I stand up and start to call John with Shawnte leaning way too close.

"He can't even hear you breathe," I hiss at her before John answers. "If he knows you're here, we're fucked."

Shawnte nods, but I'm as serious as a heart attack right now. If John even catches a whiff of what we're planning, we're toast. He's not above locking us in a literal dungeon – I'm sure of it.

"What do you want, Mel?"

"Did Sammy ever mention his psychiatrist having a dog?"

"Yeah, a damned blue-nosed pit bull with a funny name. He couldn't stop complaining about the fucking thing..."

The revelation of what is happening hits me. This dog definitely had to have attacked my mom. If Dr. Gabriel is behind all this, she must have wanted to hurt my family to get me out of the picture.

"What was its name? Can you remember?"

John sounds annoyed. I can't blame him, but my instincts tell me Shawnte might be onto something.

John answers regardless of his audible frustration. "Sounded really Southern. Not a common name for a dog. What the hell is the point of this? I'm busy."

"Relax, John. I'm trying to help."

John dismisses me. "Stay out of trouble, Melanie. Don't try anything else."

"The dog could be important. The dog could have a social media account with clues on it."

John hangs up on me. I shrug, tossing my phone on the bed as Shawnte rolls her eyes. "It's because he's *old*. He probably doesn't even understand how to use the like button," she says. At least she isn't discouraged by John's dismissal and we did get some information that we could use.

She might be right. I've never seen John use his phone to do anything other than make phone calls, and I don't even know if it's anything more than a burner phone.

"So all we know is that it's a pit bull with a Southern name."

Shawnte perks up. "That's still something. I'll search."

"There have to be a million pit bulls in America."

Shawnte ignores me and keeps tapping away into the search engine or social media account or whatever the hell she's doing. Her brow furrows as she focuses and taps away.

"4.5 million," Shawnte says. "According to this website. But that's not the point... I think I might have found it. Taylor Mae Davis?"

"That sounds Southern."

"Look."

Shawnte shows me a social media account: @taylormaedavis_thepittie

"That's kind of a mouthful..." I mutter.

"Is that her?"

Shawnte scrolls down through a few more pictures of the pit bull until she stumbles upon one of the pit bull with her owner. The woman in the photo looks exactly like the Dr. Gabriel I saw during my Google search.. She has swept back long black hair, red lipstick and large gold hoop earrings. She hugs the pit bull's face against hers and a large pink tongue hangs out of the dog's mouth. They have the same color eyes, so dark brown that they look black.

"Look at the caption," I suggest.

Shawnte nods. "This has to be her. I found her page... Look – it's a med school alumni weekend picture from Hofstra. This *has* to be her."

"Great. We found her dog's social media page and now we can stalk her med school selfies."

"It's an investigation," Shawnte says sternly. "Stop being a downer. Sit down and help me search for clues."

I don't share Shawnte's enthusiasm that we'll find anything.

"She lives in the city, right?"

"I don't know anything about this woman except that she somehow managed to kidnap a man twice her size.."

"Do you think she was working alone?"

"I don't even know why she would do this."

Shawnte furrows her brow and stops scrolling. "Look at this."

She shows me a picture of Dr. Gabriel and her dog in front of a small beach house.

"Okay..."

"Do you think she could have Sammy at a beach house?"

"Maybe. But I don't see how this helps."

"That's East Hampton," Shawnte says. "Look at the mansion behind it. The sand... What if she doesn't have him that far away? That would explain how she could even kidnap someone as big as Sammy. She could've drugged him and dragged him, but she wouldn't have been able to get him very far."

"She could have lured him with a weapon," I point out. It's not like I'm actively trying to argue with Shawnte's thought process, because she makes some good points. It's just that I don't believe tracking down Dr. Gabriel would be this easy.

"It doesn't matter how she did it. This *has* to be where she took him. She cleared out her office, so she would've had to bring him somewhere else. . This makes sense, Mel."

"It's a huge risk. We don't even know where the house is."

"That's easy. It's a small, white house in East Hampton. We can guess the square footage and look it up on Zillow."

"The internet has turned us all into stalkers," I grumble.

Shawnte nods excitedly and continues "researching" on my phone. She hisses, "Yes. I think this is the one."

She shows me a place on Zillow that looks somewhat familiar to the one in Dr. Gabriel's picture.

"That house is lime green. The house in the picture was white."

"It's not impossible to paint a house. Look at the design on the front door and the bushes on the front. It's the same damn place."

I hate to admit that Shawnte's right, but I feel something *move* in my stomach. This must be a sign considering this is the first time I've felt my baby move. I gasp and touch my stomach.

"What?" Shawnte says. "Are you getting a sign from your ancestors? Do you have a bad case of gas?"

I wrinkle my nose. "No. I just felt the baby move for the first time."

"It's a sign."

I touch my stomach again. I just want to feel the movement pushing against me and the signs that my baby is here with me. Shawnte patiently watches my stomach.

"I can't feel anything else. But you're right. That's the house. Now comes the hard part."

"I snuck past Lucky one way. I can do it again," she says confidently. "What do you think?"

"We don't have a plan. We can't just rush in and rescue Sammy without weapons or a plan. She has a dog who attacks people, remember?"

"And you have Big Tex."

"I'm *not* putting Big Tex in a damn pit bull's mouth."

"Fine," Shawnte grumbles, rolling her eyes. "You're right. We need a gun. I could call my cousin Mac, but if he helps us, he'll want something in exchange."

"Like what?"

"I don't know. Mac takes pills."

I talk Shawnte out of involving her pill head cousin with the mob.

"We'll have to steal a gun before we leave. That's all. I can get one from Sammy's room, but I don't know where he keeps the ammo."

"Who cares?" Shawnte says. "We can't actually kill some-one. We just need the unloaded gun to scare the crap out of this lady and get Sammy back."

"Sammy would say this is a bad idea."

"And? He's not your damned daddy."

"He's my baby's grandpa. And... I love him."

"Wow," Shawnte says, smirking. "You *are* completely fucked up."

"Shut up."

Shawnte laughs at me even more and helps me sneak out of the bedroom and across the hall to a room where I know Sammy keeps several handguns. It's always been an unspoken yet obvious rule that I never touch Sammy's guns.

I enter the bedroom and head straight for the closet where Sammy has a small safe with his pistols. He keeps the key underneath a pair of jeans on the top shelf.

I reach for the key and it's there… *Fuck yes.* I unlock the safe and grab one of the smaller pistols before hiding it beneath my shirt. I tip toe back to the bedroom door where Shawnte was keeping watch, and we both creep back to my bedroom and shut the door. Her eyes gleam with excitement as I reveal the pistol from beneath my sweatshirt.

"Hell yes," she hisses. "We've got this."

"Should we tell John what we're doing?"

"Sure," Shawnte says. "Once we're out of here and he can't stop us. He can play back up."

Sammy would never hesitate to rescue me. I can't leave his fate up to his angry cousin who acts like he hates Sammy's guts half the time. He protected me when I needed it and I know he thinks I'm just a stupid, teenage girl, but I'm not.

Shawnte masterminds us sneaking out past Lucky, but her plan isn't glamorous. She scouts the top floor from my bedroom window and finds a place where we can drop down from a balcony behind the house and disappear onto a neighbor's lot before Lucky notices us.

"If they notice us, they might shoot first, ask questions later," I point out. "We'll have to be quiet and we'll have to be careful with the gun."

Nothing moves her. With the baby, I'll have to be careful, but I know I can make the drop without landing on my belly. Shawnte and I have certainly done worse. I've had to sneak out *tons* of times when things got bad with my mom, like the time she threw hot coffee on me after I got a D in chemistry junior year. *That* was a bad night.

Melanie

We carefully leave the bedroom from the window. Shawnte drops to the ground first and lands quietly. I lower the gun and my cell phone to her, and then it's my turn. I make it, but the impact hurts the hell out of my knees. The baby moves again and kicks me in what feels like the freaking kidney once I stabilize on both feet.

Shawnte runs for the largest tree on the property. I can't run as fast as she can, but my training with Sammy didn't count for nothing, I'm not as slow as I expect and I only get to the tree a few seconds after Shawnte. She points to the next one and we dart across the property from tree to tree without detection until we get to the neighbor's lot.

"So this is Lucky's place?" Shawnte whispers as we walk slowly around the outskirts of the neighboring property. I nod, still afraid to speak too loudly even if I know logically that Lucky is across the expansive property, at Sammy's place. The only people here are Lucky's wife, Althea and their kids.

Once we get to the main road, we start the hard part. Shawnte uses a ride-share app on her phone to call a car, and despite the driver's skepticism, he drops us off at a house in East Hampton, several miles away from Sammy's and Lucky's, but only a few blocks away from the address where we suspect Dr. Gabriel of holding Sammy.

Once the car drives away and Shawnte tips him on her phone – which she could have done later – I anxiously remind her that we're supposed to tell John where we are now that it's too late for him to stop us.

I can't work up the courage to call John directly, so I text him the address and a few words.

Sammy's here. I'm with Shawnte. We're going to stop her before she moves him.

. . .

I TURN my phone off before John calls back and loses his damned mind. Shawnte takes the gun out of her hoodie pouch and hands it to me.

"You have the baby, you take the gun, that way you'll be safer."

"You do remember the gun isn't loaded, right?"

"Exactly," Shawnte says. "I'll need my free hand to swing on that bitch."

I don't remind her about the dog situation. We might be able to scare Dr. Gabriel with an unloaded weapon, but a loyal pit bull defending its master won't exactly cower at the sight of a fake weapon. *We'll figure that part out later, I guess.*

It's already getting dark, and the streets in East Hampton are quiet. We would stick out even more if it were summer and there were crowds of rich white folk walking through the streets. Girls from Queens don't exactly spend a lot of their free time in East Hampton, and people around here would definitely notice that we don't belong. I don't help my case by gawking at the mansions we have to walk past to get to Dr. Gabriel's house.

If she can afford a house out here, what the hell does she want with Sammy Zagarella? She doesn't want to extort him for money, that's for damned sure. One of the large white houses has a real Lamborghini parked in front of it. *Holy shit, this place is bougie.*

Shawnte and I keep walking. We pass an elderly couple out for a walk. They stare at us, but they don't say anything questionable, just a curt hello before continuing their walk. Shawnte shakes her head. "They're probably wondering what the hell we're doing out here."

Shawnte keeps track of our destination on her phone.

"We shouldn't go through the front door," she says, even

if it's risky climbing through another person's back yard. I point out that in a neighborhood this nice, folks might be more than willing to call the police.

"We got past a *literal* mobster. We can make it past a Karen with a cell phone."

Shawnte's stubbornness is almost inspiring, honestly. She encourages me to cross the backyard of a large brown house with her and then we're there, right near the bushes from the picture on the other side of the house. Now that I'm close, I see the resemblance to the pictures and I know we're in the right place.

I'm coming Sammy... I won't let you down.

Chapter 18
Out Of The Fog
Sammy

I wake up foggy and every inch of my body hurts. My quads strain against my binds. How the fuck did that woman get me up here and strap me down? She's either a lot stronger than she looks, or she had help. I groan and tilt my head to the side. I don't hear the dog panting, which means she isn't in here. Maybe she's taking the damned dog out for a walk, or planning my demise…

The last thing I remember was a pinch in my arm and then her hand wrapping around my crotch. *I don't know what the fuck she did to me.*

The door to my room swings open and I tilt my head in an attempt to hear her footsteps better. My arms jerk unwillingly against the binds. I can't allow her to do any worse to me. I'll demand my death. I'll go berserk. I'll be the crazy person they think I am.

"Don't be a fucking coward," I growl, unable to hear anyone moving in the room.. "Kill me. Get in here and kill me."

"Damn. This is all the way fucked up."

That's not Dr. Gabriel's voice. The speaker has a Queens accent, but she doesn't sound like Melanie either. I jerk my head around, but that doesn't help. I hear footsteps and then feel something against my cheek. *It's her.*

"Sammy," Melanie whispers as she starts to take my blind fold off. "She's taking the dog for a walk. We're going to get you out of here."

Fuck. What the hell is she doing here? She's nearly twenty weeks along, if not further, and in a situation like this, John ought to have her under tight guard...

"Go!" I call out hoarsely. I don't mean to sound so angry, but Melanie can't be here when that woman comes back. I don't know what the hell she'll do to Melanie if she finds her, but I can't be responsible for that.

Melanie ignores me and works on the leather straps buckling my arms to the bed. I grunt as she works the straps free. I glance down at my feet to discover the identity of the first voice I overheard in the dark. She brought Shawnte. *Melanie, what the hell am I going to do with you?*

Melanie works me free, but my limbs are stiff and swollen. I sit up and groan. Every part of my body hurts.

"She could come back any minute. You need to leave."

"Here."

Shawnte moves around to the other side of the bed and hands me a firearm. *Fuck.* I close my fingers around the pistol and it feels natural in my hands. The gun isn't heavy enough to be loaded. *Melanie...*

Still, I can't respond to this calmly and celebrate Melanie's actions when she sandangered herself and the baby. I set the gun on the bed and give her a stern look.

"Where's John?"

"I texted him. Sammy, we're fine. I needed to save you."

She throws her arms around me and for a moment, it's

hard to be angry with her. She earnestly threw herself into this rescue and although she thinks everything is fine, she has no idea the monster we're dealing with. But her touch… Melanie runs her hands through my hair boldly and I can't help myself. I wrap my arms around her and clutch her against me as tightly as I can.

Her small baby bump presses into me and a possessive urge awakens in me. I kiss her forehead, leaving me unable to resist her touch or mischievous ways. I can't stop myself as I tilt my head to kiss her on the lips. Fuck, it feels good to kiss her, even if I shouldn't waste a single second. Shawnte whistles as I kiss her, but I don't stop.

One taste of Melanie's lips and I crave more. I grab her cheeks and hold her in place so I can kiss her properly. Her lips yield to mine and my tongue presses into Melanie's mouth. She tastes delicious and I suck on her lower lip, losing myself in her scent for a few moments. *Freedom.* I'll have my freedom soon enough, as long as I get her out of here okay. That dog has a sense of smell, so if we don't leave soon…

Loud shuffling and a slamming door interrupts my thought and my kiss. Melanie drops away from me quickly and terror registers on both her and Shawnte's faces. *We wasted enough time.* I hear Taylor Mae Davis emit an unusually high-pitched barking noise. Then she barks some more.

"Did you bring any ammo?"

"No," Shawnte hisses. "Too dangerous."

Great.

"You two need to hide."

"Where?"

"Under the bed. Wherever you can… Trust me…"

Shawnte flicks off the lights in the small bedroom. I can handle this. Melanie hesitates to move, but I squeeze her hand and demand she join Shawnte in her hiding spot. She swallows nervously and tucks herself under the bed. The two of them must be packed tightly down there. My throat tightens as I expect Dr. Gabriel to return shortly. She'll want to check on me... then what?

I don't relish hurting a woman, but if I had to hurt her, shooting to injure her would have been better than the alternatives. Since that's not an option, I'll have to disable her without ending her life, despite my temptation to punish her. *I don't know what she did to me when I was unconscious, but I still feel violated.*

Footsteps get closer to the door and I hear Melanie emit a nervous yelp.

"Hush," I murmur to Melanie and Shawnte, getting out of bed and crossing to the door with the gun raised as if it were loaded. I hear the pit bull's nails against the floor and then Dr. Gabriel's softer footsteps. The gun might scare Dr. Gabriel, but I'll need another solution for the dog.

"What's wrong, Taylor Mae?" she whispers. "Huh? Are you hungry? Don't worry, you'll have your teeth in that bitch's arm soon enough..."

I hear kissing sounds as she entices Taylor Mae Davis to calm down and then Dr. Gabriel thrusts the door open, leaving me only seconds to react. I have an unloaded gun, drugs in my system, significantly depleted strength... and a pregnant woman to protect at all costs.

I move swiftly, hitting Dr. Gabriel in the back of the head with the butt of my pistol. She cries out and falls forward. Taylor Mae Davis races into the room, heading straight for my makeshift hospital bed. *Shit.* The dog barks twice, but I have to tune her out because Dr. Gabriel lunges for my legs to knock them out from underneath me.

I fight back, kicking her and then shoving her across the

room. Dr. Gabriel yelps and her distressed sound sends her pit bull into guard mode. The dog's ears lay back flat and she exposes her teeth, snarling and growling at me. She barks and then barks again. I throw Dr. Gabriel against the wall, hoping to knock her unconscious.

The dog lunges for me. *Fuck.* I took care of the doctor, but I don't have time to react to the dog. I hear my shirt fabric rip and feel an instant surge of pain as teeth puncture my skin and the pit bull's jaw grips my forearm. I can't control the scream that comes out of my mouth and I apparently can't control Shawnte or Melanie either.

They spring from under the bed, screeching as they lunge for the dog gripping my arm and try to pry her off. Taylor Mae Davis shakes her head furiously and I cry out as the pain increases and she clamps her jaw down harder.

"FUCK!" I cry out.

"Sammy, hang on!" Melanie calls out.

I don't know how the girls wrestle Taylor Mae Davis off me, but then next thing I know, the dog separates from my arm and blood spurts into the air. Melanie screams again and I cry out as the sudden appearance of blood sends me into shock. My nausea increases and I want to direct Melanie to wrap the wound, but she's holding back Taylor Mae Davis with Shawnte's help.

"Mel..." I choke out.

Flashing blue and red lights appear outside the window. I didn't hear any cars pull up but the flashing gets brighter, so I start counting. Three... four... five cop cars outside. *Fuck.* Dr. Gabriel groans in the corner. The room fades around me. There's too much blood. I can't run. I can't negotiate. John isn't here...

I hear loud fists on the front door, but I can't move. There's too much blood.

"Melanie, run…"

"I'm not leaving you!" she yells. "Are you crazy?"

"Melanie…"

Three police officers work through the house announcing themselves as they burst through the doors in each room. They'll find us soon and I don't know what they'll do to Melanie, Shawnte, or the dog…

"Run…"

"NO!" Melanie shrieks. I slump over and lose consciousness.

I WAKE up to searing pain in my arm as the cop moves me.

"We need an ambulance, but he's still under arrest."

"You can't arrest him," Melanie argues. "He's hurt. She kidnapped him and that dog bit him."

The cops ignore her. I've lost too much blood and my mouth is too dry to speak up for myself. They put the cuffs on me and I hear more sirens. *Ambulance.*

"I need to talk to her," I grunt. "Please… she's carrying my child."

The cops allow Melanie to approach me. They don't step back, so I have to speak carefully.

"John will get a lawyer, honey bun. You have nothing to worry about. You go home when he gets here. You let John handle things and… you might not see me for a while, but… I love you."

It's all the energy I have. There's too much blood. I might not make it, but I don't want Melanie or these fucking cops to know that. Tears swim in Melanie's eyes. The cops scoff, but I don't care and neither does Melanie. She leans forward and kisses my forehead.

"You're losing a lot of blood," she whispers.

"I'll be fine, honey bun. I'll be fine."

"I don't get it," she says. "Why are they arresting you?"

Bᴜᴛ I ᴅᴏɴ'ᴛ ɢᴇᴛ a chance to answer before the EMTs come and take me away from Melanie and away from freedom.

* * *

Chapter 19
Dirty On The Phone
Melanie

Sammy's been in jail for three weeks. John keeps trying to tell me this is just how it works and as long as Sammy stays out of federal prison, I have nothing to worry about. The last thing he said to me was that I was carrying his child. Not his grandchild… We never got to talk about that or anything that happened. I never even got to say goodbye…

John's wife Alexis wants me to feel better, so she's throwing me a gender reveal party at Lucky's Westhampton home with Althea's help. Althea's married to Lucky and she's fierce, with a spunky eleven year old daughter. They're doing everything in their power to make me forget the fact that the man I love is in jail and anything could happen to him.

The party starts at noon, and it's a small, intimate gathering. I told Althea not to bother inviting my mother, but she seemed so sad at the idea that my mother wouldn't want to be there that I felt too embarrassed and invited her. I know she won't come, but there's still the concern that she might show up and ruin this.

I saw her in the hospital the day after the cops arrested

Sammy. John hadn't told me the charges yet and he thought seeing her again might cheer me up. He was wrong about that, but my mom at least seemed entertained by my presence. She tore me down about how I'm carrying the pregnancy weight, how big pregnancy is making my nose, and how she also thinks Sammy will go to prison for life.

"I know that big old white fella sent that dog," she said, even when I reminded her that their family was paying her medical bills.

Yeah, she won't show up today...

Shawnte and Damzel are coming. Damzel reached out to Shawnte and we've been hanging out together since Sammy's arrest. I never told her about Javier and she's never asked. I don't know what to make of our new friendship, but it's nice to have people I can invite to a party. It's nice not to feel like the loser my mom wanted me to feel like.

Shawnte and Damzel arrive with gifts, adding to the pile Althea and Alexis put together for me. Apparently, John picked out a gender reveal gift for me on his own and Sammy sent instructions for a gift too. I also brought Big Tex to the party so he can play with the other dogs.

He's been my responsibility since Sammy's arrest and we're getting closer. I think he misses his master and we keep each other company during those lonely nights in the house neighboring Lucky's.

Althea starts the party with some smooth bachata music in the background and she gathers everyone around for her hostess announcement. Lucky and John appear from the room where they're hiding out watching football to listen to Althea's announcement. There are a few other mobsters at the party, but I don't remember all their names. I know Vinnie and I think Alexis told me a couple of John's friends are from Boston — Darragh and Callum Murray — who are hiding out in NYC because their brother's going to prison.

"We're going to play a few games," Althea says. "Then, we're going to guess the baby's gender and reveal it with a giant cake, baked by my daughter Chiara and her aunt, Alexis, who are the only two people who know the baby's gender."

"For all we know, she could be having twins," John mutters. I think the doctor would have found that on the ultrasound, but his comment sends a sudden shudder of worry through me. Having twins is one thing, but having twins alone would be hard to manage. I have two boobs… that part might work. But how would I hold two kids? Thankfully, Chiara distracts me from my mini-freak-out.

"It's coconut flavored," Chiara announces. The eleven-year-old girl is freaking adorable. She has dark curls in a pineapple on her head, a cream-colored Carhartt sweatshirt and pink leggings tucked into gray Ugg boots.

Delicious. It's my favorite cake flavor, a fact my own mother doesn't know. It's been a bit harder to move around with the baby. Alexis immediately notices my discomfort and gives me the softest plush chair to sit in.

Damzel wins the first baby shower game. John wins the next one, which pisses Lucky off a bit. Chiara wins the third game and then Althea begs us to place our guesses into a jar before I then get to cut the cake and find out about the baby. I didn't want to see the results, but they all think I'm depressed over Sammy, so I relented.

The closer we get to cutting the cake, the more I feel the bursts of excitement that Althea and Alexis want me to feel. Even if Sammy goes to prison, I'll have a baby and I can write him letters and maybe this will all have a happy ending. I can make a happy ending without Sammy, even if I'm still in love with him and even if we have to keep our love alive through love letters, phone calls and smothered gifts.

Althea and Alexis lead me over to the cake before giving

me the cake knife as they add up the guesses from around the room.

"Most people guessed that the baby would be a boy," Alexis says. "With only three votes for a girl... Let's see who's right. Melanie? Are you ready to cut the cake?"

I bite my lower lip. I don't know if I'm ready, but there isn't any time for me to pull out now. I stick the knife into the cake and slowly drag it through. I still can't tell when I pull the knife out. I cut out a slice and put it on a plate. It's pink.

I think.

"A girl?"

"It's a girl!" Chiara cheers. John cheers. He voted for a girl. I thought I would be having a boy. I never expected to have... *a daughter.* It's good news – obviously. I would love my baby if they were purple or genderless. I'll love my baby because they're mine... and I would never put a kid through what I went through.

Tears form in my eyes and I suddenly miss Sammy Zagarella more than anything. He should be here. Instead, he'll find out through a phone call. I quietly hand the cake slice to Althea, who insists that I should eat the first slice of cake. She wraps her arms around me, giving me a quick hug and congratulations.

Alexis takes over cutting the cake so I can rest, and I enjoy my cake. My mom doesn't show up, but I didn't expect her to. That visit in the hospital represented a shift in both of us. I won't stand around and be her punching bag anymore and ironically, that's what's getting her to leave me alone – abandoning her. It hurts, but I have an Italian family that accepts me more than I ever expected.

My phone rings as my mind wanders to Sammy again. I don't recognize the number.

.   .   .

This is a collect call from Nassau County Correctional Center. To accept this call, please press one.

It's Sammy. I press one and walk out onto the balcony and onto the expansive grounds of Lucky Vicari's Westhampton home.

"Hello, honey bun," he says. "Did I miss the party?"

I have to try to hold it together on our calls. *It's so hard to hear his voice and not have him here.*

"No," I whisper. "You didn't. How's your arm?"

These calls are expensive and even if Sammy's in the mob, you can get into big trouble hogging the phones too long. I don't want to be the reason he gets his ass kicked.

"Fine. Hurts all the fucking time, but John hooked me up with the good shit in here."

"Let's hope you don't get addicted to the good shit."

Sammy chuckles. "Fuck, I miss you."

"I miss you too."

"Tell me about our baby," he says.

This is the second time he's said "our baby" and I desperately want to talk about it, even if we probably have very little time on this phone call.

"It's a girl," I whisper. "Surprise."

"Holy fuck," Sammy says. "You serious?"

He sounds genuinely happy and I find the joyful tone in his voice infectious. I'm not depressed about the baby or the gender reveal. I just miss Sammy.

"Yup. A girl." I try not to cry. Why doesn't he just use his mob connections to get out of jail?

"I miss you, honey bun."

"Stop. I don't want to cry again. I nearly lost it cutting the cake."

"You miss me?" Sammy asks.

"Yes."

"I miss you too. Every day I'm in here, I think about kissing you. And fucking you."

"Sammy! I'm at a baby shower."

"Go upstairs," Sammy whispers. "Find a room and lock the door. I want to talk to you alone..."

We've done this before. It's been three weeks and Sammy has a *very* high sex drive. But he can't seriously expect me to do this here, right?

"I'm at Lucky's place."

"That house has over ten bedrooms. Find an empty one, lock the door, and put your fingers in your panties for me, babe... Please... I fucking miss you."

*** * ***

Chapter 20
Freedom
Sammy

I've worked out a way to talk to her alone. I'm lucky to get this privilege because John doesn't have to forgive me for getting into so much trouble again. He's only doing this because he's fond of Melanie and too much of a dick to admit it. I hear my honey bun walking up the stairs and imagine her picking the perfect room to touch herself. My cock stiffens in my pants.

I can't wait to get out of jail and away from a bunch of foul smelling fuck-tards who piss and shit themselves on a regular basis and have absolutely no shame. Jail sucks. I promised I would never end up here again, but I fucked up trusting Dr. Gabriel. She got busted for drug trafficking.

Her office is now closed, and the cops found her prescriptions and the cocktail of drugs she had prescribed me. They also find some other paper fudging which lands my ass in jail. John promises our new lawyer can get us out – she's a hotshot from Nashville named Meg Nigel who recently started a new law firm specializing in criminal defense. I haven't met her yet. John's handling everything because he swears it'll go faster.

I just want to see Melanie again.

"Okay," she whispers. "I'm ready."

"I'm so fucking hard for you, honey bun."

"I could get caught."

"You won't," I murmur. "What are you wearing?"

"I'm at a baby shower and I'm twenty-three weeks pregnant. It's not exactly Playboy material."

"You are much better than anything in *Playboy*," I murmur. "Now tell me what you're wearing."

"Black maternity leggings. A white top…"

"Boobs…"

"Yes, Sammy," Melanie says. "Boobs."

"I would give *anything* to see your boobs right now."

"Then come home," she says. Her voice makes me want to cum. This is pure fucking torture, but I can't come home, I can't change anything about my situation. I can just sit here and picture Melanie touching herself. I can reach into my pants and lose myself, worrying about the mess later.

"I want to," I growl into the phone. "But right now, I want you to touch yourself more. Slip your hand into those tight black leggings and touch your pussy for me."

"Sammy…"

"I want to hear you moan as you touch yourself, honey bun."

She makes a slight whimper into the phone and my cock jumps in my pants. I wish I could slide my cock into her deliciously tight warmth.

"I'm touching myself," she whispers. "Oh my God… I'm so sensitive."

"It's been too long since we've done this," I growl. I don't feel like I have any control, and just wish I had her in my arms. I miss touching her. Melanie's too far away from me right now. I reach my hands into my pants and grip my cock, stroking myself as I think of her.

"Touch yourself for me, honey bun. Imagine my tongue going down on you and spreading your sexy lower lips apart..."

Precum oozes from the tip of my cock as I grip myself. I wish I had Melanie's lips wrapped around my cock. This will have to do. An excitable moan escapes Melanie's throat. Her beautiful fingers are probably spreading her apart, teasing her entrance open.

"Put a finger in your pussy," I murmur. "I want to hear you scream as you touch yourself."

"I'm close..." she whimpers.

"Then touch yourself slowly, honey bun..."

I hear Melanie squirming in the bed, the sloppy sounds of her fingers spreading her lips and sliding between them. I don't want to control myself as I slide my palms up and down the length of my dick. Listening to her moan drives me fucking wild. *I want her to cum first.*

"Put another finger in your pussy," I whisper. "You sound so fucking hot right now..."

"I can't..." she whimpers. "I'm gonna cum..."

Melanie's whimpers drive me wild. I listen to her move again and she moans even louder than before. Despite her protest, she sounds like she added another finger to her wetness.

"Cum for me, princess," I growl. I want her to feel good. I can't be there to touch her, or taste her, or pin her hands over her head while I finger her to a climax, but I can use my voice to push her over the edge.

"Touch your pretty pussy for me, honey bun..."

"I'm cumming..." she gasps before emitting an untamed moan. She's so hot when she cums that listening to Melanie lose herself in the throes of pleasure pushes me over the edge. I grunt and grasp the base of my cock tightly as I climax. Thick spurts of cum make a sticky mess in my pants. *Fuck it, she's worth the mess.*

Melanie's heavy breathing is the only sound I can hear on the other end of the line. I feel a panicked tug in my heart as we get closer to the end of our phone call. I'll have to leave this room, say goodbye to special fucking treatment and head back to sleep on a metal bed with a thin mattress that stinks like piss and men who don't know how to fucking shower.

"I love you," I murmur.

"Yeah..." Melanie says. She sounds far away now. As I regain my senses and wipe my hands clean on my pants, I notice the pain in her voice.

"Did I keep you from the party too long?"

I don't want to keep hurting her like this.

"When are you coming home?" Melanie says with a hint of anger in her voice. This isn't good.

"Soon. I promise."

"How soon?"

"I can't make any promises."

I wish I could give her the reassurance she wants, but there's no way to know what my lawyer can do. Maybe she's right to be angry because even in our family's privileged position, the law can still fucking get you in the life. There are no guarantees.

Melanie's voice comes back tough and distant. "You keep saying this is *our* baby but you aren't here, Sammy."

"Melanie... Don't be upset. I know it's hard."

"You don't know how fucking hard it is," she snaps.

"I'm in *jail*," I growl. I bite my tongue to avoid making things worse. This place is hell. Men rape and beat each other to death over fucking dinner rolls here.

"I don't give a shit," Melanie says. "I'm pregnant and you keep promising me that we'll have a life together... that this will be *our* baby... but if you aren't home... The baby can't be yours, Sammy. I don't want my kid to have a dad behind bars."

"Melanie, don't be ridiculous," I growl. I have no power here and I have no power on the outside.

"You're going to prison for *life*," she says. "I love the phone sex but… you can't raise a kid over the phone."

"I will be there for the baby, Melanie. I *want* to be a father to *our* baby. I lost Enrico and this is a chance for both of us. I'll be there. I promise, I'll be there."

"Sammy, you're in jail," she says. "I know how your family keeps secrets. If you were coming home, you would be here."

"Melanie…"

Your collect call has ended.

THAT'S IT. The phone disconnects without the touch of a button. I'm stuck here and there's nothing I can do about this unless some lawyer or another jack off gets me out of here.

"Damn it!"

I SLAM the fucking phone down. There's nothing I can do and I hate it. I have to be with her.

I CAN'T LET Melanie think this is it – that I rot in fucking prison while she's out there.

I'M GETTING the fuck outta here.

Sammy

* * *

Chapter 21
A Knock
Melanie

I don't tell anyone about the fight with Sammy and the party ends with everyone except me, Lucky, and the nursing mamas totally drunk. Shawnte ends up leaving with one of John and Sammy's cousins from another family regardless of how much I beg her to stay late. Althea and Alexis give me all the new mom advice I could hope for, and John escorts me home at the end of the night with Big Tex.

"You sure everything's okay?"

"I miss Sammy. I want him out of prison."

John grimaces, which isn't the answer I want to hear. I've been suspicious of the Vicari brothers for a while, but I suspect they know more than they're letting on and that Sammy will have longer in jail than they want me to know.

"Good night, Melanie."

I'm RIGHT. I spend six weeks in the house alone except for Big Tex. Damzel leaves the city to go to SUNY Oswego and Shawnte leaves for Newark. Saying goodbye to both of them hurt more than I expected, but I have business in New York, even without Sammy.

Since I haven't finished high school, Alexis suggests I get my GED and apply to college. I have the GED exams in three weeks, so I hope our baby girl comes right on time and I finish my exams before the due date. Studying isn't as hard as I thought I would be and it's a lot less distracting not having to dodge school bullies and the asshole guys in my grade.

For the first time in my life, I have a favorite subject – History. I ask Althea if there are any jobs that use history and she suggests library sciences or going to graduate school and becoming a professor. The idea of working in a library appeals to me now more than ever before. With all my alone time under John Vicari's watch, I've finally discovered the magic of romance novels.

I was missing out. Period. I've devoured six of them this week alone, so working in a building filled to the brim with romance novels, where I might get to learn even more about history, definitely appeals to me. Books have also given me an obsession with baby names for my daughter.

Our DAUGHTER.

I HAVEN'T TALKED to Sammy since the baby shower. Every day I'm home alone, I keep hoping he'll appear and surprise me, but John would definitely tell me if Sammy were coming home. I wish he were here.

Big Tex sleeps at my feet as I work on some math problems for my GED. Math isn't the hardest subject, but it's my least favorite. I can't think about the numbers when I'm alone at night the way I can think about a romance novel. Math is pure repetition and pain – don't forget the pain.

Big Tex makes a low whining noise and stirs after a long nap. He rises to his feet suddenly and stares at the front door. Big Tex whines again and then bumps his nose into my thigh.

"No walk…"

The doorbell rings. Okay, so he wasn't asking for a walk. Someone's at the door? Hope swells in my chest. It's Sammy. It has to be him. I slam my book shut and nearly trip, getting my body out of the chair at the dining table. Big Tex whines and then runs off into one of the bedrooms.

Why is Big Tex acting so weird?

The doorbell rings again. I wonder why Sammy doesn't just open the door and then remember that he probably lost his house keys in the kerfuffle with Dr. Gabriel. John says she'll go to prison for years if she survives until the trial, but as far as I know, she's behind bars.

I open the front door after the fourth doorbell ring. The house is huge, so it always takes time to get to the door. Someone this impatient has to be in Sammy's family…

I thoughtlessly swing the door open.

"Mom?"

She misses my baby shower, but shows up at my house, a place I've never given her the address to. I freeze in the doorway, one hand gripping the door and the other gripping the frame as I stand frozen and unsure of what to say to her.

She glances down at my stomach and a smirk crosses her face. The smirk dissipates when she notices me watching her and her neutral, disinterested expression returns.

"I needed a ride from the hospital when they released me. I had to get all the way back to our place on the damned bus."

This is her idea of a greeting. I bite my lower lip to

prevent myself from saying something insensitive. I don't want to be like her.

"Do you want something? We haven't spoken in ages."

"It's been a struggle to work since the attack," she says. "You never sent me flowers, by the way. Clearly, you've got money now. I don't know what you're doing for these white men to get all this money, but clearly... you've got money."

Don't let her get under your skin, Melanie. You're not her punching bag, anymore. You're not anyone's punching bag.

"If you want something, ask for it."

"I lost the house," she says. "I need... I need $16,000 to get on my feet."

"Sixteen-thousand dollars?"

I know rent has spiraled out of control, but it can't require sixteen-thousand dollars. She glances at the door frame and then attempts to peer around me into the house.

"How did you find me?"

"I need the money, Melanie. I'm your mother. You don't want your kid seeing their grandma in a tent under an overpass."

"My kid? You mean my *daughter*."

"Whatever."

"Not whatever," I snap. I never thought I'd have the courage to say what I've always wanted to say to my mom. The words come out easily now. I don't even feel angry anymore. I feel... *in control.*

"Who cares if it's a damn boy or a girl? Aren't you hearing me? I don't have anywhere to *live*."

She folds her arms and I notice so much about her that I never saw before. She never looks me in the eye. When she sees me smile, her smile falters. I don't know why I make her so fucking unhappy, but looking at her now, I have to face the truth about her. She doesn't love me. She *can't* love me. I would never treat my daughter the way she treats me.

"You missed my baby shower and gender reveal," I say as calmly as I can muster. "You couldn't bother coming to those, but you could find me when you needed to ask for money?"

"I have bigger problems," she says. "I don't have time for useless parties."

"It wasn't a useless party. My daughter's uncles were there, her aunts and her entire family. We got together to celebrate my daughter's life... Even her grandfather called in and he's in prison."

"Don't you have the perfect fucking life," she says, trying not to raise her voice. I know it's only because she needs something. Before all this, I might've leapt at the chance to try to please her. She'll never be happy and nothing I do for her will ever change her.

"I'm not giving you money, mom. I don't have that kind of money and if I did, I would give it to someone who gave a crap about me and my baby girl. We matter. We're important... And even if I'm not important to you... I'm important to someone else."

She smirks again. "Look at you acting like a whiny ass white girl. Fitting in with the Long Island crowd already."

I can't let her get to me. My voice steels and I straighten my back. This may not be the happy ending everyone wants for me, but it's the happy ending I need to have for myself. I need to choose my family carefully and build the life I want for my daughter. There's no room for my mom in the life I have now – not unless she changes.

"Get off the property," I say to her. "Now."

"Bitch."

"I mean it, mom. Don't make me call the cops."

I don't give her an opportunity to change my mind. I close the door in her face and then press my back to the door. It hurts. I want to pretend that it doesn't hurt to shut the door on my mom and cut her out of my life forever, but it's like ripping out a piece of myself that I don't want to admit is completely toxic.

I don't want to say goodbye to her. I want her to love me.

Big Tex bounds out of the bedroom once I start crying. I'm pregnant, alone, my mother doesn't love me and Sammy's big stupid behind is stuck behind bars where he'll probably live forever. I argued with him during our last conversation and I've basically ruined everything.

If I don't get my GED, my life will be a waste and I will have failed my daughter before she was even born...

I hear a loud fist on the door a few minutes into my crying session and it's not exactly a welcome alternative to the doorbell.

"Go home, mom!"

"Melanie Stevens, open the door this instant."

I COULDN'T TURN AROUND FAST ENOUGH. I throw the door open and my mother isn't in the front yard anymore. Big Tex races outside and runs in excited circles.

"SAMMY!"

I don't think before jumping into his arms, even if I'm *super* pregnant, so it's probably a horrible idea. Sammy grunts as I land in his arms, but he catches me. Sammy Zagarella catches me and clutches me against his chest, pressing his nose into my hair.

"You little minx," he growls, squeezing me against his chest. "It's been *weeks*. I thought you got away from me."

I throw my arms around Sammy, forgetting all the reasons I fought with him before. He's here. He's bulkier and more muscular than he left, which surprises me because I thought jail food sucked, but I don't mind grabbing Sammy's *very* muscular bicep. Big Tex barks and puts his paws on Sammy's back before running in more circles around him.

I don't know how Sammy doesn't trip over his energetic greyhound. I lean into Sammy's chest. At least he's here…

"I didn't get away from you," I whisper. "I'm right here."

Sammy's grasp on me tightens possessively. "John told me you'd left and if I didn't cooperate with the lawyer… fucking liar."

"Why weren't you cooperating with the damn lawyer?"

"It doesn't matter," Sammy grumbles. "I'm here now. I cooperated."

He sets me down and holds my face, examining me closely. His hands feel weathered and even rougher than I remember, but I don't want him to let go of my face for anything in the world.

"You good?" he asks with his thick and eternally seductive Long Island accent. That accent makes my pussy throb and so do Sammy's green eyes.

"Sometimes."

"I pissed you off, huh?"

"I'm pregnant. I'm alone. Everything pisses me off."

"I told you I would be here," he says, his grasp on my cheeks tightening. "What the hell do I have to do for you to stop doubting me?"

He doesn't look like he's spent as many weeks in jail as he has except for his long hair, which is now long enough to have streaks of gold with the brown. Sammy's eyes are the perfect shade of green and they don't look empty anymore. *He looks like himself.*

"You were physically in jail, Sammy. That wasn't in your control."

"True," he whispers. "But I'll never leave you alone, Melanie. *I promise.*"

He says it with so much meaning that my heart jumps in

my chest. I don't want him to let go. I never wanted him to let go. But I don't want what happened to Enrico to happen to Sammy. I don't want my baby to lose both of them to the mafia… Sammy's thing.

"What happens if you break that promise? I'm stuck grieving you. Missing you. *Forever.*"

Sammy releases my cheeks from his grasp. A momentary panic surges through me. I hate that I could have pushed him away. Sammy wipes his palms on his pants like they're sweaty and then he gets down on his knees. He props one leg up so he's only on one knee and I stare at him in complete confusion.

"Sammy, I'm being serious. What are you doing down there?"

"Is there something men normally do on one knee?" Sammy grumbles. He reaches into his pocket and pulls out a box. I don't think they let you go jewelry shopping on the bus ride from prison, so I'm hesitant to reach for the box Sammy holds out. I don't want him to propose to me with a ring pop. I'd rather wait. I cross my arms and narrow my eyes at Sammy.

"Can you be patient, Melanie?"

"No. I'm pregnant. I'm impatient by definition."

"Hm."

He opens the box and that is *definitely* not a ring pop.

"Where did you get that?"

"Melanie, hush," Sammy says harshly. "You keep interrupting and I can't get a word in."

"You haven't–

"Hush," Sammy says. "I want to marry you, Melanie. I want to be in our daughter's life and I don't want her to know me as her grandfather. I know that's what I am… but family is more than who we are by blood. Family is about choice."

How does he always know the right things to say?

"Sammy…"

"I love you," he says. "This ring is from the old country. A cardinal in Rome gave my great grandfather the rubies in exchange for his protection. This ring has been in my family for years. It has nothing to do with the Vicari family… it's my vow that you will always come first. You and our baby. If you will have me, Melanie Stevens… I want to be your husband. I want to make you my wife."

"Sammy, do you really mean this? Because if this is about grief or guilt or what happened with–

"Don't argue with me, honey bun," Sammy says calmly, despite interrupting me. "I want you. I'll fight every case. I'll do whatever it takes, but I'll always come home to you."

"I'm too young for you."

"Yes," Sammy replies. He's still calm, still so sure that I'm the woman he wants. I almost pushed him away. He loves me more than anyone ever has and I almost lost him. Tears well in my eyes. It's not a response Sammy sees from me often and he visibly panics.

"Do you not want marriage?" Sammy says, his brows wrinkling in confusion. I'm crying too hard to explain myself and the more I try to compose myself, the more tears come out. It's like I'm having a hormonal reaction beyond my control now. Sammy, clearly confused, puts the ring in his pocket and even if he doesn't understand why I'm crying, he wraps his arms around me and draws me against his chest.

I don't resist him. This isn't about wanting to push Sammy away. I clutch him and weep into his chest.

"I'm sorry…" he whispers. "I didn't mean to upset you."

"You didn't. Not directly. It's not your fault."

"Explain, honey bun. Because you're very pregnant and I thought being here would make you feel… *safer*."

I'm glad he's close. I don't want to push him away,

despite how angry I've been. I didn't want him gone, I just wanted him home and I wanted absolute certainty that he wouldn't leave again.

"How can you love me this much? You didn't even want me around. I was… a burden."

"You were not a burden, Melanie. You were a blessing. I don't know if I would have been able to leave my darkness behind if I didn't have you showing me what was really important."

He draws me into another tight embrace. This one feels even safer than the first. Sammy kisses my forehead and murmurs, "I still want to marry you, honey bun."

"Yes," I whisper. "If you really want to marry me… If you're not doing it out of guilt—

"I love you, Melanie. I love you enough to make you my family."

"How is that possible? My own mother…"

"Did she come here?" Sammy asks, suddenly pulling his body away from me as his fingers interlock with mine.

"Yes. And we're done. She asked for money, so I sent her away and I had to accept that she doesn't love me. How can she not give a crap about me, but you do? It doesn't make sense."

"Love doesn't make sense," Sammy murmurs. "Neither does family. My family killed my son, but they also saved my life. They protected you when I couldn't. I know they will always look after you. This is our life… a strange little life, but it doesn't matter what your mother thinks. You choose what you want, Melanie."

"I want you."

I mean it.

"Good," Sammy says, releasing my fingers and reaching for the box in his pocket again. He opens it and hands it to me. I inspect the ring. It's beautiful. The gold ring has a ruby in the center surrounded by several smaller rubies and diamonds surrounding it in the shape of a sun.

"This is beautiful."

"It's worth millions," Sammy murmurs. "Just like you."

He takes my hand and slips the engagement ring on my finger. Something powerful shifts between us. The bond that was once just physical and then verbal becomes spiritual as we choose each other.

"I want to take you to Italy," Sammy whispers and he takes my hand again. "I want to take you all over the world with our daughter and I don't want to stop moving until... I get you pregnant again."

"That sounds incredible. But you'll have to wait until I take the GED exams."

"Are you sure?"

"Yes. I need to have a high school education. If I was taking being a mom seriously back then, I probably would have never punched Damzel."

"Luckily your punching days are behind you," Sammy whispers. "Come on, honey bun. Let me kiss you."

Chapter 22
Love Of Mine
Sammy

"How can a baby be late?"

"I don't know," Melanie grumbles. "Can you stop asking me stupid questions? I can't get my Crocs on. I'm too big."

I hustle to help, but I'm wary. The last time I tried to help Melanie, she slapped me hard across the face. I don't remember what I did to earn the slap exactly and she definitely didn't apologize for it.

"Promise not to slap me again."

"When did I slap you?"

Pregnancy has made her memory spotty too. The baby is over a week late and despite my insistence that she remain home, Melanie has finally convinced me to take her for a walk on the beach. We're only a few hundred yards from a nice beach that isn't too crowded since the hordes of tourists returned to Manhattan.

I help her get into the shoes and Melanie links arms with me, suddenly excited. She's changed her hair again with the help of Althea. I don't mean to make it sound like a conspiracy, but I last saw her with waist length black hair. Now,

Sammy

Melanie has black braids with green strands woven into the braids. She wears half of them in a little bun on the top of her head and the rest hang past her butt. They're very long and pretty.

Her braids smell nice too, but smelling her head is possibly the easiest way to earn a slap from Melanie. She looks beautiful today with the braids and with an emerald green linen kaftan that leaves her baby bump room to breathe but highlights her curves.

Her breasts are even more gorgeous than before the further along she is. She's too sensitive for me to touch her, but it's a blessing to be close to her and watch her grow like this. She struggles to walk a little, but she's so much stronger than she was before the pregnancy — and she's officially a high school graduate.

When we get to the beach, the smile on Melanie's face makes all her scowling and begging well worth dealing with.

"It's like I'm finally free."

"You're about to pop. This is risky…"

"It's not risky, Sammy. You're too worried. I bet I could race up the beach."

"If you dare attempt such a thing, I'll spank you."

Melanie elbows me. "You wouldn't dare."

DON'T TEMPT ME, honey bun…

WE WALK for a while and then I set up a large beach towel and sit with Melanie facing the ocean. She leans back on her hands with her legs out in front of her, letting her belly relax. The emerald kaftan highlights her brown skin. Her braids happen to match her dress. I wrap my arm around her shoulder.

"The baby should have come a month after my birthday," she says. "We can't plan the wedding until I give birth."

"Be patient, Mel."

She sighs and leans on my shoulder. "Do you get more patient as you get older, Sammy?"

"If my behavior with you is any indication at all, no."

"Damn. I was hoping it would get easier to always be waiting."

"No," I respond to her. "But you realize how important it is to find someone you can wait with."

"Do your cousins know you're this corny?"

"They're worse," I tell her. John's having his third kid and Lucky just brought Chiara around New England to tour fancy boarding schools where she can get recruited to play lacrosse. They've always had a craving for family stronger than mine.

Losing my son hurt more than anything and it still does, but if I hadn't lost Enrico... I might have lost my way entirely. *I'm sorry I couldn't protect my son, but maybe now I'll get a second chance.*

"Have you thought of baby names?" I ask Melanie, kissing her shoulder. She smells like baby oil. I could kiss her all day when she smells like this.

"Yes. She's Italian, right? What about Giovanna?"

"I have an Italian cousin named Giovanni... He would probably consider it a great honor."

"Is he in the mob too?"

"He's... a very wise man."

Melanie smirks because she knows that she shouldn't ask those questions or use those words. If we weren't on a beach, I would have to be more fierce in my admonishment. A little side-glare suffices. Melanie bites her lower lip and shrugs.

"It's an old-fashioned name," I tell her. "What about Gypsy?"

"Are you... Is this a joke?"

"It's whimsical."

"It's literally a racial slur, Sammy," Melanie says. "Where the hell did you get that idea?"

"Fine," I grumble, although how was I supposed to know how fast times changed. "What about Lexus?"

"You're off the baby name committee."

"She's my daughter too."

"Great. You can pick her middle name."

"Salvatore. Obviously."

"Huh? What kind of name is Salvatore?"

"It's my first name, Mel."

"Your name is Sammy," she says, rolling her eyes. "Don't be dumb."

"It's short for Salvatore. It's a nickname. We all have nicknames."

"John doesn't have a nickname."

"He's the boss."

Melanie shakes her head like she still doesn't believe me. "No way. You were always Sammy Zagarella."

"Salvatore Zagarella. I can pull out my driver's license if that's what you need."

"Yes. I'll need to see that."

Melanie doesn't believe me until she reads my license several times.

"That's a funny name," she says. "It's very old-fashioned."

"Yes. I suppose that's why I want my daughter to be modern."

Melanie rests her head on my shoulder and sits even closer to me. A breeze blows around us from the ocean. I want to kiss her so badly. She smells and looks delicious. We're finally together. It's everything I want... everything I shouldn't want but what's the point in denying myself anymore? We're good for each other...

"Naming her after a car isn't the way to handle that,"

Melanie says, interlacing her fingers with mine. "We can name her something modern *and* Italian. Like Destiny."

"That's… not an Italian word."

"Yeah, but it sounds Italian."

She's too pregnant for me to argue with her. I like the name anyway.

"Destiny. That's a pretty name."

"Yup," she whispers. "And it's how we met. Destiny. I was running away from my problems and what do you know… a giant stranger drags me off the street and saves my life."

"You would've been just fine without me, honey bun…"

Her nails sink into my arm.

"Oh my God," Melanie says. Her nails grip me so tightly she nearly draws blood.

"What's wrong?" I answer through gritted teeth, trying not to scream out from the pain of her nails digging into my bicep.

"I think my water just broke," Melanie says. "The baby's coming."

Destiny…

Epilogue
MELANIE

I clutch my sleeping daughter to my chest as I sneak out the back door into Alexis' car so she can give me a ride to Sammy's office. I love Destiny so much, it hurts.

"I'm marrying him in a week and I don't even know where he works. It's weird."

"John was all weird when I asked him about it. He has a casino. Lucky has the security company. They never talk about what Sammy does."

Alexis gives me a worried look. I put Destiny in the rear-facing car seat in the back, and sit in Alexis' passenger seat. I'm so nervous about this.

"What if he owns a creepy massage parlor?"

"He doesn't," Alexis says, but she sounds like the thought has crossed her mind. She continues with a little more hope. "I investigated John's little black book and this is the only address I found that makes sense based on the commute timeline you established via his texting routine. We'll check it out. He can't blame you for bringing your daughter to visit him at work."

"We're getting married next week. I should trust him."

"They're in the mob," Alexis says. "It's who they are. Trust him, but do your research."

"Right."

"It's not stalking if he's your fiance," Alexis continues with far more confidence than I have in the situation.

We arrive at a white building that looks like a giant warehouse. There are a few eighteen-wheelers parked out front, but the parking lot is mostly empty.

I spot Sammy's new forest green Chevy Silverado parked in front of the large navy blue garage doors. Alexis swerves her car around the back of the warehouse and we park behind a large trash can.

"Hopefully he's not a weapons dealer."

"What a perfect time to bring that up, Alexis…" I mutter. I hope she can throw hands the way Shawnte can in case we enter a situation. It's like my new future sister-in-law can read my mind.

"Don't worry, I have a gun in my purse."

"Maybe I should leave Destiny in the back…"

"I'm sure it'll be fine. We're just panicking because we know them… You know?"

"Yeah. And he wasn't in jail for being citizen of the year."

Alexis sighs. "You love him, right?"

"Too much."

She cracks a slight smile. "Then you're good for him. That man needs love so he doesn't lose his head. I can see why he gets along with John. Come on… Let's go."

I get Destiny out of the back seat. She wakes up a little bit, but when I hold her against my chest, she gurgles and her eyes occasionally flutter open. She's probably sleepy from screaming all night. Sammy stayed up with her when I wasn't feeding her.

Alexis and I walk up to what looks like an office door and we knock. A tall, pale blond man with piercing blue eyes and a white t-shirt answers the door. He scowls when he sees us, the revulsion on his face immediate. Alexis and I exchange glances. We know what that look means.

"Who the fuck are you?" he asks. Woah. He's not from around here.

"This is Sammy's future wife," Alexis says. "Where is he?"

She's more confident than I would've been. This man is almost Sammy's height and his tattoos scare the crap out of me. There's a large Celtic knot on his bicep and two full sleeves of indecipherable black ink.

I can't unravel his tattoos when my instincts tell me not to look away from this predator's eyes.

"That's Sammy's daughter," Alexis continues. "Now tell us where he is?"

He grunts. "I'm Aiden Murray. Sorry. I didn't know Sammy's family was so... diverse."

Alexis and I exchange glances again. We were right about the expression on his face. You just have to ignore people like Aiden.

"Where is he?" I ask. "I brought Destiny down here to say hello."

"He's on the warehouse floor. He's busy. I'll tell him you're down here. Come in."

He hardly looks at us again before disappearing. Once he's out of earshot, Alexis doesn't hide her disdain.

"Sammy's working with a creep. We know that much."

"Maybe he wasn't that bad."

"Did you notice he had a tongue piercing? He's dead behind the eyes. Maybe we should take Destiny out of here..."

Before I can give Alexis' suggestion any thought, Sammy flings the door to his little office open. I can't stop looking around and staring at this mysterious place. I half expect him to be angry, but he just looks shocked.

"What are you doing here?" he asks.

Alexis stands up along with me to defend me, but I can tell from the expression on Sammy's face that I don't need any defending.

I respond with a question of my own. "Since when do you wear glasses?"

Sammy's cheeks darken and he swiftly rips his glasses off. "How is Destiny? Was she crying for me?"

"She's fine. I just…"

Before I can spit anything out, Alexis blurts out, "What illegal business are you conducting here, Sammy? I know you all have your little secrets, but she's going to be your *wife*. If you hold sacred the institution of marriage, you will confess immediately."

Sammy scowls, but again, he doesn't seem angry, just confused and frustrated.

"I didn't know this was a great concern for you."

"Really, Sammy?" Alexis chimes in.

Sammy turns to me. "I run an architectural firm and construction company. I'm working with the Murray family to build a few apartment complexes in Boston. It's just… boring."

"Oh," I blurt out. This is a construction company?

"I inherited the company from my uncle," he says. "In my twenties, I owned a strip club. It wasn't the best place for a young man. For… Enrico. I worked it out."

"You never talk about this."

"It's boring. You're my fun, exciting and very sexy fiancee. I don't want to bore you with this."

Destiny makes soft cooing sounds and wriggles in her baby blanket. Sammy crosses the room and peers over at her.

"I wouldn't mind holding my daughter…"

I give him Destiny, but Alexis isn't assuaged yet.

"Are you sure there aren't cages full of people in the back?"

Sammy looks disturbed. "No, Alexis. I know you have a low opinion due to our minor disagreement…"

"You kidnapped me," Alexis snaps. "And my best friend. We both agree it wasn't minor."

"Well, I've apologized," Sammy says, bouncing Destiny a little and kissing her forehead. He takes a second to smell her head. Sammy has a weird obsession with the smell of a baby's head. "And you can tour the warehouse if you want. I'd rather you relax. We're getting married, Melanie. You're supposed to be kicking your feet up."

"She doesn't want her husband running a secret trafficking ring," Alexis says. "I don't blame her."

"No trafficking ring. Come… I'll show you around…"

SAMMY WAS RIGHT. His job *is* boring. He tries to make the tour quick, but it's not a soon enough end to my suffering. I want to jump in the car with Destiny and leave long before the tour ends. At the end, Sammy has a ridiculous smirk on his face. Alexis yawns.

"I need a coffee."

"Thank you for bringing Destiny over," Sammy says, handing our daughter back to me. "And see? No secrets."

"Except that blond guy," Alexis says.

"Aiden? Listen. I don't want you or any of my other family dealing with the Murray brothers. They come from a very traditional family in Boston."

"You mean a *racist* family," Alexis interrupts before Sammy can get too far into his explanation. "I saw the way he looked at us."

"He was just surprised. That's all. And their people have problems we couldn't possibly understand. Now, I need to get back to work. Can I trust you two to stay out of trouble at least until I get home?"

"Maybe," I tell Sammy. "If you promise to stay out of trouble."

"I think I can handle that."

I kiss him goodbye, but I don't want to let go. On the ride home, Alexis seems satisfied with our investigation and giddy about the wedding.

"You know you can trust him for sure now... as long as you're convinced he's changed and he won't run around kidnapping college students anymore."

Sammy's better than I've ever seen him. I think his college student kidnapping days are over. He's been the perfect father to Destiny and I have what I finally need – the remaining doubt I had eliminated entirely.

MY WEDDING DAY starts like something right out of a fairytale. For the first time in months, I wake up to the sound of birds in the feeder outside instead of Destiny screaming for food. Althea and a Sammy-approved nanny had Destiny for the night. Althea, Lucky's wife, wants us to focus on our big day.

I've never had to make so many decisions in my life. At first, I wanted something simple. I don't have much money and it doesn't seem fair to ask Sammy to pay for everything when he already supports me and Destiny. I'm not ready to leave her to find a job yet and Sammy wants me to consider university instead of a job if I have any interest.

So not only do I have to think about a job, colleges, and the daily care of my daughter, but I've had to pick out food selections, flower arrangements and so much more. I've never been the center of attention like this and it's weird. I want to talk to Sammy about it, but I'm not allowed to see him today. I consider sneaking out early, but when I open the door to my bedroom, John and Alexis are standing there.

"Sammy warned us you might try to escape," John says. "Alexis brought over breakfast from our place. Want something to eat?"

"I'm too nervous."

"You *have* to eat," Alexis says. "It's so nerve-wracking being up there in front of a million Italians never knowing if someone's gonna start throwing punches."

"Hey," John grumbles. "Just because we're Italian doesn't mean we're loud and scary."

"The last wedding I went to, your cousins fired shotguns into the air. I still don't know why," Alexis says sharply. "Now come on, Melanie. You need food in your system and we can video chat with Althea so you can say good morning to Destiny." Althea must have already picked up Destiny from the Nanny to get her ready for the wedding. I found her the cutest white dress for her to wear as our flower girl.

When I smell the bacon and eggs Alexis has downstairs, my appetite returns suddenly. I eat as much as possible while Alexis reviews her well-organized agenda for the wedding. The rehearsal dinner definitely helped, but I'm still nervous that somehow, I'll screw something up.

I check in with Althea Island Destiny, and after breakfast Alexis ushers me to the wedding venue. Shawnte's already waiting with my dress and the rest of the bridesmaids. John plans on walking me down the aisle. He asked about my dad, and I had to tell him the truth – my mother never told me who my biological father was. I've never known.

"That doesn't matter," John reassures me. "With us, you've got whatever family you need. Uncles, brothers, grandfathers... We'll look after you, kid. I promise."

Sammy is all I can think about as I dress for the wedding and struggle to sit still for the hairdressers and makeup artists tasked with making a regular black girl look like a princess. They curl my hair with curlers and the stylist, a Zagarella cousin, pins up my hair so half of it is on top of my head in an ornate updo with pearl hairpins.

I look so... different. Alexis balks when I tell her how weird I feel.

"You look beautiful and you'll look even better in the dress."

Shawnte agrees with her and carries the heavy wedding dress over from the rack. I needed multiple people to help me into it when I tried it on and the same holds true today. Damsel, Shawnte, and Alexis help me get into the dress. Sammy's cousin Jacinta helps lace me up and when she thinks the bust isn't tight enough, she uses as much force as possible to push my boobs together.

"He's Italian," she explains. "He loves boobs."

I can't argue with that. Sammy has never faltered in his appreciation for my breasts. Once I'm dressed, Alexis and Shawnte dramatically reveal the final look.

"I look... different."

"I know," Alexis coos. "Every day should be a wedding day. You look great."

Right on cue, Lucky knocks on the door to our dressing room.

"Is the bride ready?"

I need several bridesmaids to carry my long veil and the train of my dress. It's the prettiest dress I've ever worn and better than any of the prom dresses Shawnte and I tried on before we got kicked out of high school and kissed our prom dreams goodbye. *This is so much more glamorous than prom.*

This is the hard part – getting up there in front of everybody and becoming Sammy Zagarella's forever…

THE BEST PART of the wedding was the kiss. It was hard to listen to all the other parts about loving each other for all eternity when Sammy's olive eyes bored into me with fervor like I'd never seen before. He's not the most patient man alive and two days without each other fills him the most brazen lust.

When the Italian priest gives us permission to kiss, Sammy grabs my face and kisses me like there's no one watching. His grandmother who came all the way from Sicily coughs dramatically to get him to stop kissing me so deeply. I don't want it to stop. I want our entire night to be this perfect.

"Once we're done dancing and eating cake," Sammy whispers after the kiss. "I'll take you upstairs and put another baby in my gorgeous wife."

I don't think the priest heard him, but I can't be sure.

LUCKY HOSTS our reception and I reunite with Destiny for a few hours in between dances with Sammy, all of Sammy's uncles and cousins, Lucky, John and then a few dances with Alexis and Shawnte. Althea offers to take Destiny for the night.

"It's your wedding night," she offers with a wink. "I think you should spend that time alone with Sammy."

It's not like this will be our first night together, but it is our wedding. I'll miss Destiny, but I definitely want to be alone with Sammy tonight. *Definitely.*

He drags me away from the party at midnight. We sneak out the back and instead of driving home like normal people, Sammy takes my hand and we drunkenly sneak across Chiara's lacrosse field to get back to our property. Sammy unlocks the back porch to let us into the house and we don't make it three feet into the house before Sammy pounces.

I haven't dragged my dress completely in the house and of course, Big Tex comes tearing towards the door as fast as possible, trampling the train of my ivory dress. Sammy grabs my hips and swirls me around, nearly tripping Big Tex as he presses me against the wall.

"My dress!"

Sammy chuckles and instantly presses his lips to my neck. "I'm ripping that dress off you tonight one way or another."

"You spent ten thousand dollars on it," I remind Sammy as I stifle a moan from the pleasure of Sammy's tongue running along the length of my neck.

"That will make it much more fun to fuck with."

He reaches for the ribbons cinching in the base of my corset and pulls them loose. I gasp for air as the tight corset finally allows me to breathe.

"Your tits look amazing in that thing," he growls. "I've been staring at you all fucking night, Mel."

Sammy bends his head to kiss the tops of my breasts and the tiniest touch from his lips sends a shivering sensation straight through me. *Holy fuck, his tongue and lips are even warmer than I remember.*

Our lips remain locked in an eager embrace as Sammy fumbles with the ribbons and eventually pulls them loose so the back of my dress spreads open. The skirts stand up on their own and I'll definitely need help to slide out of the enormous dress completely.

Sammy reaches in through the open corsetry and runs his

hands down my back before he reaches for my butt. I bite my lower lip as I wait for him to discover one of my wedding surprises.

"Are those pearls?" Sammy growls as he slides his finger beneath my ass cheeks and pulls out the string of my pearl thong. I wriggle in his grasp and from the naughty sensation of the pearls between my legs as Sammy fondles the thong.

"Yes," I whimper as Sammy teases me more with his fingers.

"Fuck," he growls. "Those pearls in your ass are making me want the dirtiest things… let's get those off."

Sammy postpones stripping me to kiss me more, touching my hips and every part of my body until he can't stand to wait anymore. He helps me out of the dress and then he loses control. Sammy lifts me out of my wedding dress and I wrap my legs around him wearing nothing but a pearl thong with a white bow at the back.

"That sexy white thong looks incredible against your skin," He whispers. "But I want to make our babies in my bed. That's where I want you."

Gripping my thighs with ultimate control, Sammy carries me upstairs easily and slowly presses me into our bed.

"It feels like a do-over of our first time," Sammy murmurs. "Where I'm not hurting you."

He pushes hair out of my face and runs his tongue over my nipples. His lips move to my stomach and when he reaches my mound, his lust takes control. I cry out as Sammy gives my lower lips a very wet kiss. I moan and reach for his hair as he licks my clit in slow circles, and I don't hesitate to tug on Sammy's thick brown hair as I get close to orgasm.

He slides the pearl thong to the side to lick my pussy to orgasm. I can't control my urge to cum. I plead with Sammy for mercy, but he ruthlessly flattens his tongue against my clit and licks me to another three unceasing orgasms. I nearly forget my own name, I cum so hard.

Sammy kisses my inner thighs and then kisses all over my legs before he moves his weight on top of mine and brings his face close to mine. I don't mind the signs of age on Sammy's face. He has lines from pinching his brow in frustration too much and the deepest smile lines ever from his dark sense of humor.

He's handsome... not just for a guy in his forties. Sammy's handsome for anyone.

"I want to make a baby with you," he whispers. "I understand I'll never be Destiny's real father but–

"Stop," I whisper back, pressing my hand against Sammy's chest. I love feeling his heartbeat and his heart races now the same way mine does. "You're Destiny's real dad. You will always be her real dad."

"But..."

"Enrico's dead, Sammy. It hurts. I know it hurts you more than I could ever understand, but you're here to help his blood and you're here to become the father Destiny needs. We can have another baby, but you *are* her real dad. Never forget."

"How did a troublemaker like you get so wise?" Sammy murmurs, giving my lips the softest kiss. I can feel his hardness pulsing against my thighs.

"Life. This life."

Sammy smirks. "Yeah. That'll do it."

We kiss sensuously as I slowly strip off Sammy's tuxedo. He's happy to be free from the clothes and in his natural, naked state. I caress his muscular body and grab the base of his cock to guide his stiffness to my entrance.

"I love you, Mrs. Zagarella," Sammy murmurs into my ear as he nibbles my ear lobe and slides every inch of his cock inside me with one smooth stroke. *Holy fuck, I'm full.*

I wrap my arms around Sammy's neck and grab him tightly as I lose complete control. Our hips join together in the perfect mix of pleasure and pain. It won't take long for me to orgasm again.

"Yes..." I whisper. "I love you... I want a baby..."

Sammy's hips move ardently at my pleading for a baby. His smooth rhythm makes it easy for me to cum from penetration. He cups my ass and holds my body against his as he plunges into me slow and deep to make me cum. We both get soaking wet after my first orgasm and I feel Sammy's dick stiffening inside me as he slows down.

"I want to fill you up," he murmurs. "I want to get you pregnant..."

"Cum inside me," I whisper, stroking Sammy's cheek and goading him to act on his urges. "Please... cum inside me."

He groans and thrusts his hips forward one last time as he finishes. Satisfaction spreads through me as Sammy's climax gives me an orgasm that matches his. Our bodies intertwine as we ride the sweaty, sticky and oh so perfect wave of euphoria together. I feel Sammy's sticky seed between my legs and the perfect warm gush only makes me want more...

I wrap my thighs around him and hook my ankles around each other.

"Don't you dare leave this bed," I whisper. "We have to make sure I'm pregnant."

"Hm," Sammy agrees. "That'll require at least three more rounds."

"AT LEAST THREE," I whisper back, raking my fingers through Sammy's gorgeous light-brown hair. "Maybe even four..."

* * *

The End

Click here to order the next bwwm dark mafia romance series
by Jamila Jasper.
https://bit.ly/bostonirishmafia
The Boston Irish Mafia Romance (5 books)

About Jamila Jasper

The hotter and darker the romance, the better.

That's the Jamila Jasper promise.

If you enjoy sizzling multicultural romance stories that dare to *go there* you'll enjoy any Jamila Jasper title you pick up.

Open-minded readers who appreciate **shamelessly sexy romance novels** featuring black women of all shapes and sizes paired with smokin' hot white men are welcome.

Sign up for her e-mail list here to receive one of these **FREE hot stories**, exclusive offers and an update of Jamila's publication schedule: bit.ly/jamilajasperromance

* * *

Get text message updates on new books: https://slkt. io/gxzM

Mafia Playmate

https://bit.ly/bostonirishmafia1

Boston Irish Mafia Romance Series

Mafia Playmate

Mafia Property

Mafia Surrogate

Mafia Possession

Mafia Stalker

* * *

Click here for the complete collection:

www.jamilajasperromance.com/catalog

Content Awareness

Read this passage if you require content warnings for sensitive material. I do not give detailed content warnings that will spoil the plot, but be aware of this note.

This is a mafia romance story with dark themes including potentially triggering content of **all** varieties, violence, frank discussions and language surrounding bedroom scenes and race.
All characters in this story are 18+
Sensitive readers, be cautioned about some of the detailed romantic material in this dark but *extremely hot romance novel.*

Description

A large pink box arrives on Aiden's doorstep with a woman inside.
His mail-order bride arrives in her birthday suit and tied up in knots with a pretty pink silk ribbon.

Aiden never requested a dark-skinned beauty...
His family would never approve of such an impure connection.

Who is this woman? What does she want?
A note in the box reveals the truth...
The woman in the box - *Valentina* - is a gift from an anonymous sender who wants something dark and twisted in return.

Chapter One
Aiden

You have one job in the Murray family. You grow up, you get your marks, you listen to Pa, you marry a nice Irish girl, preferably a blond or a redhead with lighter features.
You do what Padraig Murray asks.
You pray everyday and you keep your rosary wrapped in your pocket.
You stay loyal. You keep our bloodline strong.

Pa demands a meeting with me now that I'm back in the city. He claims it's important, but it can't be that important if he wants to meet me during the Red Sox game. It feels good to be home. There's something special about Boston, but maybe that's just it – paradise is wherever our family is.

After Pa, I'll go home and see Roscoe, my Rottweiler. Then get my shit together and call my younger brother Darragh to check in on his training and find out if Rian's around. Over the weekend, I'll head to Leominster to visit Callum and then Sunday after church, stop by to see Ma and

Odhran. I brought a gift home with me for Tegan, Rian's daughter, and I can't wait to see my niece's face light up when I give it to her.

If there's one thing I don't miss about being home, it's a never ending list of shit to do.

I meet my father at our usual casual meeting spot, Mulligan's, a place where we aren't afraid to celebrate Irish pride. A place where you can catch the Red Sox game and no one can catch your conversation. *It's as much home as anywhere else.*

I spot my father hunched over the bar from the street, his face illuminated by a warm orange bulb as he watches the pre-game announcer talk. I prefer football to baseball, but Pa bets on all their games, so he likes to keep his eye on the Red Sox each season.

When Pa calls, you answer, and he's desperate to know about the affair with the Italians – what the fuck happened, have I found the renegade cousins who pissed off the Italians, and whether I've killed them yet. *I haven't.*

It's all bad news and my ass is on the line if I don't find a way to sort out all the shit that happened in Long Island. At least we're guaranteed peace with the vicious Italians. *Those greaseballs aren't any better than the blacks. 'Trust 'em as far as you can throw them', Pa told me. But for now, we have peace and that's what matters. At least to me.*

I enter Mulligan's and the conversations fall to a hush. *Aiden Murray's back.* I clear my throat and the conversations continue. But there are more phones pulled out than before and two guys sitting in the back leave. I don't hate the reputation I have. Most of the bar fights I earned this cutthroat reputation in were Darragh's fault, but that doesn't change what people say about me.

Darragh, my younger brother, can still throw his weight around in the ring, but he got his practice here, in this fucking place. Our last fight here was over a girl. Darragh kicked some Puerto Rican's ass and a few of our boys jumped him outside... I don't know what happened to the guy after.

My father slides a twenty-dollar bill across the bar to the bartender, Finnegan O'Malley, a one-eared ex-hitman, who in turn fills up two glass pints of amber Sam Adams. Pa's already several drinks ahead of me. *Great. The news can't be that bad then.*

I pull out a bar stool next to my father, who barely acknowledges me, although he must've caught me entering the bar through the reflection on the glass behind the bartender. He shoves one of the pints across the bar towards me. He knows I prefer Guinness, but I don't mind starting with this. I can see my dad's reflection in the glass. He looks older than I remember. He's pushing 70, so I shouldn't be surprised by the large streaks of gray through his slick hair which was once blond, but changed color throughout his life, settling on a dark chocolate brown, like Rian's.

I glance at the television to check the score, but the game hasn't even started yet. I can smell the alcohol coming off of him already.

"You can have a Guinness after you drink this," he says. "I heard you did good work with the Italians."

He sounds raspy, but calm. My tension dissipates. This is just a normal, father-son meeting. Nothing to worry about.

"I didn't find Eoin or Robert. Haven't heard fuck since they all screwed with Vicari," I say as I take a sip of my beer.

"Maybe the Italians killed them," he says. "They're a violent, vicious group of people."

"Yeah."

Like we're ones to talk. Pa's done with his Sam Adams already and waits patiently for me to catch up, as if I could catch up to a man who's been drinking for an hour. At forty, it's not so easy for me to keep up with long nights of drinking. I don't know how he does it.

He waits for me to have a few more sips, his eyes glued to the television. Chris Sale throws the first pitch. It doesn't go so well. My father glances down at his glass and sighs. "It's going to be a long night."

"That bad this season?" I grunt, glancing up at the Detroit batter sliding into second.

I've been too busy to keep up with baseball. My father grunts. Yeah, it has been that bad.

"Any other news?" I ask him, finishing off the Sam Adams. Dad grunts and snaps his fingers for the bartender, Finnegan. The buff, tattooed bartender hustles over as dad orders two Guinnesses without opening his mouth. Bad news if he's drinking Guinness.

"Cops got Rian last week. They're charging him with manslaughter."

Manslaughter?

"What did he do?"

"What the fuck do you think he did?" Dad responds calmly. "He killed somebody, they caught him. That boy's not careful enough and I have to pay to get his ass out of trouble. Maybe some prison time would do him good."

"That's what you said the first three times," I grunt. Sale throws a good pitch and my father's face visibly brightens.

"If it weren't for Tegan, I'd let him spend a few extra years behind bars," Dad confesses. "Your mother won't let me do that to his daughter."

"What's going to happen to her?"

"I don't know," my father says. "No one has seen the kid in a week."

"What?" I growl, sipping at my beer and hoping this is my father's idea of a joke since he sounds dangerously unconcerned.

"What do you mean no one's seen her? Is she with her ma?"

My father shrugs.

Rian's notoriously bad taste in women landed him with a child he should have never brought into the world. She's a sweet girl, but doomed by a mobster father and a whore mother.

Her ma doesn't live in Boston anymore. She wants nothing to do with Rian.

"Where does he say she is?"

"Last time he saw her was the night he got arrested," Pa says before taking a sip of his beer.

"What about the cops? Did they give her to his lawyer or something?"

I don't have a single paternal instinct in my body, but my mind courses with worry over Tegan, despite my father's calmness.

"She'll turn up," he says, pouring more alcohol down his throat.

Fuck, Rian. My brother must be an even worse parent than our father. His daughter's missing and he's behind bars and there's no one else to look for her except...

"I can find out where she is. Once I get Roscoe and take care of–

"It would serve him right if something happened to her," my father says coldly. "Her mother isn't Irish. He keeps fucking up. I'm tired of cleaning up his messes. Now *drink*. This is not why I asked you here."

I bristle at his comment, but it's just Padraig Murray. This is who he's always been and my brother should have had the good sense to keep his dick in his pants. I made it to forty without fathering bastards all over Boston. Rian should have been more careful. I drink a few more sips, but I can't let this go. *Who else will worry about the fucking kid if not me?*

"How the hell did Rian let this happen? Can I talk to him?"

"Best that none of us talk to him. The cops listen to everything. I can get messages into the prison and messages out, but I don't want you talking to him."

"Fine," I grunt, finishing off my first round of Guinness and ordering us another. I try to pay, but my father stops me and then finally answers my other question.

"Your idiot brother trusted a woman," he says. "He wants a mother for that little girl so badly, that he's willing to do anything. He's willing to kill for a woman who doesn't deserve him."

"I didn't know he had a woman," I grumble.

"*Had* is correct," Pa says. "She's dead."

I wish I could tell you a chill ran through me, or I had some other human response to my father's announcement. I don't need a university degree to understand what he's implying. Rian had a woman, she got him locked up, so my father had her killed.

"Will that affect his case?"

"No," Pa says. "It was very clean."

"Who?"

"None of your business, Aiden. You worry about your shit, I'll worry about your brother."

I want to feel sorry for Rian, but he deserves it for crossing our father. This is what happens when he pisses off Padraig Murray. More problems for all of us.

"How much time is he facing?"

"Three years since he's been in jail before. I tried to get that stupid motherfucker to get his life together, but your brother just wants to be a fuck up."

"Who's the lawyer?"

"Someone from Nigel & Bancroft."

At least he isn't cheaping out like he did for Rian's first case. I don't want to push my father's buttons, and despite his outward calm, he must be furious at Rian for drawing more attention to us, but Rian has his uses.

"It's Rian," I remind him. "Crazy fucking Rian. We need him out soon. There are some jobs only Rian has the balls to handle."

Padraig snorts. "He takes after my father. Too proud and too violent for his own good."

We created the monster Rian Murray is. He's our responsibility.

"He needs another woman."

"He needs a woman who isn't a fucking spic," my father spits. "At least the child looks white."

"What about this previous woman? What'd she look like?"

"It doesn't matter," he grunts. "She's dead. Now drink. We have more important things to talk about than your idiot brother and his shitty taste in women."

I drink because Pa commands it. I do everything he commands and have since I was a child. I have the burns and scars to remind me of what happens when you disobey my father. At first, I hated him for what he did to me, but to keep an organization like ours together, you need to inspire fear.

You HAVE to be cruel to survive – that's just how the world works. I can't let Tegan go. The second I see Darragh, I'll ask about her and track her down.

I DRINK SO I don't lose my temper. He doesn't give a fuck about Tegan. No one does. Maybe he's wrong and one of my sisters took her in. But who would do that? Evie's saddled with her drunkard husband and two unruly kids of her own –

Katie and Patrick. Kiara's off at university and Maeve's sixteen, too young to have any involvement.

"I need to tell you something important," my father says somberly, as if there could be something more important than my missing niece right now. I'm burning with desire to leave, but if I get up without my father's dismissal, he'll hurt me. Or someone I care about. Not like there are many of those people yet. It's foolish to get close to people in this life.

"Then tell me."

If he notices my tightening tone, my father doesn't acknowledge it.

"There's a plot against my life. I don't know who. I don't know why but... there's someone out there trying to kill me," my father says, the faded tattoos on his knuckles even more wrinkled than I last remember. He's getting older, but aside from his physical appearance, he shows no signs of slowing down. If anything, he's desperate to prove himself more. If he wasn't ordering more killings than necessary, maybe Rian wouldn't be locked up.

I don't want to dismiss his concerns as paranoid, but he's the leader of our family. There's always a plot against his life. It comes with the territory. My father doesn't have to worry because he has us. *Family*.

"Fuck that," I grunt. "No one would be stupid enough to try to kill you. April 2013, four days after the bombing. An entire decade ago. That's the last time anyone tried."

I was thirty back then, old enough to be the one who ended that war before it started. Back then, we only killed when necessary. I got five tattoos that year, one for each kill. Each a painful release, each representing a necessary act to keep my family safe.

My father smirks and keeps drinking. He shrugs. "That's what I thought. But I'm serious. This time is different. This time the bastards might just get me. I'm getting old, Aiden. Most guys in our line of work don't make it this far."

"What happened?" I grunt, urging my increasingly drunken father to get to the point. His cheeks blaze tomato red with alcohol and his blue eyes swim with tears, again brought on by drinking rather than any emotion. He grunts and knocks his biggest gold ring against the bar's surface contemplatively.

If anyone tried to kill him, surely Darragh would have mentioned it. He's responsible for keeping our father alive.

"I feel it in my bones," Pa replies. "Someone wants to destroy our family."

"Yes," I grumble. "Our cousins. But they're gone and if they were anywhere near this city, we would have heard about it."

"I don't know. Something big is coming for us. I feel it."

"We can make decisions based on feelings now?"

"Cut the shit, kid. You know my instincts are good because you're like me. You can smell shit before it hits the toilet bowl."

"I'm home. If anyone tries to kill you, they'll have to get through me, Darragh, and Callum."

My father smirks. "My boys. I'm proud of all of you. Except Rian. He's a piece of shit."

Ah, Padraig. Honest as fuck, especially when he's drunk.

He might not be proud of Rian, but he still loves my brother enough to spring for decent lawyers and to make sure Tegan goes to the best day school in Boston. Once she's old enough, she'll go to Milton or Dana Hall, or another nice private school where she can meet someone to untarnish her sullied blood, that is as long as I can find her. If Rian's behind bars, she could be anywhere. Hopefully not with her mom's people.

She belongs with us, even if Rian made mistakes. She

looks like us and that's good enough to cover up his shameful behavior. I don't know what Rian was thinking with that Puerto Rican chick. Tegan's mother was low class.

Let's hope my brother's behavior doesn't come back to haunt all of us. Let's hope his daughter is safe, sound asleep somewhere and protected.

"Thanks, Pa," I mutter, uncomfortable with even this much emotional closeness between us. I love my father, but trusting him too much is dangerous. Rian found out the hard way that it isn't worth it to defy our family beliefs, and it definitely isn't fucking worth it to screw around with the wrong women.

"And Aiden? I need you to hurry the fuck up and find a wife. I'm getting old and I want to retire, but I need a family man to lead this family. You're the oldest. Why the fuck can't you keep a woman? Do I have to send you back to Galway?"

He wants a real answer.

"Not interested in chasing after girls, dad. All they want to do is take your money and ask where the fuck you're going. I've had enough."

"That old dog won't take care of you when you get old."

"Neither will some Boston snob who could take my ass to the cleaners in a divorce."

He laughs, which is the best reaction I can hope for. He quickly moves along to talking about the game and his plans for the business, and then asks me questions about Long Island. They're a mess out there, but doing better under John Vicari's leadership. We're developing a few buildings together and are prepared to make a lot of money in the real estate game. John does cleaner business than his father. Too bad the old man died of a heart attack... that's the word anyway.

"I need you to find a nice girl," my father reminds me once he's almost blackout drunk. He can barely keep his head up. *Great*. I'm not dragging his ass outta here tonight. If he wants to get so wasted he can't sit up straight, I'll leave him for Finnegan.

"We have this conversation every time we talk."

"This time, I'm serious. I want to retire. I don't want you bringing home no spics either like the Duffy boys."

"Fuck's sake, Pa. You can't talk like that around here anymore."

"I can say whatever the fuck I want. I want Irish children. Irish fucking children and I need you to have a wife so I can retire."

"Retire any old fucking day you want," I growl. "It'll be good for you to stop worrying about who I fuck or marry or the fate of the fucking family."

"The fate of the family matters," he says, taking another sip of his newest glass of beer before rubbing condensation off the sides with his napkin.

"I'm too old to have kids," I growl. "I'm too old to get tied down. You and mom were lucky you even found each other."

That's bullshit and we both know it. They stay together because they're Catholic, because back in the eighties, my dad killed someone for her father and won my mother like a prize. He also put a baby in her quickly and then kept her pregnant. There's nothing romantic about their love story or marriage in the Murray family.

"If you can't find a girl, I'll find one."

"The last girl you found me was a crazy fucking redhead who wanted to bring Roscoe Jr. into the bedroom. No thanks."

My father shrugs. "She was white. Do you know how hard it is to find a white girl around here who hasn't been fucking ruined by some fucking Puerto Rican or black guy?"

"What do you want from me, Pa?"

I know what I want. I want an end to this conversation,

and I want my father to give me a fucking break about women and dating. All the Irish and Catholic women in Boston know to stay away from us, and the ones who don't learn their lesson pretty fucking quickly.

"Find a nice white girl with big tits and blond hair and get her pregnant so I know you're fucking serious about family. That's what I want."

"Give me time."

He continues, getting to what I suspect was the original point he wanted to make before the liquor got to him. "And get your ass to the site in Back Bay tomorrow bright and early."

"Why?"

This is the first I'm hearing about something wrong at the Back Bay construction site. I know something's wrong because my father doesn't do anything bright and early unless there's a problem to solve.

"You'll find out tomorrow. You just got back. Go home. Pet the dog. Your mom's tired of walking that big fuck. He nearly knocked her over near Harvard Square."

"How is mom?"

"Pissed off."

"Why?"

"Eh. Upset about another woman. It's nothing."

It's nothing. Dad just got his second mistress pregnant and even if we all know about it, we're all supposed to pretend it's no big deal that our elderly father knocked up a Irish teenager who he supposedly hired to clean the construction company office.

I hate how he treats our mother. What's the point of having a family or a woman if you hurt her? There's no getting through to him, but I have to try for my mother's sake.

"You treat her better, pa. Seriously. She needs you."

Chapter One

He grunts. "Get your ass home kid and get a white girl pregnant."

"Thanks, dad."

"If you can't find one, I'll find a good Irish girl who needs a green card and bring her over to you!"

My father is the last person I want picking my romantic partners. I mutter something to him about cutting back on liquor, then I pat my father on the back and leave the bar. This is the closest we've felt in years, but there's still a wall between us and there always will be. I felt closer to him when I was younger, when it was easier for me to justify the life I led. I know I'm a screw up, I know I don't belong anywhere near a woman or a family or any of the fucking things my father wants from me.

He knows it's wrong to bring a kid into this life, but he did it anyway. He knows that we're villains, but he doesn't care. Fuck, I don't care either, I suppose. I'd just rather not ruin a perfectly good woman.

I drive out of the city listening to rock classics on the radio. Just as I turn down my street – I live at the end of a cul-de-sac – I notice the large box on my front step. There are only five large houses at the end of this cul-de-sac, all of us with wide open well-maintained lawns around traditional New England colonial houses.

The box on my front step is fucking enormous – and I don't remember ordering anything for delivery. My hand moves swiftly to the pistol under my seat. I feel no fear as I reach for the gun and slip a mag out of my pocket. I feel ready.

Leaving the city for any amount of time always carries a risk, especially since I didn't exactly leave the place with a house sitter. The last time my teen brother Odhran house-sat, he trashed the place and had a threesome in my bed. I hop out of my black GMC Sierra with the gun under my coat and approach the box slowly, glancing furtively over my shoulder for anyone who might have eyes on me.

The box has holes in it. It's large. Pink. Wrapped in a bow. I reach for the bottom of the box and try to lift it. *Fuck.* It's heavy. I drop the box and I swear I hear a sound coming from inside it. *Is that possible?* I try to peek through the holes but it's too fucking dark and something's telling me opening this box will be a shitshow. It has to weigh about a hundred pounds. Maybe more. I'm no weakling, but it still takes a measure of back strength to lift a box that fucking heavy.

I open my front door and greet Roscoe Jr., my rottweiler, as he bounds towards the door to greet me. His coat looks shiny, the nub of his docked tail wags back and forth. Pa's choice, not mine. He runs up to the box and sniffs at it a bit.

There's definitely something in there and it gets his attention because Roscoe utters a low bark.

"Roscoe, go lie down."

Once he heads off to his bed, I throw my doors open wider and eye the giant box to decide how to carry the fuckin' thing. I would call Rian if his stupid ass wasn't in jail. I could call Callum, but he's still hung up on some fucking girl and won't answer my calls because I won't sugarcoat my opinion of him. Then there's Darragh... He's probably twice as drunk as Padraig. Not a good option either.

I'll have to carry the box myself. I stretch a little and then grab the edges of the box and grunt as I carry it a few feet inside my doorway. I set the box down more gently. *Is there something alive in there?* If it were an animal, I suspect Roscoe would be barking from his spot in the house, but he's laying down as I commanded, gazing at me curiously and wagging his tail.

He's probably wondering why I'm not taking him for a walk since I'm back. *At least he didn't bite the sitter this time.* I close my front doors and then search for an opening on the giant pink box. Finding none, I start with the ribbon and peel it away. The box comes up to my waist. It's *enormous*.

If it didn't weigh a hundred fucking pounds, I would assume it's a novelty gift or something extra special from one of my brothers. Which of my piece of shit brothers would get me a welcome home gift? It's not like either of them are here with a six pack of Guinness right now…

I peel the top of the box open and there's another box inside it, also pink. I open the second box and stumble backwards as I expose the contents. I don't mean to act like a fucking idiot, but I nearly fall over, because this is the last thing I expected to find on my doorstep. I just got back to Boston… How long has that box been out there?

Holy fuck, why isn't she screaming?

I GAIN control of myself and approach the box again, heart pounding because my second assumption is that the human female in the box might be dead and that's the reason she hasn't made a sound. The sick thought twists my stomach into an unyielding knot.

I slowly approach the box again, ignoring my heavy breathing, focusing instead on taking in as much information as possible about the situation. I move the flaps of the box open and stare at the woman's face.. Suddenly, her eyes snap open before swiveling around and looking me directly in the eye..

Holy fuck, this woman is alive.

"What the fuck is this?" I grunt to myself. Not to myself. I'm not alone. I dry swallow and run my fingers through my hair. She's black. Someone tied up a black woman in a pink ribbon, wrapped her up like a gift and put her in a box on my doorstep. This has to be a sick joke.

I'm almost too scared to reach into the box and touch her, but I have to touch her to get her out of the fucking box. Whoever this woman is, she ran into the wrong fucking people and ended up in the wrong living room.

I have tattoos and vows of loyalty to prove how I feel about people like her. "Don't worry. I'll get you out of there."

I don't know why I'm bothering with comfort. I reach into the box and grab her at the base of her spine before hoisting her out of the box and gently setting her on the ground. My stomach lurches. This is some sick, twisted shit. Whoever did this to her stripped this woman naked, bared every inch of her dark skin, the color of Arabica coffee, and wrapped her in a pink ribbon, contorting her limbs and running the ribbon over her bare breasts, between her thighs and in loops around her body so she's wrapped up like a chocolate present.

My body has an unconscious, primal reaction. I could unwrap her like the present she's been wrapped up to be, but I need answers quickly.

She has a gag in her mouth, a round white ball that keeps her lips spread open and hooks at the back. Her eyes roam around the room in terror as I reach into my pocket for my knife. I've killed people with this knife and now I'm using it to save someone.

Her skin prickles with goosebumps as I touch her. I apologize, but I need to brace myself against her to get her free. I press the serrated edge to the ribbon and make the first cut.

I cut her legs free. She groans as her legs fall in a curled heap. She cries out and tries to jerk them again, but however long she's been in that position was far too long for her to have full control of her legs and hips.

"Don't move," I remind her. I touch her skin again and

my stomach lurches. Fuck, her skin is so dark. I look pale as fuck touching her and even putting my hands on her drives guilt through me. She's black. She's the wrong kind of person. I run my tongue piercing over my lower lip as I focus on all the parts of the ribbon I have to cut free.

When I have her limbs mostly free, she rolls onto her side, groaning in pain as her arms and legs curl in an awkward and splayed mess next to her. Even her wrists bend at an unnatural angle. I know she's alive, but the woman still looks dead.

I swallow slowly. What the absolute fuck is this?

"I'll take the gag out, but you can't spit or bite or do anything of that nature. Do you understand?"

She stares at me, but she can't say anything. I approach her mouth slowly and reach around her to find the clasp of her ball gag. I unhook it and take it out of her mouth. She groans again and winces in visible pain as she attempts to close her jaw. She slowly moves her hand to her face and rubs her cheek, groaning.

I crouch next to her, staring at her in awe, knowing that I shouldn't but am completely incapable of taking my eyes off the naked woman in front of me. If her nudity makes her uncomfortable, that hasn't sunk in yet. My cock stiffens inappropriately in my pants and I clasp my hands in front of my dick, refusing to take my eyes off her.

Her breasts are small, but they protrude forward in tiny, dark orbs with nipples that are even darker than her extremely dark skin. Holy fuck, I didn't know nipples came that dark. My eyes widen inappropriately and I pray she doesn't notice my leering. Who sent this woman to me and what exactly did they send her for?

Christ, Aiden. Get a grip. You're staring at her crotch now and it's obvious.

She's waxed completely and my gaze snaps to the bare,

dark brown lips. I wonder what this strange woman conceals between those lower lips and what color her flesh is between those thin, toned legs. I clear my throat.

"Who are you?"

"Read the card with the gift," she manages to say, with a raspy voice and an accent I can't place.

"I asked you a question."

"Read the card with the gift," she repeats.

I raise an eyebrow and walk towards the box. There's a large card at the bottom, about 8 x 10 inches, printed on thick paper. I pull it out of the box and read the note, muttering it out loud to myself. *What the fuck is this?*

Dear Mr. Murray,

We hope you enjoy your object. Your task is simple.

Use the object wisely. Have unprotected sex with the object and film a 4K quality video.

Compress the video file and send it to the email address below.

The object may be initially unwilling but both of you will face strong motivation to comply. The object understands that documentation of her existence belongs to us and if she fails to comply enthusiastically, we will destroy her identity.

If we do not receive the video within one week of today's date, you will both lose what's most important to you.

Chapter One

Tegan Murray counts on you to succeed. We have possession of the girl and you would be wise to listen to our orders if you or your family want to see her safe.

Do not call Padraig Murray. Do not call anyone else, or you will both suffer.

It takes less than a second to fire a bullet.

You must comply. When you're finished with said object, it is yours to keep.

Sincerely,

Your Benefactors

OA

"WHAT IS THIS SICK SHIT?" I growl, throwing the card back into the box, causing the woman still kneeling on the ground to flinch. My heart thuds.

These people have Tegan and this woman might know where she is and who they are. I won't be a part of this sick fucking game.

* * *

Chapter Two
Valentina

"You have to do what they say," I say to him. *"Please."*

It's not what I want to say, but these were my instructions if I wanted to survive. I never saw the people who put me in the box, but I heard their instructions and their threats clearly.

My throat burns raw as I attempt to plead with the man in front of me, hoping that he'll spare me. *He's involved with the people who took you. He's dangerous.*

The more I talk, the quicker he'll piece the truth about me together. I don't want this man to know *anything* about me. My voice. It's bad enough that he's seeing me naked. It's bad enough that he's about to take a part of me that I never wanted to give to strangers, that I always wanted to *mean* something.

I want to keep a piece of myself to myself. I've never had that privilege before. I won't have it tonight. He's an utter stranger to me and a terrifying one at that.

The gigantic blond man glowers at me, his blue eyes enough to melt me in place. He's 6'4", his hair looks slightly unkempt. Black ink swirls around his pale skin in a variety of Celtic knots, cursive Bible verses and symbols that I don't understand. *Lots of tattoos. He must be a gangster. Something like that.*

I hate that I'm naked, but I'm glad that I'm free. There was nothing but pain in that box. The drugs helped at first, but they didn't last thirty-six hours. That's how long it took to get here from Idaho. Technically, the drive takes twenty-five hours, but I tried to measure time – I have a good sense of it because of the piano – and I know they took thirty six.

There's no getting out of this. Maybe this one won't be as wicked as the first.

"Who are you?" the man growls at me. "Who did this and what the fuck do you have to do with this?"

His anger sends a surge of terror through me as his face reddens with frustration. He has absolute control over this situation and he knows it. I can't afford to freeze and make it worse by proving to him what he already knows – I'm vulnerable, weak and utterly at his mercy.

I position myself to cover my breasts as much as possible as well as my *other* parts, but he's already seen every bit of me. Modesty is entirely pointless.

"My name is Valentina," I rasp out, my voice getting stronger as I tell him my name.

"Is that your real name?" he growls, stepping forward and towering over me.

I'll never know if I had another name. I've been called Valentina since I was a little girl. Sometimes Val, but never anything else. I must've had a life before, but I don't remember any of it. All I remember is Pulsifer. He was my father, my abuser, my everything. I wouldn't call this freedom, but there's still a weight lifted because this is the closest I've ever come to leaving the governor's mansion.

The blond man is even taller than I thought he was. I'm

more vulnerable naked and despite wanting to stand up for myself, I shrink back from him.

"Yes," I say as firmly as I can manage.

"Who sent you? Because I'll be damned if I screw around with a n–"

He stops himself, but my skin feels a flush of outrage and humiliation as his lips hover over the n-word. I want to hit him, but I don't know what type of man my new master is yet. A racist. That part I understand. He's not the first racist I've had to deal with. He might be the richest though. *He lives in a mansion.*

"Who sent you?" He roars. His face reddens as he screams and his creepy blue eyes look bloodshot. I shouldn't cross him, but I stopped giving a fuck about what happens to me a long time ago. I've already experienced the worst.

"I don't know. All I know is they want you to do what's on that note."

I don't want that. I have to go through with it, but I definitely don't start off wanting that monster anywhere near me.

"No," he growls, his jaw tightening. "I... This is fucking ridiculous. Tell me who sent you, woman."

His anger mounts and my fear intensifies. I'm no stranger to racism, but for the word to nearly fly off the tip of his tongue like that. *How can someone who looks like that be so ugly inside?*

He reaches into his jacket and I know he's reaching for a gun before he pulls it out. The men who sent me here weren't any better than the man who received me as a gift. My throat tightens and I try not to lose control of my bladder as he pulls the pistol out of his jacket and points it straight at me.

Men are all the same and they're all violent disgusting pigs who will put a bullet in an innocent woman's head if she gets in their way.

They'll use us up and spit us out and there isn't a man alive capable of real love...

"If you shoot me, you'll die," I state plainly, trying to sound like I have control of the situation. I'm not lying, but I'm also not stupid enough to mean that as a threat either. "And whoever you love enough for them to threaten will die too."

"I don't give a fuck," he snarls. "Who sent you?"

I don't believe that he doesn't care. I sense a crack in this man beneath his outrage. His anger cloaks his genuine concern. If he wanted to kill me, he would have done it already.

"Do I look like I was in control of the situation? You have their instructions. Are you going to do it or not?" I say to him sharply. Talking to him like this could be dangerous, but he doesn't react to my strengthening voice or sharp tone.

"Am I going to rape you?" He growls, lowering the gun. "Is that what you're fucking asking me?"

He has a thick accent which I can finally place. *Boston.* I'm in Boston, or close enough to Boston that men sound like Matt Damon in *Good Will Hunting.* I don't know anyone in Boston, but maybe that's for the best since I don't know any good people. Never have.

I don't respond to him. He reads the card to himself again and mutters a long string of curse words. I'm already naked and despite his apparent hesitation, the man hasn't offered me clothes. He doesn't know if he's going to do it yet, but I do.

He's going to have sex with me.

. . .

Chapter Two

"YOU HAVE TO FOLLOW THE INSTRUCTIONS," I say to the terrifying blond man pleadingly. He still hasn't told me his name and I don't know if he will. He might worry I'll go to the police. "At least according to them." Hopefully he thinks of another solution since he's clearly some type of gangster.

I've been through enough shit to know that the police don't care about women like me. The police have *never* cared.

"This is a crock of shit," he hisses, spittle flying from his mouth as his face reddens with pure vitriol. "I have *never*..."

He glares at me like I'm responsible for this. Every inch of my body aches and I have little patience for this bastard acting like I'm the fucking problem.

"Never what?"

He glowers. "I've never been with... I don't... I don't fuck black women."

His voice drips with disgust, but I don't mind because I find this man's racism equally repulsive. He's more bothered by my race than the fact that I arrived on his doorstep naked, wrapped in ribbons, and sent to him in a box.

"You have to follow their instructions. I don't know what happens to you if you don't, but I know what happens to me."

I'll be lost to my past forever.

"Who fucking sent you?"

"I don't know."

I should have expected his next actions. He's a sicko, because the people who sent me only send gifts to sickos. My boss... My *old* boss was probably worse than this man. He was certainly much uglier, but all cruel men are the same.

He quickly racks a bullet in the chamber before re-leveling the gun to my face so I am forced to stare directly down the barrel.

"Kneel," he commands without wavering. I can see in his

eyes that he's capable of shooting me. He runs his long pink tongue over his lips. He has a piercing through his tongue, a giant gold knob with a Celtic knot in the center. *What the fuck?*

My knees ache and I can't stop myself from groaning as I obey him. I have no choice but to listen to him despite the pain shooting through me. My stomach turns and if I'd eaten anything in the past 48 hours, it would've come up on this rich white man's hardwood floor.

My head lolls forward and I struggle not to cry out as more pain surges through my legs.

"Who sent you?"

"I don't know," I answer truthfully. If I had those answers, I would disappear in the middle of the night and find some way to get my real identity from the people who own me, or I suppose owned me before him.

"You must've come from somewhere," he says, his finger hovering near the trigger. It never occurred to me that he could do worse than hurt me, that he could kill me. *But he might. The men who did this to me never considered that.*

"My master sold me."

"What the fuck?" he snarls. "What the fuck does that mean?"

"I grew up… I grew up in a house with an older man. He sold me when I turned twenty-five."

"Sold you to who?"

"I never saw. I just know… I know what kind of company he keeps."

"Who was your master?"

"Governor of Idaho. Ezekiel Pulsipher," I respond as calmly as possible, even if just saying his name brings back flashes of horrific memories that still torment me every night. Who needs sleep, right?

"I don't know who the fuck that is," he spits. My chest

swells with odd satisfaction that there's a corner of the universe not entirely ruled by Ezekiel.

In any other situation, his confusion would have been confusing. Old Zeke was a king in his universe and I wasn't the only girl in his harem. *He owned me since I was six years old. I don't want to tell this criminal about that, but I wouldn't feel sorry if this psychopath turned on my old master. I wouldn't feel sorry if these modern slave owners met this monster.*

I glare at him. I'm not here to give him an explanation. He's not the victim here, I am, and judging by his accent and other cues slowly coming into view, I'm on the other side of the country with no identification, no proof of who I am... Nobody knows I'm here.

It doesn't matter that I'm alone, I have to survive. I don't know what life will be like on this side of the country, but this is the best chance I've had to escape my entire life. *I can fool this white man. I know I can.*

"Why would someone do this?" He snarls.

"Maybe you're a criminal. Maybe they want revenge," I offer, perhaps pushing him too much with my attitude. His body tenses when I say the word *criminal.* Men. They think they're so careful with their emotions, but they get careless when they're underestimating you. Men get careless when they think they have the upper hand.

"I can't do what they want," he says, keeping the gun fixed at my head. This does little to warm me to him. "I can't screw... If my father found out... he would paint the sidewalk with your brains."

Charming. Now I have a definitive answer about the extent of this man's criminality.

He sets the gun on the table behind him and re-reads the card for the third time. His face turns several shades of red.

"This is sick," he spits, glowering at me with familiar, racially motivated revulsion. In most situations, I can't actually know if a man is racist. I have proof about this man.

"You have to. Whoever sent me paid a lot of money. You messed with powerful people," I tell him. "And they have someone you love and if you don't do this–

"I haven't messed with anyone," the man growls, interrupting me. "Get up."

I thought the pain shooting through me would knock me unconscious, but I had too much pride to ask him for relief. I slowly rise, my limbs barely cooperating. I look and feel ashy. I hate that I missed my routine. Spend a any amount of time in a box and you will miss the most damning prison you had before. My body still aches.

He looks me in the eye and I'm too scared not to meet this man's gaze. He's a predator and showing a predator fear gives them permission to pounce.

"My name is Aiden."

Aiden. I shouldn't care what his name is, but hearing it makes me consider him differently. The name sounds forceful and as rooted in his heritage as his Celtic tattoos.

"Great," I reply softly, unclear about what to do with the information.

He clears his throat and speaks again, "I thought you should know before we…"

"So you changed your mind?"

I shake before my body knows I'm shaking. This has happened before. Men have *taken* my body several times. Ezekiel *owned* me and believe me, he made good use of his property. Aiden. The name sounds Irish, but the man standing in front of me is All-American. He's 6'4" tall with *very* pale blond hair, but a thick crop of it. It's nice to see a man who isn't bald and who clearly works out. He's very muscular and the gun is out of the way, which sets me at ease.

"I don't know who sent you, woman. But I intend to find out. Seems like the best fuckin' way to do that is follow their instructions."

I knew it.

Aiden reaches for me and I fight my gut reaction to flinch. I don't want him to know how much I fear him. I want him to worry that I'll stab him in his sleep. I want him to feel like he's risking his life every time he rapes me.

Aiden puts his hand on my shoulder. I expected his touch to be rough, but it's very soft.

"Do they have anyone you love?"

I don't want to tell him, but his blue eyes harden and I sense that I'd better tell the truth if I want him to get this over with. His hand cups my shoulder too gently for me to describe. After the sharp angles and the pain of having my body squeezed into a box, his softness is surreal.

"I... I don't know."

"I don't want to hurt you. I won't rape you."

"If you don't have—

"I know," he growls. "But I won't hurt you. You have to consent. I..."

"I belong to you," I tell him, refusing to look away from him. I want him to gaze into my eyes and see a human being. A part of me desperately wants to shame him. It's hard to stare into those eyes and not feel something. He has intense and expressive eyes.

"No," he whispers. "You belong to yourself and once this is over, I'll have to let you go."

I fight back laughter. He won't let me go. I know men like Aiden better than he can even understand. I've lived my entire life in a world of pain and depravity.

"They'll hurt you if you don't do it. Surely my life isn't as important as yours."

"You're right," he growls. "But I've never fucked one of

your kind and I don't intend to rape you either. That's not *my* thing."

He says it with the implication that he knows someone who prefers rape. And there he goes with the race talk again. *One of my kind...*

"You have to do it."

"Then agree to my terms."

"Terms."

I don't phrase it as a question and I don't want to sound too eager either.

"I'll give you money."

"So I won't be a slave, I'll be a prostitute."

His face reddens. "I'll send you away. You said they have someone you love. So you have a family?"

"No. I don't."

His hand drops from my shoulder and I glance down at his crotch. Despite Aiden's assurances that going through with this is the furthest thing from his mind, his dick bulges from his jeans. The bulge sends a deep surge of discomfort through me and my head swims.

There's no escape. All my smart-mouthed comments and my internal pleas that I might be able to survive this... I have to go through with it.

"What do you want, then?"

"A place to rest my head for a few nights. Time to get on my feet."

"Done."

He clears his throat. "I'll film it on my phone. I just... I've never..."

Aiden suddenly leans forward and kisses me. His lips surprise me with how soft they are when they first make contact. I want to scream, but it's a good kiss that draws me into Aiden's world instantly. His smell consumes me. His fingers claw at my cheeks as he holds me suddenly and keeps me still so he can kiss me.

Before Aiden, kisses felt like... cottage cheese. I want to push him away but the kiss is too fucking good for me to break away from it. I don't want to upset him, anyway. When he breaks away, his cheeks are red.

"I'm fucking dirty," he says and the revulsion in his voice tells me that he means it.

He doesn't look like he hated the kiss despite the words coming out of his mouth. He leans forward again and kisses me. This time, he spreads my lips apart and slides his tongue into my mouth. The piercing teases my tongue, sending a shiver straight through me. It's better than the first kiss and I kiss him back. He's the first man I've ever kissed back, the first man who has kissed me well enough for me to even try.

Men have done so many horrible things to me in my life and not one of them has kissed me properly. Aiden pulls away again and he pushes hair out of my face.

"We'll do this in my bedroom. Go upstairs. Third door on the left. Shower first."

Shower first. I don't like his tone, but I can't exactly blame him for it. I've been trapped in a box for several hours in a row and I probably smell exactly like it. At least he isn't pointing a gun at me anymore, and doesn't kiss me like a gross, perverted old man. He kisses me like... he would be a good lover.

That's another experience I've never had, another sad truth about my life that I never want to dwell on.

It hurts to walk up the stairs, but my body revels in the most freedom I've had in days. I almost want to race up the stairs to get to the bathroom quicker, but I walk patiently to the top and follow Aiden's instructions to find his bedroom. I can hear Aiden talking to his dog, telling him to stay on his bed for the next little while while he's busy. His house smells new, even if it's an old colonial that has probably been around since Boston's founding.

The bedroom is *extremely* neat. The floor smells clean and as my bare feet touch it, I feel like Aiden's right to wrinkle his nose at me. I'm the dirty one. *But he's sexually aggressive, and a racist one at that.* I can hear him following me up the stairs. He walks slowly, but he has a heavy gait. That may come in handy later if he tries to sneak into bed with me when I want to sleep. If I need to fight him off. That type of thing.

I had to fight off Pulsifer sometimes. That got easier as I got older. Aiden's a lot bigger than some decrepit governor of Idaho.

I find the bathroom door open and I walk inside. He has a clawfoot tub that could hold seven people. Judging by the perverts Pulsifer normally deals with, Aiden probably has had seven people in this tub at once. It sickens me to think what other secrets he could have. I flinch as he appears behind me. For a man with a heavy gait, he can apparently walk quietly when necessary.

"Get into the shower. Take your time. I'll set up the camera."

He sounds nervous, which makes me nervous. I imagine him being completely cruel. A monster would be crude and quick. Monsters *really* want you to cry. Aiden doesn't have any of those traits. He glances at my breasts, his cheeks redden and he swears under his breath.

"I can handle the shower," I say to him. He stares at me for a few seconds before leaving the doorway. I relish this alone time. I'm too grateful for my survival to think about escape. I wish I could tell you otherwise, but this is the truth. I grew up being passed around America's dirty underworld. Escape stopped being a real consideration when I turned eighteen and realized this was my destiny – permanent sexual slavery.

I clean myself as best as I can and try to ignore the numb feeling spreading over my body as I anticipate Aiden's actions. Most men are very rough. You can close your eyes and do your best to block out the pain, but nothing stops the dirty feeling of being powerless and having another person use you like an object.

Once I'm clean and have spent as much time in the shower as I think I can get away with, I step out and grab one of the insanely fluffy white towels hanging from the rack. As soon as I put it on my skin, the luxurious warmth spreads through me and the towel is so soft that I get a momentary feeling of safety.

I've carved out a life for myself despite my circumstances. I don't want anyone to feel sorry for me. I've learned how to play the piano. All the men who owned me had books that I enjoyed reading. I write poetry too, though none of it is good enough to share. Who would read my poems, anyway? Certainly not this blond hunk of muscle. His brain is probably the size of a pea.

He returns to the doorway and scowls as he watches me dry myself, reminding me that he's oversized and perpetually disgusted by me. I'm not shy about him seeing my body. He's seen it all anyway and he's going to have sex with me on camera, so there isn't a point in pretense.

"I took a vow that I would never touch a woman of another color," Aiden growls, sounding angry with me, like it's my fault that I'm black and he's racist.

I don't respond to him.

"I don't know if I can get hard," he says. "You might have to work to get me off."

I purse my lips. I have to ignore his suggestion that I'm too ugly to arouse him. White men. I try not to generalize them, but it doesn't help that all the men who have hurt me have had brilliant blue eyes, just like Aiden's. He has more of a pretty boy look, but he still has those cruel blue eyes.

"Have you done this before?"

"Yes."

I'll respond to his direct questions, but other than that, I have nothing to say. It's not like he cares.

"I'm sorry."

I give him a curious look, but I don't say anything. It's smarter not to say anything.

"If it helps, I'll make it good for you," he says in a gruff and gravely voice.

Don't bother. I want to say something cutting, but I don't want to anger him. Violence and sex are intertwined in the male brain, especially men like Aiden, a giant clearly used to getting what he wants.

This time, not responding to him provokes cheek redness. White men are always turning red when their feelings are about to take over. I brace myself for another racist comment.

"Whoever sent you must know my family. They must know about our beliefs and I want you to be clear about mine. I know my history and my heritage. I believe firmly in the superiority of my people over all others. This will not change because I stuck my cock in you," Aiden says, his voice trembling with rage as he stares at me.

I drop the towel. I'd rather him finish this than continue listening to his racist tirades.

I don't flinch, even if I want to. His words cut me deep, but Aiden, for all his complaints, still reacts like a man. His gaze drops decisively to my breasts and his teeth instinctively sink into his lower lip. His supposedly difficult to rouse cock bulges forward in his pants. *It doesn't look like he's struggling to get hard at all.*

He's even redder than before and his left hand clenches

into an angry fist. I hope he's not the hitting sort. Those are always harder to deal with.

"Get on your knees," he commands, asserting power over me as my naked body renders him powerless to continue his racist little speech. I don't defy him. Despite my complete disgust with Aiden, pleasing him represents my best chance at survival, so I consent to his commands.

Any position on my knees still hurts. If Aiden cares, he doesn't show it. He walks towards me and crudely thrusts his hips into my face. His trousers smell like cigarettes and beer. His pants pockets bulge with car keys and a few other objects I can't identify. A simple, brown belt cinches over his dark blue denim.

His thighs are thick and muscular, barely held back by his pants. My heart quickens as he shifts his stance to his left side, cocking his hip. I glance down at his shoes. Brown boots. The tips are probably steel, so I don't want to do or say anything that could provoke him to kick me. I'm in enough pain as it is.

"The camera's over there," he says. "We'll have to move. I just wanted to see if you would obey me."

He leans forward and kisses the top of my head. *He's fucked up. It aches down here on my knees and I'll have to get up again.*

Aiden commands me to my feet and I follow him back out into his bedroom. He shows me where he has his cellphone set up on a bookshelf right in front of Sun Tzu's *The Art of War* and an extremely tattered copy of *The Holy Bible*.

"Kneel there," he commands, pointing to a spot in front of the lens. "It's already recording."

I obey him and quietly kneel before Aiden, facing away from the camera. He walks into the frame and commands me again, "Look up at me. I want to see your face."

When I gaze at him, he frowns with that mixture of revulsion and disapproval I already recognize as his gut reaction to me. Despite his cruel facial expression, he's still hard. I can still see the bulge in his jeans and it's terrifyingly huge the closer he gets to me.

"I don't cum from getting head," he says. "But I doubt you can arouse me without it. Take my dick out."

He's so full of shit. This man has the biggest erection I've ever seen. *He doubts I can arouse him? Something is making him unbelievably stiff and there's no one else in the room but me.*

Taking my time to remove his cock from his jeans is the only way I can postpone it. I've seen dicks before, and most of them are completely unpleasant to look at. Many of the ones I've seen are shorter than my pinky finger. The governor called some of the world's most depraved men his friends.

Aiden remains resolutely planted in place, glowering down at me as I unbuckle his belt and then slip the jean button through the loop before unzipping his pants. Because of his muscular butt, I can't rely on his jeans to fall off on their own. I hook my fingers through the back, making contact with Aiden's ass as I pull the jeans down. As I ease his jeans over his ass, I can't help but notice how deliciously round and muscular his ass feels. My hands fight the urge to cup his firm glutes and focus on the required task - getting his dick out of his jeans.

His breath catches as the jeans slide down, revealing an equally toned and muscular pair of thighs. He has tattoos everywhere, but the thigh tattoos are the most alarming. *Choose death.* He has a skull, several Celtic knots, Bible verses, and intricate designs woven together in a tapestry of a criminal's life.

A pair of crisp white boxer briefs cling to Aiden's thighs. More details of his bulging cock become apparent to me. The monster curves slightly in his briefs, the thick head oozing fluid that creates a wet spot where the tip touches the fabric.

The elastic waistband of his boxer briefs sticks to his hips and as I remove his underwear, I expose more tattoos and worse. He has scars and partially healed wounds all over his body, not to mention more muscles. He's the most muscular man I've ever seen this close and it feels wrong to notice.

All the men who fucked me were ugly and cruel with bodies and tongues that failed to arouse me. This man might be a sick motherfucker but at least he's handsome. It's a small comfort, but I've never touched a man with such well-defined muscles, and the least I can do is appreciate it.

His cock springs free and juts forward with all the arousal Aiden claims he doesn't feel. His body doesn't lie. I haven't even touched him yet, but his cock already protrudes with pure enthusiasm. Once I get the briefs over his ass, they remain taut and stretched around his thighs.

I can't help but stare at Aiden's dick. I've never seen one as big as this. His dick is nearly the length of my forearm and it's thick, with a dusky pink color. The tip reddens immensely, like he's sore from how hard he is. *His dick is so red.* Tufts of trimmed dirty blond hair cover the base of his cock and his shaft is so heavy, his erection leans to one side.

Clear fluid oozes from the tip.

"Don't just stare at it. The camera's rolling."

He probably doesn't mean to be insensitive. He's nervous about this too. It's not like he wants me in this position. I grasp the base of Aiden's cock to hold it up and he makes an uncomfortable grunting sound. He pulses with heat and saliva pools in the corners of my mouth against my will.

He's huge. I run my tongue over my lips so I can get them wet enough to stretch around Aiden. I lean forward and he grunts, nearly jerking back.

"I can't..."

I grasp his shaft tighter. It's too late to back out of this. Before Aiden can pull away from me and deny both of us a chance at survival and escape, I run my tongue over the head of his cock and lick up every drop of the clear fluid emerging from the tip. Aiden's next groan sounds more like an uncontrollable moan of pleasure.

Pleasing him is good. Pleasing him will bring this to a quicker end and I'll have a much greater chance at survival if I please him. The thought occurred to me that once my use has run out, he'll kill me, but I can't dwell on that. If pleasuring this man ensures my survival, it's what I'll do.

I tighten my lips around the smooth, bulging head of Aiden's big cock. He makes an ungodly pleasurable groan as I get his dick head wet with my spit and prepare myself to take the length of that enormous thing down my throat. If I gag, he could hurt me. I have to make him like it. We're being filmed, aren't we?

I tighten my lips more and get Aiden's dick even wetter. His next groan is even louder than the first and he touches the top of my head instinctively before remembering himself and jerking his hand away from me.

Men enjoy having lips around their cocks, but this man really likes it judging by the moans coming out of his mouth. I flatten my tongue along the underside of Aiden's shaft and then slide the full length of his dick into my mouth.

Tears prickle in the corners of my eyes as I stuff every inch of Aiden's dick in my mouth. He groans with pleasure again and I tighten my lips around the base of his cock as I feel the tip tickling the back of my throat, threatening my gag reflex to erupt. I squeeze my eyes shut and focus on breathing slowly through my nose.

As the tip of Aiden's cock touches the back of my throat, he moves his hips slowly with one thrust, and then he erupts. His climax happens so quickly that we're both equally surprised. The tears threatening to pierce the corners of my lids fall freely down my cheeks. I make a gagging sound as Aiden pumps thick ropes of cum into my throat.

The first warm gush fills my mouth and as Aiden tries to remove his cock from the sticky deposit of fluid between my lips, even more spills from the tip and he leaves my lips, face and mouth a mess of cum as he stumbles away and gains his composure after a few steps, making the conscious choice to put as much space between us as possible. There's surprise evident on his face, especially his eyes. *They're terrifying.*

I cough once and try to swallow the cum in my mouth, but that does nothing to remove the thick ropes coating my face and lips.

"Fuck," he says. "I've never…"

"I'm fine…" I whisper, leaning forward, trying to wipe the cum off my face and not wanting to look Aiden in the eye out of pure humiliation. I look ridiculous, I'm crying and there's cum all over me. I worry he won't go through with the instructions on the card. Then what? I'd rather stay here, thousands of miles away from the governor than to *ever* return. If Aiden doesn't finish this, I don't know who might come looking for him.

Aiden crosses the room, standing straight in front of me with his cock hanging limp. My body tenses with uncertainty. I can't predict how he'll react. He crouches in front of me, forcing me to gaze at him with concern. *Is he going to hit me?*

We're face to face and Aiden takes his finger, places it beneath my chin and turns my face so I'm staring him right in the eye. We're still on camera, but it doesn't feel like it. This moment is just for the two of us.

"That was the best head of my life," he whispers. "Once we make this fuck tape, I'll pay you back for that with my tongue. I owe you."

The touch of his finger and the intense blue gaze feel romantic, but Aiden's words emerge with a business tone.

There's no romance here. I nod slowly and he rises to his feet.

"Get up," Aiden commands. "Get on the bed and face the camera."

He won't look at me as he commands me this time. I don't want him to look too closely. He's seen more than I would show a stranger, if I ever had control of my life enough to make the choice not to. I avoid gazing into the camera lens directly, but I obey Aiden and position myself in all fours on the bed.

I feel lewd on display like this. I tilt my head downward so my hair falls down over my shoulders to cover my breasts from the camera's view. It's not exactly modesty, but it's the closest I can manage given the circumstances.

I glance over at Aiden through my peripheral vision. He's hard again, with barely any time between this and his previous orgasm. The way he spoke about his ability to cum, I expected a man with some type of sexual dysfunction, not a seconds-long refractory period.

My throat tightens as I imagine my body stretching to accommodate that thing. I nearly choked on Aiden's dick in my mouth. That enormous thing could make me bleed if he isn't careful.

"Arch your back," Aiden whispers. "I want to see your ass."

It might be my imagination, but I swear his voice shakes like he believes the words emerging from his mouth represent the worst taboo. He approaches the bed slowly with that gigantic cock jutting from his hips.

"I've never filmed something like this," he murmurs as he draws closer. Aiden presses his large hand to my lower back tentatively. His hand is so fucking warm. His warmth spreads through me and I squeeze my thighs together to avoid any biological reactions to his touch.

Chapter Two

I can't control my response to him. Aiden moves his hand down my lower back over my ass cheeks, his palm curving around my soft cheek. He makes a low growling sound in the back of his throat as he touches the inside of my thigh and discovers my wetness.

"That will make it much easier," he murmurs in response to my wetness. I think that'll be it, but Aiden slides his finger through my juices, swirling his index finger in slow circles through the juices on one thigh before moving to another. "But this is the only time. I don't fuck around with black women. Understood?"

I don't answer him. I just nod. If I'm going to have sex with this racist, I want to get it over with quickly. Judging from what happened before, maybe this won't last long. That's my best hope.

* * *

Click here to order Mafia Playmate:
https://bit.ly/bostonirishmafia1

Forced To Surrogate

Sample these chapters from my Amalfi Coast Brotherhood Italian mafia romance series while you wait for the next mafia romance series.

If you enjoy dark & twisted mafia romance stories, you can binge the entire completed series on your eReader.

Enjoy the free chapters.

A BWWM DARK MAFIA ROMANCE

FORCED TO
Surrogate

JAMILA JASPER

Description

The last thing Jodi remembered was a shot of tequila.
Next thing she knows,
Italian sociopath Van Doukas has her chained in his
basement...
And he's claiming she agreed to become the mother of his
child.

There's a detailed contract and everything... with her
signature.
Jodi will do whatever it takes to get away from him...
But she doesn't count on the 6'7" Italian Stallion being skilled
with his tongue and excellent in bed.

* * *

Click here to read *Forced To Surrogate*:
https://bit.ly/amalficoast1

Series Titles

Forced To Surrogate
Forced To Marry
Forced To Submit

Content Awareness

Chapter 1
Produce A Pure Italian Heir
Van Doukas

There aren't enough cigarettes in the world for meetings with my father. The boss. Tonight, I meet with him to discuss something 'very important'. He calls everything 'very important', but tonight, I know exactly what he wants from me.

He wants me to kill again, this time for my foolish sister, who can't seem to keep herself out of trouble. Everyone in the family heard about what happened to Ana by now. That idiot Jew was foolish enough to put his hands on her with witnesses and expect nothing to happen? That's not how the Doukas family works, which he'll soon learn.

You mess with the Doukas family, we retaliate. If the Jew had any wits about him, he would disappear from the Amalfi Coast and head for the mountains or Sicily, or somewhere we don't have ears. He could go to Albania like Matteo. Maybe then we wouldn't find him. But fuck, I don't want to carry out another hit. Why can't that lazy fuck Enzo do it? Or better yet, Eddie. I carried out my first hit when I was two years younger than him. We spoil the new generation and wonder why our family falls apart.

None of this would be my responsibility if Matteo would get over himself and come down off his fucking mountain.

I stop my motorcycle and approach my father's front door. The all white old European style mansion sits on an excessive and opulent lot on the coast, right above the cliffs with a long path to the beach, a 'fuck you' to the tax collectors and the government who want to stop us from doing business.

Most of my siblings still live here, but I prefer keeping myself far away from papa and his... associates.

I can hear the party from the entrance. Seriously? On a fucking Tuesday afternoon? I assumed he called this meeting because he was working for once. He's intertwined in a different business based on the noise filtering outside. Please, Lord, let me not walk in on my father having sex with a model... *again.*

I open the front door to our old family home without knocking and immediately regret it when a completely naked foreign woman runs giggling toward the door, too high and drunk to feel self-conscious, exposing her completely nude body to a stranger. At least I didn't find her twisted in bed with papa, although this isn't much better.

"Oh! Good afternoon, sir!" she teases me in crude Italian, spinning around to show off her assets. *Whore. Foreigner. Her tricks possess little interest to me.* My brothers Lorenzo and Matteo would sway more easily.

"Where's my father?"

She giggles and spins around again. Fucking hell, I wish the ground would swallow me up. My father's prostitutes do not interest me.

"Your papa?" she says, standing to face me with her legs slightly apart, daring me to ogle more of her body. I have no interest in whores and I want her to answer my fucking question.

Before I can answer, another one of my father's toys saunters into the foyer, naked. This one is young—she looks eighteen just about—far too young for my father. I grimace and keep my gaze firmly fixed away from the nude females. Just because the men in my family are bastards doesn't mean I have to follow suit.

If we don't conduct ourselves with respect, how can we expect the respect of the Amalfi Coast?

"Yes. My father. Sal," I grunt, failing to hide the irritation in my voice.

The woman ignores my irritated tone with her response.

"Oh, he's in the back with Boyka. I can take you there after we take you to bed upstairs."

How much is he paying these women? We're still struggling to get Jalousie off the ground and he spends all his money on Slavic hookers.

"Not interested. I have a meeting with him."

"Are you sure?"

I don't dignify them with a response. I walk past the girls, keeping my eyes away from their bodies. Where the hell is my father? I pass the long hallway with the family portraits and follow the loud music and the louder giggling from near the pool. The familiar sound of pool jets betrays papa's location.

He's in the fucking hot tub again, I know it. He spends all fucking day in the hot tub, dishing out orders and expecting work to happen without him lifting a fucking finger. It's a fucking miracle anything gets done around here.

My father chuckles loudly, and I brace myself before approaching him. He's the boss and you don't question the boss, even if he's your father and even if he cares more about partying and women than our family — than our future.

When I enter the back patio, the pungent smell of tobacco and marijuana surrounds me. Judging by the bottles of vodka on the ground, the piles of cigarette butts and the other piles of detritus, they've been at this fucking party since last night.

Fuck. I put the cigarette tucked behind my ear into my mouth and approach my father's outdoor speakers, unplugging them and stopping the little dance party happening around his hot tub. Three women, each wearing next to nothing with their tits out belly dance for him while he chuckles loudly, his fat stomach causing waves in the hot tub. When the music stops, they stop too and look up at me indignantly.

They don't have to ask who I am. The ones who don't know Van Doukas can tell that I'm related to Sal. I have my father's eyes, but thankfully, I don't have his overweight body or his bald head. The girls make booing sounds at me, but I brush them off.

"I'm here for our meeting," I say sternly to papa.

He chuckles and nods. "Yes. The meeting. I almost forgot."

Almost? He doesn't look like he's fucking prepared for a meeting.

Papa dismisses the girls, except for one — Boyka. She slides into the hot tub next to him, twirling his thick plumes of chest hair around her fingers and sliding his freshly cut cigar between his lips. Nauseating. Papa coughs after a puff and taps the cigar over the edge of the hot tub.

"You're early."

"I'm twenty minutes late."

"Oh?"

"Papa, you said it was important. Shouldn't we conduct this business alone?"

None of the girls are dumb enough to rat on Salvatore Doukas, but unlike my father, I don't see the sense in taking risks.

Boyka's hand moves down my father's chest and I don't

want to imagine what sorry shriveled part of him she touches next. I just want my orders so I can get the fuck out of this bachelor pad.

"I'm getting old, Van," he says. "I'm getting old."

He didn't call me down here to bitch about his old age. I furiously puff on my cigarette, waiting for him to get to the fucking point. Papa grunts as Boyka touches something... sensitive. Cristo...

Watching my father grunt through a hand job might be the only thing worse than watching him stick it to a woman.

"Do you mind postponing your fucking hand job until later?"

Boyka's hand rises guiltily from the water and I choke down bile. She really was touching the old fuck. I shouldn't swear at him or set him off. Papa might seem old, but he can have me killed. Any of my brothers would do it if he gave the command. Tread carefully, Van.

"Maybe I should leave," Boyka says, giving me a flirty glance as she plays with her tiny pink nipples.

"Yes," I snap. "Please get the fuck out of here."

Papa scowls. "Be respectful, Van. Boyka is a very dear—"

"I said please."

Papa smirks. "Boyka, return in thirty minutes. If we're not done..."

"We'll be done," I interrupt, glowering at my father. I don't have all afternoon for his games when I have the club to attend to.

Boyka reluctantly leaves.

"Are the women in this house allergic to fucking clothes?"

"None of them are allergic to fucking anything."

I'm not doing this with the old man today.

"Why did you call me here?"

I start another cigarette. I keep swearing I won't touch

another, then I spend five minutes around papa and change my mind.

He leans back in the hot tub, displacing several pints of water over the edge.

"I'm tired, Van," he groans, leaning back and rubbing his forehead.

"From working?"

My father doesn't pick up on the sarcasm. He hardly leaves his fucking hot tub anymore, and he hasn't done anything even remotely resembling working at either of the nightclubs, restaurants, apartment complexes or construction sites around town.

If it wasn't for me and Enzo, he wouldn't have the fucking time to boink Boyka or whatever the fuck he does with all these young Slavic women.

I still have to tread carefully around him. He's still my father, my boss, and I must obey him.

"Yes," he says, coughing. "From working. I need someone to take my place and lead the family soon. I want to retire, Van. You and I both know I need a break."

He spends every fucking day on vacation while his sons and nephews run his businesses. Vacation? We're the ones who need a fucking vacation.

"Perhaps you should contact Matteo about that."

My older brother spent his entire life preparing to be the boss. It's not my fault he fucked off, leaving his worthless children with us, I might add. I'm already halfway through my fucking cigarette and he hasn't closed in on the point.

Papa scoffs. "Matteo hasn't left Albania in four years. He left his children, his business, his fucking money, and he's not coming back. Give up on him."

"You're the one who trained him for the role. Send Enzo after him. Better yet, send his fucking son."

I don't want to go into the mountains to bring my jackass

older brother back and I don't want to have this conversation with my father.

"Why don't you go to Albania?"

"Every time I'm in the same room as Matteo, he tries to kill me," I remind papa. I love Matteo, but he isn't exactly easy to get along with.

I'm surprised a woman tolerated him long enough to allow him to give her Eddie.

"Fair. But I need a replacement, Van. I don't want to be the boss anymore. I can't take the stress much longer."

Stress? What stress? Does my father seriously think sitting in his fucking hot tub banging whores counts as a job?

"Have you considered the role?" He asks before I can spew something disrespectful in my father's direction.

"Why would I want to be the boss of this fucking family? It's filled with degenerates, fuck-ups, people who need more violence to be kept in line. I kill enough as it is. You don't want me to be the boss and nobody in this fucking family wants me as the boss."

"People respect you, Van."

"People fear me. There's a difference."

Papa nods. "Exactly. Personally, I think you would make a good boss."

"I disagree."

But I don't completely. Yes, the job would be horrific and I'd have even more blood on my hands than I do now by the end. I could bring honor back to our family, clean the streets of our scum, stop the Jews from fucking with our shit... but I can't. Not with Matteo gone. Even in the fucking Albanian countryside, he would find out what I did and Matteo would kill me.

"No," Papa replies calmly. "You don't. But I agree with your assessment that you're not quite ready."

"I never said that. I said I didn't want the job."

Nobody smart wants my father's job. He spent twenty years walking around with a target on his back before he built up enough trust, enough loyalty, enough captains in the streets of Italy to ensure his safety. I don't want to lose my freedom.

"You didn't have to say anything. I know my son."

"Hm."

Arguing with my father is entirely senseless.

"You need an heir, Van."

"What?"

"I will give you the leadership of this family without the ritual, without the sacrifice and without the financial investment required. All I want is an heir."

"Why don't I go up to fucking Albania, then? Because I can't produce a child out of thin air."

Papa chuckles. "Don't you have women? If you want a woman... I filled this house with them. I have very young ones too. Eighteen. Nineteen. They make good mothers."

"I am not interested in fucking teenagers."

"Then find a whore like that old Greek Pagonis fuck. I don't care how you get the heir. You can prove how serious you are by giving me a child. I'll be generous. I'll give you a year."

"I don't want this role," I snap. "So the likelihood I'll produce an heir is slim."

Papa laughs, which only infuriates me further. There's nothing funny about bringing a child into the world.

"You can't lie to me, Van. You were always the most ambitious child. Maybe it's because you were smack in the middle and we didn't pay any attention to you. Who fucking knows?"

My father spent little time raising any of us, except for Enzo, and look how that fucking turned out.

"Thank you for the psychoanalysis."

Every time I visit my father, my desire for alcohol increases exponentially, along with my cravings for nicotine. He brings the worst out of everyone, especially me.

"No problem," he says, again ignoring my sarcasm.

"What happens if I don't produce an heir? Eh? You still need someone to take your place."

"I make this offer to Lorenzo if you don't produce what I want."

"What?" I would have at least expected him to mention one of our cousins, one of the very obedient captains from the northern coast, or even fucking Eddie, Matteo's 18-year-old son, would be better than my irresponsible fuck of a brother. That old fuck really knows me well because he just said the only thing that could get me to reconsider his stupid fucking offer.

"You heard me."

"Lorenzo would ruin this family. For fun."

"I know. And it would become your responsibility to save it. You would have to act as the boss to save Lorenzo from himself. You might as well earn the position."

Fuck this old man...

"I don't want a family life, papa. I don't want the fucking wife or the fucking family. I want this life. It's what I'm good at. Business. Killing. More killing. That's who you taught me to be."

I'm not a man who can picture himself kicking around a football with my children or taking them to the beach. I'm not built for seducing women for more than a night and dealing with the danger of introducing them to my life or worse, hiding it the way papa did with our mother.

He can pretend it's not his fault what happened to her, but we all know the truth. No woman deserves our life. I can't afford to react. He loves when he can draw a reaction out of me.

Papa continues, as if my reaction is irrelevant. "Part of this life means having a family. I can't expect my other children to carry on my bloodline."

"Matteo has a son. You have a fucking bloodline. Why don't you make him the fucking boss?"

"Eddie? Eddie will not survive long the way he lives."

"That's a way to talk about your grandson, eh?"

"Have another cigarette, Van."

I'm already on my fucking third. But I'm not in a position to turn down his offer, considering the shit he wants me to deal with right now. An heir? I thought he wanted me to kill someone. Producing an heir in a year... It's just fucking impossible. I stick the cigarette in my mouth and light it.

"You can't let the family fall apart. We aren't the only people who would suffer. What would happen to our people, good Italian people, when the only people around they can get money from are the fucking Jews, who hate our guts?" He says.

I can't let his guilt trip work on me.

"I want an heir."

"Hm."

"Consider what you would sacrifice by turning down my offer, Van. It's not just about the family. It's power. You act like you're a fucking saint, but you are my son. You enjoy power. You're just too much of a stuck up cunt to let yourself enjoy it."

"Thanks papa."

"You're welcome. Now, onto the matter of the Jew."

Fuck. I hoped my father would only piss me off one way today, but if we're discussing the matter of the Jew, I won't leave here tonight without an assignment. Someone else could easily do this job, but he wants me to kill. Because I'm good at it.

"I suppose none of my other brothers have the free time to do this?"

"I don't care. I need you to do it. The cunt offended this family."

"Perhaps we waste too much time retaliating for every offense. Ana told you to drop it."

I'm taking a risk just questioning his order, but he's pissed me off so much that I stopped caring.

"Decision making isn't women's work. It's our work. The man signed his own death warrant. I want it done soon. Call me when you finish the job."

"Hm."

"If you don't like the way I run this family, Van, you know what to do. I want to retire. Make an old man happy."

Drugs and whores are the only things that make my father happy.

"An heir," I scoff. "You want me to have a fucking bastard child to continue your bloodline? A bastard won't have any loyalty to his family. Children have a mother and a father, a mother they spend all their time with. If I fuck some poor woman, you won't have an heir. You'll have a problem on your hands."

"Then get creative. If you need to get the baby and kill the mother, do what you must."

What's happening to this family? When did we lose our way and talking about murdering women for our own ends? Papa… This life changed him. It was slow, but it changed him completely. Too bad there's no getting out.

"Thank you for the advice."

"You're welcome. Now get Boyka back in here and get the fuck out. I need relief."

"Good evening, papa."

I drop my cigarette on the ground without bothering to step on it. Maybe my father's right — it's time for him to retire. But how the fuck will I get an heir? I need help.

There's one person I can call on for assistance in these matters. I don't like involving the Greeks in Italian business, but... they're our cousins. She answers after a few rings and it sounds like she's at a nightclub. She has an inordinate amount of time for parties...

"Ciao?"

I can barely hear her over the sound of the music.

"Miss Pagonis. It's Van."

She giggles. "Duh. What's happening? You finally have work for me?"

"How soon can you come back to Italy?"

Chapter 2
Single AF On The Amalfi Coast
Jodi Rose

I'm the last single woman in my family.

Three months in Italy, and I haven't had so much as a kiss, but my younger cousin Raven gets married to her college boyfriend and he looks like a dream. I drop a congratulatory comment on her photo, but my heart sinks.

You ugly, Jodi. Get used to it and stop chasing all these men out of your league. Settle with Kyle. He's the best you can do. Maybe mama was right. I'm not the marrying kind, anyway. I spent all my dating years focused on school and look at where that got me...

"Edo!"

The bartender gives me a sympathetic look. Ugh. Edo is so hot. Too bad all the hot guys are gay, especially in Italy, apparently.

"What happened?"

"Look at this."

I show him my phone and Edo cracks a smile. "Beautiful! Is she your sister?"

"No, my cousin. She's getting married and here I am... single... again."

And I'm running away from my problems with a one-way ticket to Italy. When my family finds out I'm not coming back, they're going to lose their minds. Everyone already thinks I'm crazy for leaving Kyle...

"Fuck your ex, Jodi. Seriously, fuck him," Edo says with all the passion of a best friend, even if we barely know each other.

I have major regrets about getting drunk my first night here and spilling all the drama about my ex-boyfriend to a bartender, but at least it made us fast friends. Although I'm not sure if Edo just likes the fact that Americans tip, unlike our Italian friends. He always has a way of scamming some extra euros out of me. At least he's a damn good listener.

I groan and dramatically lean against the bar as I make a proclamation that I wholeheartedly believe.

"I'm never going to get with another guy again. This is it. I'm dying alone."

I've read the statistics. Or at least I've read what women on Lipstick Alley say about the statistics. I'm a thick, well-educated black woman who is tired of the dusties and has real ass standards — according to the internet, I'm dying alone.

Edo grins and shakes his head. Since he learned I was American, he's done everything in my power to take me under his wing since I got here. I just hate getting too far out of my comfort zone, so I've ditched all his invitations to visit the local clubs in favor of spending my nights drinking cocktails alone and checking social media. I'm in Italy. I should have daily adventures and bread. I can't forget the delicious ass bread.

"You will not die alone," Edo says. "At least not without trying... my latest cocktail creation."

Edo does a dramatic dance before revealing some clear

beverage that looks like some horrible mix of vodka, vermouth and orange juice.

Good. I want to get completely fucked up.

"That looks... clear."

"You'll love it, I promise."

"Will drinking really make the pain go away?" I muse, twirling the glass around so the little orange peel swirls inside it. Kyle. Why do you always miss the ones who fuck you up the most?

Hopefully, this drink will get my ain't shit ex off my mind, but let's be real. What I really need is a summer romance. Ha. Like that's going to happen in a country where half the people think I'm a prostitute because of my skin color.

"Yes. It will. Absolutely." Edo replies with a wink.

"Cheers." I swirl the drink around despite Edo's repeated claims I ruin his creations by doing that. I pour it down my throat and taste a pleasant citrus flavor before a powerful vodka burn. It takes everything in my power to get the rest of the drink down my throat. Whew! That was a damn burn.

"What the hell did you put in that?"

Edo winks, but offers no response. Tricky ass Italian.

"My shift ends in ten," he says. "I'll take you out tonight to Jalousie. No getting out of it this time to watch *Empire* in your apartment."

How the fuck does this skinny ass white boy know me so well already? I shake my head, prepared to reject his offer to take me to the club, but Edo won't let it go. He wriggles his brows suggestively.

He loves regaling me with stories about all the shenanigans that go down at the Amalfi Coast nightclubs. I'm not really a nightclub girl. Small bars like this one fit me better, but didn't I come to Italy to have fun? Meet someone? I should put in some effort.

The only men who give me any attention are the creeps

on the beach who say so much nasty shit to me in Italian that I'm glad I don't understand.

Maybe I'll meet better men at the club, especially a club with a fancy ass French name like this one. Jalousie. Wait... Edo's mentioned Jalousie to me before in the past.

"Ain't that the club with the mafia shootout you told me about?"

I don't believe half the shit that comes out of Edo's mouth, but he loves regaling me with stories about the real Italian mafia, which he claims is apparently far worse than any mafia in Long Island or Staten Island. How could anyone who lives in one of the most beautiful parts of the world hurt and kill other people? I think he likes telling tall tales to impress tourists.

I get people on Staten Island killing each other, but the Amalfi Coast? Hell fucking no. The sea is perfectly blue, the air smells fresh constantly, and it's plain peaceful out here. Italians have a rich culture, amazing food, better wine and the guys here are hot.

Not every guy, but when you walk down the streets here, you definitely encounter more than a few hotties. They all dress like supermodels, too. I've never seen so many regular ass people sporting Gucci and Fendi.

"Yes," Edo says. "But you're here for 9 more months, right? Have a fling. Don't tell him your real name... and disappear. You can find a hot and incredibly rich man to spoil you during your trip."

"Wait... is this a gay club or my type of club?"

Edo chuckles. "The guys are hot. I didn't say they were gay. You haven't earned your way into going to a gay club with me yet."

"Wow, Edo. I thought we had something going here."

Edo shrugs. "My private life is my private life. That's how it is in Italy. Your private life, on the other hand, is my playground. I'll introduce you to people. I know people who frequent Jalousie."

"Hot guys?"

"Eh…"

"Hot straight guys?" I correct myself before he answers. I don't want Edo tricking me into going out for nothing.

"Not exactly… I have a girl friend in town who goes all the time — Cassia Pagonis."

He says the name like I'm supposed to know who the fuck that is.

"Who the fuck is that?"

Edo chuckles. "A very fun girl with very hot brothers."

I perk up a little until Edo tells me they're all married. Great.

"Great. They're married…"

Before Edo can reassure me (again) more customers wander into the bar and Edo scurries to the other end of the bar to take orders.

I gaze into my phone again, looking at pictures from Raven's wedding. My cousin looks gorgeous, but I can't help a twisted pang of envy. I know it's wrong but… will that ever happen for me?

My homegirls from college keep sending me articles about the sorry state of marriage for black women. Alyssa says that we need to divest completely from marriage and just have fun.

My idea of fun isn't keeping a collection of all "my dicks" in a private folder on my phone. I want the real fucking thing! Even if the world loves reminding me that 'the real thing' only happens for white women or black women with the lightest dusting of melanin… I want to believe in love.

I scroll past Raven's pictures and my feed is all babies, new puppies, new jobs, new houses, new apartments, new husbands… new everything. Before Italy, I was just doing the same old shit. I wanted to shake things up. I don't know why my life hasn't transformed entirely. I'm in the prettiest place on earth — the Amalfi Coast.

Edo's shift ends, and he calls my name from the other end of the bar, beckoning me over to the cash register.

"Any tip for me today?"

"I saw you slip that five euro note out of my wallet. I think we're good."

Edo shrugs. "Sorry, this job doesn't pay well."

"I get it. I'll pay for our drinks tonight. Happy?"

"Incredibly."

I shouldn't be offering to pay for anyone's drinks, honestly, but I tell myself that I'll worry about all the damn money I'm spending once I get back to America. I have nine months of freedom and then I can worry about these damn bills and loans and everything else.

Edo drags me off my stool, and we step outside into the cobblestone street. I'll never get over how beautifully blue everything is here. The streets smell like the ocean, pastries, wine and cigarettes, of course. People sell jewelry and fruits on the streets and the Italian accents are… gorgeous. My Italian's still crap, despite Edo's best efforts to teach me a few phrases.

At least I don't have to hear all the street harassment thrown my way, which is plentiful. Edo replies defensively to a grey-haired man who calls something lewd in my direction and grabs me tighter. "Fuck these guys," he says. "You aren't that fat."

I swear, I'll never get used to how fucking blunt they are. But I appreciate Edo doing his best to defend me. We can hear the music from Jalousie echoing down the street before we get close.

"Isn't it early for the club?"

"Why are you so fucking American?" Edo asks, linking arms with me. "Relax."

"EDOARDO!" A shrill voice with a strange accent calls from across the street. I know Italian accents by now, at least how people from the Coast sound when speaking English, and this girl sounds different.

"That's Cass," Edo says to me, a smile breaking out across his handsome face. "Chin up. She'll love you."

Edo waves to the girl across the street and she struts over to us, sticking her hand out to stop the cars making their way down the cobblestone streets. They don't even honk as she passes.

The first thing I notice about her is how striking she is. She's tall, with curly dark brown hair pinned up out of her face and flowing down her back. She's wearing crazy high heels, like all the European girls do, a short leather skirt and a tight black leather crop top.

With her dark red lipstick, she looks like a film noir femme fatale… and she stares like one.

"Edo… is this your American friend?"

She turns to me and smiles. Shit, her accent might be strong, but her English is perfect. Cass's hair falls over her shoulders, her curls carrying a soft eucalyptus scent.

"Jodi Rose," I say, happy to have some female company around here, not like there's anything wrong with Edo. "Nice to meet you."

She takes my hand, three silver Cartier bracelets sliding down her wrist. Wow. Her bracelets aren't the only expensive item of clothing she has.

"Cass Pagonis. I'm sure Edo has told you all sorts of horrible stories about me."

"I did not!"

Edo definitely did. But Cass doesn't seem like a crazy party girl. She rolls her eyes and brushes him off.

"I'm here on the Coast working for my cousin's family," Cass says. "I'm from Thessaloniki. My idiot brothers want me back next week, unfortunately. But I could use a night out before I go."

Edo claps his hands. "Yay! Party time. Too bad Jalousie only caters to the most chauvinistic mafia pigs you can imagine."

"I thought you said they were hotties?!"

"They are," Edo says. "But they might be assholes."

Now he tells me. Edo would have said anything to get me out of my damn apartment. I hope I don't regret it.

"Watch it," Cass cautions, an impish smile on her face. "Those chauvinistic mafia pigs are my cousins and brothers."

Edo shrugs. "Fine. Fine. But I need dick too. Gay rights."

Cass swats his shoulder.

"Edo, why don't you let me take her for the night? There's no one at Jalousie for you, and you can go meet up with Klaus or… that other one."

Edo suddenly straightens his back and reminds both of us that just because he's gay doesn't mean he's given up on old world chivalry.

"I can't send Jodi off with a stranger," he says.

I appreciate the sentiment, but I don't know if Edo would do much damage against… any man who weighed more than his slight 108 lb frame.

"I'm fine," I tell him. "Seriously."

"I'm armed anyway," Cass says. I think she's joking, but neither of them laughs. Is she serious? She doesn't look armed, and she looks more like a model than someone who knows how to use a weapon.

I could use a female friend in my life over here. I've got plenty of female friends back home, but they all want to talk about Kyle and my "healing journey". They don't want to hear that I'm still lost after all these months.

Edo shrugs. "If you insist."

"I insist," I tell him. "You've done enough taking care of me. Plus, I'll get to know my new friend… Cass."

"Exactly," Cass says. "Jodi… I think we can become wonderful friends. We can swap stories about Edo."

"There are no stories about Edo," he chimes in. "Because Edo is an incredible friend and a better bartender."

"Shoo," Cass says. "I can handle things from here."

Edo doesn't quite walk off, but he checks his phone and begins texting furiously to plan his next move.

"It's the last time they have DJ Fat Camel playing here. We'll dance, drink and later, I'll take you home, yes?"

"That sounds good to me."

"Well, you have my number if Cass abandons you on the top of a Ferris wheel," Edo says as he swipes four times quickly across his screen and then shoves his phone into his pocket.

Cass rolls her eyes. "I have done nothing of the sort. Get out of here, you big drama queen."

"Ciao!"

Cass and I say "Ciao!"

Edo walks down the cobblestone streets and lights a cigarette before disappearing around the corner. Cass breathes a sigh of relief and turns to me.

"I just think you're perfect," she says.

Weird comment to make, but I mumble a gracious thank you, assuming something got lost in translation.

"Do you have friends with you?" Cass asks, taking out a hand mirror and fixing her bright red lipstick.

"No. I'm here solo tripping. Had a quarter life crisis and… here I am."

"Do you like Italy?" she asks genuinely. Her eyes are so intense.

"It's beautiful."

"Not as pretty as Greece," Cass says. "But I agree. Shall we go in?"

"We should head to the back of the line," I say, my stomach knotting as I see the line stretched around the block. I hope we can even get into the club.

Cass grins, unperturbed by the growing line outside Jalousie.

"My cousin owns the place. Come on, we go in through the back."

Before I can protest, she takes my hand and we walk around a back alley that smells like trash, vomit and again — cigarettes. Cass drags me over to a door and surveys me once before touching the handle.

"Very proper outfit. Excellent. Let's go. Ready to dance?"

I nod, even if I'm nervous. Sure, I'm trying to have an adventure tonight, but I just met this chick. How do I know she isn't crazy? Well, she has Edo's backing, so at least she'll be a good time. Edo definitely knows how to have fun if his clubbing stories are even 55% true.

Cass punches in a six-digit code and the back door to the club opens. I can smell the club before I hear the music and Cass drags me in through the back before I can second guess myself. What am I really doing? I don't know this chick at all and I agreed to go clubbing with her? Is Edo's word really enough?

Once we're in the back door, a man appears. He's tall, with dark brown slicked back hair, tattoos all over his arms and grey eyes. He has broad shoulders, but is otherwise lean and very muscular. He's handsome, but it's too bad he smokes. I can smell the cigarettes from a distance.

"Cass? What the fuck are you doing here?" he asks, seeming genuinely upset.

"Shut the fuck up, Enzo," Cass snaps, her expression

changing suddenly into a disapproving scowl. "I have business here."

The man smirks. He's around Cass' height, but he looks… greasy.

"Is that her?"

"Mind your fucking business."

Cass pushes him hard so we can get past him. The grey-eyed man's eyes land on me and he runs his hand over his jawline before snickering.

"He's going to kill you."

"Shut up," Cass snarls. Enzo laughs and raises his hands in defeat.

"Enjoy your night," he says to me in a sing-song voice. For the first time, I feel real hesitation. But Cass grabs my hand and drags me inside of the club.

Cass drags me all the way to the tables and chairs surrounding the dance floor, chatting excitedly and peppering me with questions about America. I struggle to understand her accent at first, but then I get into the rhythm of her voice and it's easier for us to communicate.

I have to listen in so hard that I barely scan the room we enter. At least the nightclub has a nice interior, and it doesn't seem like any ghetto shit might pop off. Another Edo exaggeration, it seems. I relax as Cass sets me up at a small, two-person table.

"I'll get you a drink. Wait here. If anyone comes to talk to you, tell them you are with Cass Pagonis. That will shut them up."

Before I can protest, or offer to come with her, Cass disappears. Shit. I guess I have to wait here. I already have five texts from Edo about the hotties he met at the club a few doors over. Damn, he moves quick. I've been here for weeks already and I still haven't met a heterosexual male who hasn't been an incredibly old and excessively horny man offering for me to be his 'African prostitute' — offers I have obviously declined.

Cass returns quickly, before I have any time to worry with two shots, each one with some blue flavoring at the bottom.

"Okay, Jodi. This is to a long and beautiful friendship between us, starting with one crazy night, yeah?"

I nod. "Hell yeah. I've never done anything like this before."

I blurt out the last part nervously, but Cass has a way of soothing me. She just smiles and nods. "Don't be scared! I'm a good Greek girl. Now come on… we'll take the shots together."

She counts us down.

"1… 2… 3…"

I take the shot — and it's the last thing I remember about that night.

Chapter 3
Not An Italian Woman
Van

"What the fuck? Cass!"

"I did what you asked. I have a girl in the back of the Escalade. I did an excellent job. She took the pills very well."

I slam the door shut. Cass must have given this girl elephant tranquilizers because she doesn't even fucking flinch.

"I gave you a list of characteristics, you Greek bitch."

"Careful, Van. Gal's in a boat a few miles off the coast. Don't make me call him on you."

"I said blonde. I said twenty-one. I said 5'4" tall, and I said thin. Does the woman in the back of this fucking Escalade look anything like I told you?"

My voice trembles with rage and that irritating Greek cousin of mine just smiles and fishes a hand-rolled, loose cigarette from her skirt pocket.

"Do you have a lighter?"

"You sound bored. Don't you understand I could shoot you dead and drop your fucking body in the sea for this?" I growl.

Cass snickers. "You could try. Now, do you have a fucking lighter or not?"

I slam the lighter into my bratty cousin's outstretched palm. She lights her cigarette, that impish smile across her fucking face. Never trust a Greek bearing gifts. Why the fuck didn't I remember that before calling her? I only called the little brat because she likes money enough to keep my secret.

"What were you thinking?"

"Men don't know what they want," she says. "That's what I was thinking.'

"No! I know exactly what I want. I wanted a small, blond woman who belongs in the life, not a foreigner... not an African."

"Ignorant cunt," Cass snaps, slamming the heel of her boots into my calf. "She's African American. They're very cultured."

I want to break her in half. If she didn't have three of the most annoying brothers, perhaps I would.

"I don't want her."

"Too bad. She's what you get."

That little shit... Cass nonchalantly smokes. Doesn't she have a child now? That poor baker's son must be at home caring for her brat while she fucks with my life across the sea. If she didn't have a child, I would have at least attempted to smother her by now.

Instead, I'll give my bratty Greek cousin another chance to do the fucking job right.

"Go out again and find exactly what I asked for."

"You idiot. I drugged her and set her up for this. If she wakes up, she could go to the police, and this happens in your new nightclub? I'll be in Greece and your stupid club will be bankrupt. Does that sound wise?"

"Fuck, Cass. How could you fucking do this to me?"

"I didn't know you were so racist, Van."

"It's not racist. Fuck. I don't expect you to understand."

"Do you know any other words besides fuck? I'm leaving. I did what I came here to do. Sandros is waiting for me on the boat."

"I'm never hiring you again."

"You always say that. Why don't you trust me, cousin?"

"Because you're an evil Greek bitch. That's why."

Cass laughs like I paid her a compliment.

"That's going to be my next tattoo. Her name is Jodi, by the way. She seems very nice. I think she has a good curvy shape too. But what do I know? Ciao, Van."

She leans forward and kisses me on the cheek, leaving the red print of her lipstick behind. I rub my forehead as she walks off. Fuck. I've made a huge mistake and now I have a drugged woman in the back of my fucking car.

I call Enzo. Because he's the brother you call when you have a drugged woman in the back of your car and you need to go kill a Jew.

"What do you want?"

"Meet me at the beach."

"What part?" Enzo huffs. He wants to know if this is for a murder or a party. He'll know by my answer.

"Southern shore. I have a problem."

"Killing David tonight?"

My jawline clenches. "Yes. But I have another problem. I can't do this alone."

"Can't you get Eddie to do it?"

"No. I need you…"

Enzo can be a lazy fuck sometimes.

"See you in ten."

"Be there in seven."

Fuck. I get into the car and glance behind me at the woman laid across the leather seats of my Escalade. Jodi. I've never seen a woman like her in my life. She's confusing, and she's definitely not what I wanted. I need a woman I can produce an heir with—a surrogate to give me a child and then disappear. What the hell was Cass thinking disobeying me?

She's more proof we need to tighten the hold on our family. Nobody respects the Doukas name anymore.

She's still asleep when I get to the beach. I peer into the back seat at her chest rising and falling. At least she isn't dead. I don't have the stomach to dispose of two bodies tonight. Enzo rolls his car next to mine, rolling down the window and expelling an enormous cloud of marijuana smoke.

"You showed up high?"

"Relax. I also brought Eddie."

"Ciao, Uncle Van."

"Why the fuck did you bring Eddie?"

"Didn't you bring someone?" Enzo smirks, which means he probably noticed Cass at the club earlier and pieced everything together. She's still in the back of the Escalade and I don't need my fucking brother or my idiot nephew involved with this.

The last thing I need is Enzo dragging out my personal business for his habitual mockery.

"Shut up. Where's David tonight?"

"Gambling. As usual. Does Ana know we're doing this?"

My brother irks me sometimes. "Do you think Ana fucking knows?"

"Why so upset, brother? Working with the Greek cunt didn't work out? Who could have predicted that…"

"Shut up, Enzo."

Eddie glances up from his phone for the first time.

"Either of you have a cigarette?"

"You're too young to smoke," Enzo says.

"Fuck off. You're only three years older than me," Eddie

protests, throwing a powerful punch on Enzo's shoulder. My brother doesn't flinch.

"Doesn't matter. He's your superior. You listen to him," I growl. If papa had taught them discipline from the beginning, neither of them would be like this. Now it's my responsibility whenever we go out to remind these fucks what *cosa nostra* is really all about. Our way of life is falling apart.

Eddie shrugs, and Enzo hands our nephew a cigarette, giving me a knowing look. After what we do tonight, he'll need more than a cigarette. We both remember our first kill and it wasn't pretty.

After two puffs, Eddie grins. "Are we working or what? I have more cunts to catch tonight."

"Quiet, Eddie," Enzo grumbles, tapping away on his phone. "Okay. I've got him. He's five blocks away."

I wonder what weapons my brother and nephew brought tonight. We'll need more than my pistol.

"Who is he drinking with tonight?" I grunt. How many motherfuckers will we have to take out?

Enzo shakes his head. "You won't like this."

"Five other men from his family. We can't be sure he'll leave the place alone."

"We need someone to lure him out," Eddie suggests. "A prostitute. Or a woman who can act like one. I'll get my girlfriend."

"You're still seeing Zara?"

I told Eddie to leave Zara alone after the last incident. I don't want to deal with another domestic problem.

"Why should I stop? She always takes me back."

"At least she makes a believable prostitute," Enzo says, shrugging. Eddie laughs, not even bothering to defend the woman he claims to love. Yes, she's a foreigner, but that shouldn't matter if he's chosen her. Love. This is what papa wants me to fight so hard for? Whatever he has for this family isn't love, and I have no intention of repeating his mistakes. I'll leave love for the younger generation, although Eddie doesn't leave me with much hope.

"Show some respect," I growl. "We're not using Zara."

Eddie puffs out his chest, but he's careful not to push me too hard. I'm just as likely to put out a hit on him as anyone else.

"Why not? She's mine to use," he says defiantly until I raise my eyebrow and silence my nephew.

Unfortunately, my idiot brother speaks up in Eddie's favor.

"We don't have a choice," Enzo says. "Unless you have someone else for us to use?"

The smirk on his irritating fucking face tells me he knows exactly who and what he's asking for. Bastard.

He knows what Cass did for me. Either that, or he suspects. My face betrays nothing. Unlike my father and Matteo, I don't let Lorenzo get under my skin.

"I have nothing for you."

"Except the unconscious immigrant in the back of your car," Enzo replies calmly, stealing another cigarette from Eddie's shirt pocket. All they fucking do is smoke and run women. Maybe my father's right and I need to take control of this family. My stomach lurches at that thought, combined with the knowledge of the woman in the backseat of my car.

"Why bother drugging and kidnapping a prostitute if we can't even use her?"

"If he doesn't want her, I'll have her," Eddie snickers, taking the lit cigarette from Enzo and taking a huge puff.

"Put out the fucking cigarette. We don't need a lure, we need patience, something you stupid fucks know nothing about. We drive to the Jew and we wait for him to exit alone. We trust he will exit alone. If we can't get him tonight, we get him tomorrow night. Understood?"

My tone sets them straight this time. Enzo puts out the cigarette. They can't disobey direct orders. Even if they might not fear me, they both fear papa. Then again, judging by Eddie's averted eyes and sheepish glances, perhaps I'm more terrifying than I thought. Matteo would have whipped them into shape. I hope Albania is worth it, you stupid fuck.

The boys get into Enzo's car and he drives away first. I want to take my time out here on this beach, with this woman, and assess this mess of a fucking situation. Never trust a Greek bearing gifts. How many fucking times has papa warned me about the Pagonis family? They're tricksters. I wipe my sweaty hands on black jeans and open the back of the car.

Fuck you, Cass.

She couldn't have made a bigger effort to deviate from my exact specifications for what I wanted in a woman — and, more importantly, what I wanted in a womb. How am I supposed to produce an heir with... her? I specifically said blonde. This woman couldn't possibly come anywhere close to blonde. And her skin color...

My stomach twists in an incomprehensible knot as I stare at her unconscious body, a tight party dress barely covering her thick thighs. Her thighs are... large. Everything about her is larger than the typical Amalfi Coast club girl. She doesn't look like she's afraid to eat anything denser than lettuce, to start. She has curves. Very full curves. She's not my type, but my cock doesn't appear to get the message. I feel like a fucking teenager.

She isn't suitable for this job, but perhaps she'll have her uses. I'll examine my prize later. I have to kill the Jew before the woman wakes up. Considering how little Cass obeyed my instructions, I may not have much time. I follow Enzo's route to the bar where the Jews hang around, shooting dice and drinking like the rest of us. I have nothing against the religion — it's the people. It's tradition.

Our families have been at war for generations. They blame the past on our people, even if two generations ago, they were the ones bankrupting humble Italian families and taking ears and noses as collateral for unpayable loans. Without the family, without the protection and organization under papa and his trusted advisors, they would have owned all of us, kept us no better than slaves.

So no, I don't hate the Jews — but I have pride in myself and my family. I am an Italian man. Nobody owns me.

Enzo texts me when he's in position. This is the boring part. I stop the car and allow everything to settle into pure silence — except for a soft sound in the back seat. Snoring. I find the sound unsettling. I spend nearly every waking moment that I can alone, so her soft noises remind me that there's a stranger, another fucking problem, lying in my back seat.

The crowd around the Jewish bar thins shortly after our arrival. It's late enough that couples and foreigners and groups of students on vacation spill out of the bar and onto the cobblestone streets. Foreigners don't care who owns which bar or which club. They just want to spend their money, blissfully unaware of the work that goes into keeping Italy their playground.

I know the man I'm going to kill. We're friendly. In public, us Italians hold nothing against the Jews and they hold nothing against us. Our war happens in secret. I attended school with David. We played football together in high school. Tonight, I'll chop him up into several pieces and... well, you'll see how it goes.

After an hour, Enzo finally messages me. Eddie saw him and he's leaving through the back, drunk and stumbling home alone. Eddie has eyes on him, but we'll need to move the cars to get him. Easy. I command Enzo to pick him up since he has Eddie on the street. We'll take him to the beach. It's the best place for a born and raised Italian to die.

We drive thirty miles up the coast to the beach where we work. You don't shit where you eat, right? The woman sleeps peacefully in the back seat the entire time. It's for the best. Enzo and Eddie wait for me to get there, only pulling the Jew out when I leave my car. They might be fuckups, but when it's important, they make an effort at obedience.

He doesn't struggle and not just because of the gun Eddie presses into his stomach. He knows his time has come. Everyone in the life knows this is most likely how we're going to die, a bullet to the fucking head that's had our name on it for years.

"Take his hood off. He knows who we are."

Enzo obeys, but Eddie keeps a tight grip on the Jew before removing the cloth hood from the man's head. He raises his gaze instantly.

"I don't want to do this," I tell him.

"Don't give me the speech, Van," David chokes out. "Just finish it. Don't draw it out."

"You know what you've done and why this is happening. We have to send a message."

"I have money, Van. Enough money to set the three of you fucks free. You could leave Italy. Forever. Money. Information. I have anything you want."

Every man behaves differently when he faces death. Death isn't pretty. You piss and shit yourself in front of other men. You cry for your mother. You deny what's happening — and with the Jew, you attempt to strike a bargain. You attempt to give your killer what he wants, hoping he sets you free and allows you to disappear. Believe me, you get this far and free yourself, you want to disappear.

The Jew has made a grave miscalculation. I will never and

would never choose money over family. Even if it's just my sister Ana, who I strongly dislike.

"We don't need money from you people anymore."

"I know. I know… But Van… we have history."

"Fuck, I'm tired of this. Uncle, can I shoot him?"

"Eddie, no. That's not how we do things."

Enzo puts his hand on the man's shoulders and nods. "Yes," he says. "We give them time to pray to their God and whisper any last words before we gut them and stuff their dicks in their mouth."

Now the man takes a piss. I swear I could fucking kill Enzo for scaring him. That's the last thing we need.

"I promise we won't desecrate your corpse. Now pray if you must."

"I have a request," David pleads.

"Hm?"

I don't like the idea of a dying man making requests, but considering Enzo just pushed him to the edge of fear, I feel a touch generous. Just a touch.

"My chain. Give it to my daughter. Please. That's all I ask. I want her to know that I was thinking about her."

"Your daughter is three. She won't remember you," Enzo says. Fucking hell, I want to kill my brother.

"Don't listen to him. Eddie, take the chain. We'll do what the man says."

"Take my gun off him?"

"He won't run," I say to him, but of course, I can't exactly make these assurances. It's just a guess. He's alone with three armed mafiosos on the beach. He would have to be an idiot to run. I make a very incorrect judgment about our captive's intelligence. As Eddie lowers his gun and begins removing the man's star hanging around his neck, he shoves his elbow into Eddie's side and throws a hard kick toward Enzo before taking off down the beach.

Stupid fuck… I take off after him, pulling out my gun as I run. The poor bastard isn't quick — something I would have considered in his position. He played football with me. He should know who he's dealing with. I throw my leg out and catapult the Jew to the sand. He cries out as his body goes flying. Enzo and Eddie catch up with me as I trip and roll over, holding my gun aloft. I can't stop what they're about to do now. The Jew made a mistake by running.

Enzo throws a hard kick into the man's side. Eddie laughs as blood spurts from the man's face. They beat him for a while until he can't make any other sound except a whimper and a prayer. When he prays, I stop them with my hand.

"Before you die, we'll be needing that information you promised?"

He looks up at us as if he won't say anything. Then I watch the defeat flow from his face. Information. He'll give it up to us. The Jews have strong bonds, but not as strong as ours. They don't kill the way we do, so their people don't fear giving up information. At least I can justify this to myself.

I killed a man for information sits better with my conscience than killing a man for Ana. If I don't follow orders, I'll be the one kneeling on the beach next. I can't have that happen.

This isn't exactly going in the order I planned it, but I still need that information. The man gazes up at us, blood in his mouth, his eyes glued shut and swollen. He's already half dead.

"What do you need to know?"

Enzo whispers the question in quiet Italian. The man shakes his head.

"You're messing with the wrong people."

"Thanks for the advice," Enzo says. Before I give the order, he empties his gun. Two in the man's head and one in his chest. My stomach tightens. Even Eddie's eyes spark open, stunned. The worst part of all happens after the gunshots — a loud, blood-curdling scream. The three of us turn around to see her standing there, wide-awake and screaming her head off like a banshee.

My woman...

Fuck.

* * *

Click here to read *Forced To Surrogate*:
https://bit.ly/amalficoast1

Extremely Important Links

ALL BOOKS BY JAMILA JASPER
https://linktr.ee/JamilaJasper
SIGN UP FOR EMAIL UPDATES
Bit.ly/jamilajasperromance
SOCIAL MEDIA LINKS
https://www.jamilajasperromance.com/
GET MERCH
https://www.redbubble.com/people/jamilajasper/shop
GET FREEBIE (VIA TEXT)
https://slkt.io/qMk8
READ SERIAL (NEW CHAPTERS WEEKLY)
www.patreon.com/jamilajasper

JAMILA JASPER

Diverse Romance For Black Women

More Jamila Jasper Romance

<u>Pick your poison...</u>

Delicious interracial romance novels for all tastes. Long novels, short stories, audiobooks and more.

Hit the link to experience my full catalog.

* * *

FULL CATALOG BY JAMILA JASPER:
https://linktr.ee/JamilaJasper

Patreon

For a small monthly fee, you get exclusive access to over 375 chapters of my first completed bwwm dark and spicy serial romance, as well as the spin-off serial...

Despicable

The second serial, despicable has 300 chapters available for all Patreon subscribers to access instantly and... we officially have a **third completed spin-off bwwm romance series.**

And yes you get access to all of this at the $5/month tier with more benefits at more pricey tiers.

The third serial is about Clover + Thomas. Thomas has a shocking connection to a character in the second serial and Clover is an all-new African American female lead.

Powerless

This series has three *very long* "seasons" of chapters, the length of five full-length novels all-together.

You will probably have over three months of binge-reading before catching up to current content, making this one of the most 'bang for your buck' author Patreon subscriptions out there.

Don't take my word for it.
Check the post history:
www.patreon.com/jamilajasper

Patreon has more than the ongoing serial...

⚡ **INSTANT ACCESS** ⚡

- NEW merchandise tiers with **t-shirts, totes, mugs,** stickers and MORE!
- **FREE paperback** with all new tiers
- **FREE short story audiobooks** and audiobook samples when they're ready

Thank You Kindly

Thank you to all my readers, new and old for your support with this new year.

I look forward to making 2023 an INCREDIBLE year for interracial romance novels. I want to thank you all for joining along on the journey.

www.patreon.com/jamilajasper

* * *

Thank you to my most supportive readers — my Patreon subscribers!:

Carla
Jonathan
Kelly
Jessica
Jasmine
DARSHELL
Dawn
Tiabuena3
Leigh
Yvonne
Ashlee
Crystal
Marshybabyyy
Shout

Quaniquequia

TK

Kayla

Shronda C.

Ma-Eyongerie

Kayla

Chantell

Kheiara

ophelia

Vickie

Cass

Kamil

Kaela

Love

Miryam

Charlene

Summer

Lola

Eryn

DD Davis

Symone

Deborah

Beatrice

Valescha

Khadija

makhalaab

Kaya

Glitter Garden

SavageSam

sybil arroyo

Ncsportsfan79

Jessica G.

Danielle

Yola

Joslin

Alexciz

Stacia

Ayanna

Asia

Hailey

Kaya

Nikki

Naomi O.

Jessica J

Chakiya

Noelle

kourtnee

Martha

Nikki Valentina

xjkpop

Valeria

BlkBae

SweetS

Msteeq

Rhonda

Darrah

Killa

Shavon

Misty

India

Kassandra

Imani

Nala

Chantell

Benvinda

Roger

Lexi B

Zapphire

Vbrooks

Tasha G

Kiera

Valencia

Stacy

YANITZA

Texansgurl76

Emma

Tinette

Jenny

Mariah

Nale

Tanisha

Trenita

Shelle

dulcemaria413

Shanice

Letarsha

Tania

Neeka

Julia

Linda

Lisa

Jiannie

Jillian

Tameka

Asia

Scarlette

Olwyn

R W

Fayefaefee

Brianna

Tiffany

Katie

Diamond
Kera
Tia
Love Reading
Dominique
Sheria
Jennifer
Georgette
Monique
Wendolyn
King Turtle22
Jessica
Nic M.
JustChill
DJC
Atira
TheeLastHokage
Yvonne
Chrissy
Janelle
Rian
LaRonda
LaRonda
Deanna
dlawson382
Jasmine
Haley
Belinda
Sercee
Yvonne
Jadelock
Farah
Tamiya
Quin

J.Payton
Geek Girl
Ashley
Rubi
Pilar
Sandra
Jurnee
Anni
Shannet
Joneesa
GlitzyHydra
Amanda
Barbara
Brianna
Jamica
Lyons
MARY ANN
Marketia
SarahD
LoverofHawaiiHearts
ceblue
Yolanda
MonaGirl Lewis
Dianna
Mary
amna
Nysha
fayola
Ty
Abria
Shyra
Andi-Mariee
Jamila
Naee's World

KEISHA

Jennett

Fredericka

Candece

Chante

Pholuv

Lydia A

Sabrina

JM

Jackie

Mo

Natrilly83

Ashaunte

Tolu

Margaret

Wendolyn

Lori

Dionne

ZLB

Kristina

Nicol

ELBERT

A. Harris

Jesi

Brenda

Desiree

Angela

Frances

LaShan

Only1ToniD

Debbie T.

Tiffanie

April L

shawnte

Kay

Lisema

Yvonne F

Natasha

Colleen

Julia

Amy

Jacklyn

Shyan R

Kiana B

Pearl

Javonda

Sheron

Maxine

Dash

Alicia

margaret

Love2Read

Juliette

Monica

Sandhya

MaryC

Trinity

Brittany

June

Ashleigh

Nene

Nene

Deborah

Nikki M

Dee

TyKira

Kimmey

Laytoya

Shel W

Arlene

Judith

Mary

Shanida

Rachel

Damzel

Ahnjala

Kenya

momo

BJ

Akeshia

Melissa

Tiffany

sherbear

Nini J

Curtresa

REGGIE A.

Ashley

Mia

Tink138110

Phia

Sharon

Charlotte

Assiatu C

Regina

Romanda

Catherine

Gaynor

BF

Perpetua

Tasha G

Henri Ann

sara

skkent
Rosalyn
Danielle
Deborah J
Kirsten
ANA
Taylor R.
Charlene
Louanna
Michelle
Tamika
Lauren
RoHyde
Natasha
Shekynah
Cassie
AnnaBooms
Keitheena
Nick R
Gennifer M
Rayna
Anton
Jaleda
Kimvodkna
JaTonn
Jazmine
Anoushka
Raynischa
Audrey
Valeria
Courtney
Donna
Patrisha
Jenetha

LaKisha J.
Ayana
Taylor
Christy
Monica
FreyaJo
GRACE
Kisha
Christine
Alexandra
Amber
Natasha
Stephanie
LaKisha
kristylove7
Cynthea
DENICE
Latoya
monifacd .
Doneishia
Mariah
Gerry
Yolanda T
Yolanda P
Susan D
Phyllis H
Alisa K
Daveena K
Desiree S
Kimberly B
Robin B
Gary S
Stephanie MG
Georgette A

Kathy
Marty
JanetDaniels
Megan
Shelle
Delores
Janet
Lydia
Phyllis
Freda
Charlott R

Join the Patreon Community.